ARCANA

Edited by Rhonda Parrish

http://www.poiseandpen.com/

Publisher's Note: This is a work of fiction. Names, characters, places, and incidents are a product of the author's imagination. Locales and public names are sometimes used for atmospheric purposes. Any resemblance to actual people, living or dead, or to businesses, companies, events, institutions, or locales is completely coincidental.

Book Layout © 2014 BookDesignTemplates.com

Cover art and design by Philippe McNally
Interior illustrations by Marge Simon

Arcana/ Rhonda Parrish. -- 1st ed.
ISBN 978-1-988233-81-9 (print)
ISBN 978-1-988233-82-6 (electronic)

CONTENTS

Introduction

Rhonda Parrish

It was some years ago that I first considered dipping my toe into the world of anthologies. Like, really trying it out. I'd done a couple print versions of Niteblade (which you could argue were anthologies but were mostly print versions of Niteblade) but I had an idea for an actual anthology I wanted to do and no idea where to start in making that happen. I didn't know how to pitch it, where to pitch it, none of that stuff.

So, in 2011 I called a friend who knew a thing or two about anthologies, invited her to lunch and picked her brain. She was very encouraging, said my idea was a good one and offered to help in a handful of ways. I remember leaving the lunch and practically skipping back to the bus stop I was so excited.

That friend was Candas Dorsey and that conversation changed my life.

The idea I had was to do an anthology called *Arcana* which would contain one story for each of the major arcana cards from a tarot card deck. The story wouldn't have that card in it but its theme would match the meaning of the card. So the story in the slot of The Fool would be about innocence, optimism and/or a fresh start, and the one representing The Hanged Man would be about Sacrifice, surrender, prophecy and/or submission. You get the idea.

The tricky thing with a topic like that is you can't just do a traditional open submission window because people need to be writing to a different theme for each slot in the anthology. And I couldn't specifically invite people to send me stuff for it because no one had any idea who I was. Couple that with the fact anthologies are notoriously difficult to sell to publishers in the first place and what I ended up with was a great idea for an anthology which I couldn't possibly put together. So I shelved it for a time and worked on other things.

On other anthologies.

And I had some success in that arena.

But *Arcana* was always there in the murky back of my mind just waiting to be brought to life.

And so now I have.

I love the fact that it features interior illustrations by Marge Simon—the artistic force of nature who did all the artwork for Niteblade as well. Niteblade was where my editing career started and was the direct link to my deciding to try my hand at anthologies and since *Arcana* was the first anthology I ever wanted to do so it feels a bit like coming full circle.

All that is not meant to imply I'm done with anthologies, but I am super excited that the first one I conceived of will finally have a chance to find its audience. And I hope you enjoy it.

Rhonda
Edmonton
2/19/21

Finders and Keepers, Its and Not-Its

J.G. Formato

I'm not the hoarder—Granny Keeper is. I'm just the finder.

I found her the day I lost everything. My boyfriend, my wallet, my job. I had no idea where the boyfriend or the wallet went, I just knew they weren't there when I woke up. Will's stuff was all gone, from his Xbox to his nose hair trimmer, so at least I knew he wasn't kidnapped.

Maybe my wallet was, though.

On the other hand, Trisha the Manager was crystal clear on why I lost my job. You're supposed to write the customer's first name on the ticket, not bitter identifiers. *Codependent Hipsters. Sugar Daddy and the Sidepiece. Short-Term Engagement.* Yeah... that stuff ends up on the receipt, and people don't really like it.

At aggressively cheerful chain restaurants like mine, such shenanigans are the kiss of death. Termination effective immediately.

Termination's so harsh. I prefer to think of it as a release.

She was sitting at the kitchen table in the dark when I got home. I didn't see her, of course, until I flipped on the lights. But there she was, complacently knitting a bright red scarf. She later gifted it to me as a memento of our first meeting, and I love it now, but at the time it was garish and eerie. I mean, who knits in dark other-people's-kitchens? Usually psychos, I'm guessing.

I didn't say anything at first, I just watched her. She was round and soft and friendly looking, like Queen Elizabeth's approachable twin, and she hummed *That's Amore* to the click of the needles. I thought maybe she had wandered off from her family, and I tried to recall the faces of the missing people I had seen posted at Wal-Mart. She didn't look familiar.

At first, the humming and knitting was kind of nice. Soothing. But then it started making me nervous again. Needles and all. "Hi," I said, and waved. Which was kind of awkward since I was only two feet away.

"Hello." She laid her knitting down in her lap and folded her hands. "How was work today, dear?"

"Well, I got fired."

She clucked her tongue at me, a disapproving mother hen. "Well, now, that's too bad." She patted the chair next to her, and I dropped into it.

She invited me to sit in my own chair.

"Do you want to talk about it?" she asked.

"Not really." I shrugged. "But we should probably talk about what you're doing here." That was important to get out in the open.

"Why, I'm from Craig's List." Wispy grey eyebrows, aged rainbows of surprise, soared into the delicate lines of her forehead.

"Craig's List?"

"Your new roommate?"

"My new roommate?" Echolalia, the long banished, obnoxious childhood habit was bubbling up. Ms. Jess, my poor speech teacher had worked so hard to break me of it. In her honor, I bit my tongue (literally, front teeth vivisecting quite a few taste buds) and forced myself to listen, without interjecting, while my elderly trespasser explained herself.

"Your ad." She spoke the words deliberately and slowly, as if to a very small child or high-strung teen, which wasn't really fair, considering the circumstances. "I'm taking the extra room. We'll split rent and utilities right down the middle, but from the looks of you I imagine I'll be taking over groceries. You're skin and bones." She dug around in an enormous patchwork bag, and pulled out a package of Fig Newtons from beneath a tangled web of multicolored yarn. "Please, have some," she said, brandishing them at me.

Dismissing an irrational fear of being fattened up for Baba Yaga's oven, I took one and chewed on it thoughtfully. I guess it was nice of Will to put an ad on Craig's List for a new roomie. It would have been nicer if he had just told me he was leaving. Or nicer still if he'd just stuck around.

On second thought, a Craig's List ad is a pretty crappy farewell gesture.

"So, how come you were sitting here in the dark?" I asked.

"Don't talk with your mouth full, dear. No one needs to see that," she admonished before answering my question. "It would have rude to barge in here and turn on all the lights as if I owned the place."

"Right," I said, making sure I swallowed every last crumb first. "What's your name?"

"You can call me Granny Keeper." She resumed knitting and humming.

"I'm Bree."

"I know, dear." She patted my hand. "It was in the ad."

Granny Keeper was flipping pancakes when I came downstairs the next morning. Like, literally flipping them. A procession of them soared from the spatula, stopped just inches from ceiling and spun, hurtling back to their blistering doom.

I hadn't eaten breakfast in five years, but that was all about to change.

"I need something blue," she said, handing me a plate.

"Something blue?" I repeated. *Gah*. I bit my tongue, gathered a thought, and tried again. "What do you need?"

"I'm not sure yet. It's just so empty in here. We need something blue. After you eat, you can run out and get me some things. And then I'll see which one I want." She unclasped a dainty beaded coin purse and pulled out a crispy new fifty-dollar bill. "Get as many as you can."

I don't know what was in those pancakes, but I said yes.

At first, I planned on going to Goodwill, but Granny Keeper had said to get as many blue things as possible, so I kept driving. A couple of twists and turns behind the Goodwill is the junk shop. It doesn't have a proper name, it's not "The Junk Shop" or anything. It's just a big room overflowing with crap, like an above ground basement or a floor level attic. It's mostly Goodwill rejects, but sometimes you can make a really special discovery. Once I found this amazing Christmas wreath, a little smelly and dusty, but totally festive.

And anyway, you pay for stuff by the pound at the junk shop. So I could get a ton of blue things.

I slid a cracked plastic shopping basket up my arm, dangling it from my inner elbow like a designer bag. An azure tea cup capped a pyramid of broken and mismatched plates, its chipped glory beckoning me with its blueness. Old ladies like tea, right? Especially old ladies that call everybody dear and make pancakes. I grabbed it quickly, as if somebody else was actually contemplating this fine bit of pottery, and nestled it into the corner of my basket.

I poked around in the bins, gathering more items, until my basket was full. Everything was organized into a neat little spectrum of blues, from the deep navy sock on the left all the way up to a powder blue onesie on the right. I was reaching for a bright cobalt bandanna I had spotted beneath a rusty teapot, when a voice snuck up behind me.

"You entering a Blue Period?" This guy asked, arching an eyebrow. I'll bet he does that a lot and people think it's cute. I silently blessed Granny Keeper for making me brush my hair and put on lip gloss. And change into a clean shirt. And put on deodorant.

"A blue period?" I echoed, stalling until more words tumbled out. "No, not really. I mean, my boyfriend ran away and I lost my job. But I wouldn't say I'm having a blue period, though, that's kind of dramatic."

"I meant your basket." He pointed, his lips twitching. "It's like Picasso's Blue Period in there, I thought maybe you were working on a project."

I nodded. It was more like a fool's errand than a project, but that's splitting hairs.

"Me, too. I'm grabbing some ceramic for a mosaic." He proudly displayed a basket full of cracked plates and cups, in all kinds of colors.

"Okay." I said. "Well, good luck with that." I took my basket to the checkout/weigh station and paid, looking like a total baller with my fresh fifty.

As I was getting into my car, the eyebrow-arching artiste was climbing into the rustiest old Ford I'd ever seen, and I've seen a lot of rusty old Fords. He started blasting some old Prince, rocking out to *Little Red Corvette*. It looked so funny.

There were about twenty bucks left after visiting the junk shop, so I stopped at the convenience store on my way home and bought a couple of tubes of toothpaste, Airheads, Cool Ranch Doritos, and two blue raspberry Slushies. I wasn't sure if the Doritos were cheating or not, since really it's the bag that's blue, not the chips themselves, but it was worth a shot. And Doritos are manna from heaven.

I thought Granny Keeper was going to be more impressed with my stuff, or at least tell me what it was for, but she just said "That's nice, dear," like the old lady from the memes and politely declined the Slushee. A little deflated, I dropped my bags on the counter. A plastic Easter egg rolled out, hiding itself behind the microwave. Reaching back to grab it, my fingers brushed against something hemp and familiar.

"My wallet!" I crowed, waving it triumphantly over my head. It was nice to know that Will was only a thief of love and not a thief of cash.

"Oh, you found it. How lovely." She patted my shoulder, then frowned at me. "You drove all day without your license?"

I was going to look for a job the next day. I was actually going to look for a job all the next week, the week after that, and the week after that— but it never happened. Every day, Granny Keeper had a new eccentric goose chase for me. It always started with pancakes and segued into nonsensical requests.

"Bree, darling, I need some soft things."

"Bree, dear, how about you run out and grab me some wooden things?"

"Bree, sweetie, I would really love something shiny."

She never would tell me why, or what she really wanted. She just said to get as much I could, and she would know it when she saw it.

So far, no good. I hadn't found the *it* yet and my house was quickly disappearing beneath the mounds of *not-its*.

Janae came by to check on me. That was surprising— I'd begun to think I'd lost her in mini-divorce.

"Will's worried about you," she said, tucking a braid behind her ear.

"Will?" I guess I did lose her in the break up, since she was here by his decree.

"Yes, Will. He thinks you've gone a little crazy since you guys broke up."

"Crazy?" I bit down on my tongue, determined not to speak again until I had a real, original thought to express.

"Yes, Bree. You're not working or dating or anything, and all you do is buy random crap from thrift stores. And you keep posting selfies of you and your grandma having tea and eating pancakes. I'm not going to lie to you, it's weird."

I liked to think that we look like Queen and Kate Middleton as we sip our tea, so I was more than a bit offended by that last remark. My mouth screwed up into a sideways knot and I rolled my eyes.

"That's fine, you can roll your eyes at me. You never did like to listen to me. But you need to be rolling them around this house and taking a close look at what's going on. You're going buried alive in here, and Will and I are going to be kicking back, watching you on a very special episode of Hoarders."

"I'm not hoarding. I'm looking. I'm looking for something."

"Looking for what?"

"I'll know it when I see it." I waded through a pile of old quilts and tattered baskets and threw open the door. "And what do you mean 'Will and I?' You're a Will-and-I now?"

Now it all made sense—every time she came over, they always stayed up giggling, "kicking back" or whatever, when I went to bed. Guess I was right to be "paranoid" or whatever he called me.

Jerk.

Janae didn't answer me—she just grabbed her purse and shuffled to the door.

"You can tell Will that if doesn't want to look at my face, then he sure doesn't need to` be looking at my Facebook. Please let him know that my mental state is just fine, and no matter how much you guys would love it, I am not pining for his company. Or yours!"

After a completely satisfying and house rattling door slam, Granny Keeper stepped into the room, gracefully navigating the debris. "That's nice, dear. You found it," she murmured absently, patting my arm.

"Found what?"

"Your self-respect. I knew it was around here somewhere."

I met Corrine at the Safe House thrift shop, hunting for things that were purple. She was hunting for things that were t-shirts. Tiny ones to be exact. Her own clothes were really nice, brand names and classy colors. She wasn't wearing any make up, though, and warm brown roots sprouted from her very meticulous part.

She only found two tiny shirts, and I felt bad for her because she obviously wasn't very good at this game.

"What size?" I asked.

"I beg your pardon?" she said in lovely, clear tones. I'll have to remember that. Instead of inanely repeating people, I'll just say 'I beg your pardon?' Way more elegant. Like Kate Middleton.

"What size shirt are you looking for?"

"3T."

I dug through a couple piles, including the ones marked swimsuits, husky girls, and men's sweaters. I am awesome at this game, and wound up with an assortment of 3T's in a wide array of styles and colors.

"That was amazing." She grinned. "I'm Corinne."

"I'm Bree. So, what are these for? Some kind of project?"

"They're for my son," she said, grin fading. Her face tightened into a defensive mask as she unzipped her Burberry bag, pulling out a handful of dimes and quarters. "Thank you for your help," she said coldly and took her shirts to the register.

I watched, feeling rude and awkward, as the cashier refused her quarters and slipped a couple Dr. Seuss books and a worn teddy bear into the bag. They hugged briefly and Corinne hurried out the door.

I followed her. "Hey!"

She stopped, turning with an impatient look on her face. "What?"

"I'm sorry if I said the wrong thing. I'm not good at talking sometimes."

"Me, neither." She smiled. "I'm just a little oversensitive, I suppose, my life's changing and it takes some getting used to." Unwelcome tears blanketed her eyes, and she blinked the blink of a woman desperate not to cry in the middle of the road. I know that blink.

"Do you wanna get some coffee with me? My treat." Coffee usually distracts me.

Granny Keeper was waiting for me on the sofa, surrounded by empty picture frames and throw pillows with the regality of a duchess. She cleared a patch of couch for me, and I sat, resting my head on her shoulder.

"I guess I'm lucky Will ran away. With some people it's totally the other way around." She listened without commenting, as I told her about Corinne, about how she came to live at Safe House, leaving her home with nothing but her toddler and a suitcase. How she was trying to build a new life from the ground up. How she had given up everything to find herself.

"I wonder what made her come to this decision," Granny Keeper said.

"She said her counselor helped her. Corinne started seeing her because her husband said she was too moody and difficult, and that's why he acted the way he did, but then she realized that she wasn't the problem at all."

"That must be lovely for the counselor," she mused. "To be able to help other women like that."

"Absolutely," I agreed.

"So, what did you find today?" Granny Keeper asked briskly.

Months later I ran into the *artiste*. I had stopped at the junk shop after class to find some things that were broken. He arched his eyebrow at me and examined my basket of cracked plates and pottery fragments.

"So, what are these for?"

"I beg your pardon?"

"What's all this for?" he asked again.

"I'm not sure yet," I said mysteriously. At least I hope it sounded mysterious and not just lame.

"But you're not an artist?"

"I'm a psychology major."

"Oh, I get it, mending broken things."

"Yeah, that's it." I headed over to weigh my junk. He followed.

"Can we go to dinner sometime? Or get coffee?" Instead of arching, his eyebrows drew together seriously. He looked a little nervous, which was endearing.

So I said okay, we exchanged numbers (and names!), and I told him I'd see him Saturday.

Before he left, I gave him all my shattered stuff. He promised to make something pretty for me and jumped into the rusty Ford, once again blasting some Prince. *The Most Beautiful Girl in the World.* He grabbed his chest and pointed at me like a total goober. It was really sweet.

The house was spotless when I got home. Granny Keeper sat at the kitchen table, knitting by the light of my laptop.

"Where is everything?" I asked.

"What did you find today, dear?" she countered.

I blushed and shrugged. "I don't know."

"It'll be fun to find out," she said with a wink. I slid into the chair next to her and my eyes were drawn to the glow of the screen. Even though I'd been expecting it, Granny Keeper's recent web search just about broke my heart.

"You're looking at Craig's List." My throat tightened and I started blinking in sad Morse Code.

"Oh, dearie, you've found so much." She patted my hand. "It's time I went looking again."

"For who?" I swallowed all the ugly jealousy and tried to be happy for the next girl.

"I'm not sure yet. I'll know her when I see her."

Palimpsest

Kevin Cockle

She killed herself in Vegas.

Looking back, he should have anticipated that she might. The town has a replica pyramid, a replica sphinx. An Eiffel tower where no Eiffel tower should be. Venetian gondolas, and gondoliers; man-made volcanoes; a pirate ship on a man-made sea.

The city itself put the truth in front of her; she couldn't help but see it. And once she'd seen it, it was all much too much for her.

Twenty-five stories to an outdoor pool.

She missed the water.

Rorshach red. Splatter patterns on concrete. A strange alphabet only he could read.

"You know you look like a perv, sitting here—right?" She said as she sat down. Kid noise rose from the mall's child-park nearby: squeals and shouts and nonsensical hollering; the odd shriek or wailing sob; woo-woo siren noises; automotive vrroom vrrooms; high-pitched, staccato arguments over imaginary items of unfathomable import.

Mike smiled. "Suppose I do, now that you mention it."

She crossed her legs, looking into the "park": a room enclosed by a waist-high, padded wall, containing more fun per square inch than anywhere else in the city. A kid in a blue jumper was heading face-first down a little plastic slide. The girl winced.

"Yours?" Mike asked.

"That's my little hellion, yes."

"You don't look like a mom."

"Thanks? I guess?"

"You know what I mean."

"I could assume. Why don't you tell me?"

Mike exhaled a speculative breath, narrowing his eyes as he took her in. "Bored socialite. Husband's a... uh... arms dealer. Government approved but still a little shady. You're afraid of him, but he treats you well. Nothing's for free though. You come here to distract yourself, get out of the house—strike that—gated mansion. You like people, and conversation, but you don't get much of either any more," he paused, then said: "How'm I doing?"

She smiled. "You must be a writer."

"Jesus: that obvious?"

"Your slumming attitude, too-cool for the mall. Your grungy, out-of-style levis. Your unshaven, uncaring face, and the naturally curly hair which saves you from having to do anything with it. Luckily for you. Handsome, but not leading man material: more interesting than hot. Yep: a writer. How'm I doing?"

"I'm a writer all right. Mike." He extended his hand.

"Constance." She extended hers. A squeal from the park distracted her: her kid, hitting some other kid on the head with a foam bat. Why the hell would they put those things in there?

"So, Mike. Why are you hanging around a kid's park in a shopping mall in the middle of the day. Trying to get arrested?"

"You know—that's really tragic, that attitude. As it happens, I like the noise. I'm done for the day—I work alone—and I come here for

the harmless craziness of it all. I like seeing kids playing. I don't have kids. It's… different here.

"You're done for the day? What do you write?"

"Porn mostly. Some Poli-Sci or English papers at a $100 a pop. Grant applications. Resumes. Closing speeches for litigators. Wedding speeches. But porn pays the bills."

"Your touching story about hanging around a kid's park for the amusement and novelty is wearing dangerously thin, Mike."

"Whatever: it's a job. Seriously: it's not what you think. I make people's fantasies real… real-ish, anyway. Real as they can be. But, Connie—can I call you Connie? It's a job with weight attached, I find. Call me a perv, but there's something cleansing about the mall; kids jumping around all mindless and wound-up. You wouldn't believe some of the requests I get."

"You're serious, aren't you," Constance said, now truly fascinated.

"I started out technical writing, copy-editing… all the shit jobs you can do with your English degree—aside from waiting tables. Starved doing it—wasn't organized enough. Not professional enough. But people who read their porn—people who can't get what they want from video—they're educated folks for the most part, have money to pay for what they want. It's just too easy—naming your price, and having it met without a lot of bullshit. I write for a few hours in the morning, send a pay-pal invoice, and screw around for the rest of the day. When I see the bill's been paid, I email the story. Badabing."

"Incredible. What does that pay, if you don't mind me asking? I mean… I have to ask, you know? You just don't meet pornographers in the mall every day."

"Pays as much as you want it to, I guess. I don't want to do much more than one contract a day—so it's about a thousand dollars a week, give or take. Four grand a month, plus all the free time I can handle."

"But… it's porn. I mean… doesn't that bother you?"

"I'm here aren't I?" Mike showed a false grin, with just the hint of truth in the practiced irony of his gaze. "Yes. It can bother you."

Constance shook her head, processing. "Why would you tell me that?" she said.

Mike shrugged. "Taking advantage of you being a total stranger, I suppose; why not be honest? I can't make up anything better."

She chuckled.

He continued: "So... was I right? <u>Is</u> your husband a shadowy arms dealer?"

Connie's smile grew small, her eyes suddenly older than her face. "No," she said. "But let's say he is."

"You want your husband to be an arms dealer? Did you catch the 'shadowy' part?"

"Yeah. I like it. It makes me poignant instead of cliché."

Mike didn't know what to say—just looked at her too-perfect profile.

"You're staring," she said—mischievous, looking into the park rather than directly at him.

"Lot of pressure on me not to say something cliché right now. I'm thinking." Connie laughed—light, Breakfast at Tiffany's laugh.

Mike knew a high point when he saw one, knew it was time to go. He thanked Connie for the conversation, gave her a smile as he left, got one back in return.

Outside, on the walk through the parking lot to the train station, Michael was struck by one recurring thought: <u>why the pornography angle</u>? It had played well—the yarn he'd spun had seemingly written itself... but he'd never so much as visited an internet porn site, let alone produced the stuff. Closest he'd ever been to anything even remotely pornographic was leafing through Playboy's 20 Questions at the barbershop.

<u>Maybe what I actually do isn't all that different</u>, he considered.

He thought about that on the quick rail-ride downtown.

Whoa Mikey—hold the pen loosely, like this.

Like this?

Yeah… give yourself control, but leave a little room for your body to take over. Can't clamp down too hard. Free up your wrist there.

Uncle Theo… is this magic?

Not sure Mikey. Not sure what it is. Partly it's magic… partly, I think it's just letting go.

Later, at his shop in Inglewood, "Riverbend Calligraphic", Mike mulled over events in his mind and concluded that things had gone very well indeed.

She was captivating, Connie was. And the addition of sadness/intelligence to her avian features and aerobically trained body had been the perfect touch. In high school, to be perfectly frank, the girl had been a bit of a ditz.

She hadn't recognized him, which was understandable. He'd filled out a bit, carried himself differently, spoke with more assurance. She had been a year ahead of him in school—had no reason to ever acknowledge him. He was now, and had been then, a stranger.

Spreading a sheet of 140lb watercolour paper out flat against his drafting table, Michael arranged his work area. He took a moment to trim the nib of his Norfolk quill, getting the angle just right for the job ahead. Out front, in the store proper, he displayed his art—books of calligraphy, on hand-made paper, with hand-bound bindings. Beautiful things—some of them award-winning—many of them illustrated as well as sumptuously scripted. He did commissions, as well as producing painstaking volumes of his own choosing. The Canterbury Tales was there; Shakespeare's sonnets; A.A. Milne; Stevenson: the Jekyll and Hyde was one of Mike's personal favourites. He earned a modest income from his singular talent, or so it appeared. "Don't try to make a million dollars happen," his uncle had warned. "Don't do anything crazy. Too much changes Mike, the bigger you go. You can't control it then."

That had been the fire lesson, Mike remembered: the night Theo had shown him the alphabet. "Celtic designs," Theo had said, "originally Druid. Sneaky bastards."

Mike had read about druids. He thought about British savages, running around in animal skins and blue faces, ambushing Roman soldiers. "What I'm writing here is English, Mikey," Theo continued, moistening his nib, "but in an alphabet not too many guys know about nowadays. Maybe just you and me. It's the alphabet that matters, kiddo. Think of it as druids hiding in plain sight: they folded their secrets into our language with these letters. Snuck in on the back of the Uncial - curled themselves into the whorls of Roman capitals - then kind of just slipped sideways when no one was looking."

"Are you a druid?" Mike said, leaning in just past his uncle's shoulder, getting a good view of the writing surface; getting a good whiff of sweet tobacco and bitter brandy.

Theo laughed. "No Mike, I'm a drunkard. Here: check this out."

Theo's hand flowed with the writing. Later, Mike would understand that the very intricacy of the alphabet—the spidery, sinuous ascenders and abrupt descenders—the vine-like curly-cues and varying line widths—all of that signified in ways your conscious mind couldn't be aware of. Subtle demands were made on your mind and body to draw those letters—and in the act of drawing them, real power was released. But at that moment, on a summer's night in his twelfth year, at his Uncle Theo's log cabin in the middle of BC... he saw his uncle script the words "Fire, in the hearth: small, crackling, pine-scented."

And when he was done—when the last letter had been exquisitely shaped—almost carved and slashed into the page the way his Uncle was working the pen—a fire began in the fireplace. It popped and hissed in mature flame, though it was of cozy proportions.

The cabin filled with the heartwarming scent of burning pine.

And Mike had stared, with his mouth wide open—sure as hell he'd just witnessed magic.

"What do you think just happened there, Mike?" his uncle asked.

Mike swallowed. "You wrote the words, and... um... you made a fire."

"Yeah, maybe. That's what it looks like all right."

"But it's not?"

"Could be I made a fire. Or could be I made a world with a fire in it. Either way—it's a good idea to keep things small."

A grinding guitar solo jarred Mike out of his reverie—brought him back to the present. The shop's sound system carried a live stream from the University of Edinburgh's student radio: an eclectic mix of alt rock, classic rock made new again, European techno-pop, and live, awkward, irreverent, student commentary throughout. Mike liked it, related to it, though he was a few years removed from his university days. And he liked it when the DJs had to explain that David Letterman was a talk show host in America—little foreign touches like that.

An arms dealer husband. That would be tricky. This was Calgary after all; not exactly the center of the international arms trade. But, Mike thought, we do have an airport. How hard would it be to run such a business from Calgary? Probably no harder than any other global business, these days.

He dipped pen to ink, and began to craft letters. It was all-consuming, precision work, writing this forgotten alphabet that was English, but looked almost like a wildly stylized Arabic from a distance. Mike's breathing deepened like a diamond cutter's before that critical first tap, the intervals between breaths lengthening. The shapes of the words had to be exactly right, to make a reality happen. It was the shape, the calligraphic embellishment, which contained all the nuanced elements of reality his conscious mind couldn't account for. The shape of the letters, the negative spaces within and between them—the form of the alphabet—the width and weight of the lines, and their curling aspects—all these things would insure the integrity of the story.

Connie's husband an arms dealer. Legit, but dangerous all the same.

Connie a beautiful, trapped, lonely woman, drifting into an affair with a charming stranger.

Mike worked carefully, and slowly, feeling the letters form in his shoulder, in his forearm, as his body made micro-adjustments of which he wasn't altogether aware.

"It's your body that does the magic," Theo had been fond of saying. "Your subconscious, your nervous system. All you can do is point the way."

Mike had long fantasized about being with Connie, ever since he'd first seen her leaving the gym with her girlfriends after P.E. class, all those years ago.

He'd already made a couple of slight adjustments: shaping her; contextualizing her. Over-writing her.

Mike couldn't say if what he was doing was pornography or not. Perhaps there wasn't a word for it.

There was war in Africa—spreading like a grass fire on the Savannah, and it was out of control. Connie's husband Mitchell worked out of his Brussels and Marseilles offices full time to meet the endless demand for small arms, ammunition, training, and logistics support.

Mike often wondered at the convenience of the African wars, but came to conclude that they were a coincidence. Violence was endemic there: war had been inevitable whether Mike had needed Mitchell to be out of town, or not.

The affair started as affairs do: a second meeting at the mall, then a third. Connie hired a full time governess, left the child in the woman's care much of the time.

The city was dangerous for obvious reasons, but Connie had money - condos in Aruba, Costa Rica, Hawaii. Taking separate flights, they could meet in exotic locations, escaping the cold of Calgary's winter for the warmth of each other's bodies.

One night, on Maui, laying together in a huge hanging hammock under a canopy of tropical stars, Constance whispered: "I need to tell you a secret."

"I need to hear your secrets," Mike muttered, glorying in the weight of her upon his body.

"I'm a terrible, wretched mother," Connie breathed, barely audible. "I am. I only had a child because Mitchell wanted it. And I've tried to love Bryan… I've tried. But he's nothing to me. Honestly. Sometimes I can't stand the sound of him."

Michael felt her sobbing, though he couldn't hear it.

He decided that this too, must be a coincidence.

Connie just didn't look like a mom, and lo and behold: she wasn't one after all.

Vegas had been her idea. "Four days. We'll get separate rooms. I can't believe you've never been. Oh my God, I'll show you around!"

They lay under a hot desert sun alongside the big Caesar's Palace hidden pool—the one that looked like Caligula's bathhouse. Historically, the pools were closed in February, but had stayed open in recent seasons due to the unrelenting, unseasonable heat. Everyone blamed global warming. Nevada was setting records.

Ivory pillars and Grecian statues stood in marked contrast to the young, ultra-modern guests who lounged in chairs, and occupied the

cabanas. Waitresses in togas prowled back and forth; attendants offered everything from bottle-service to on-the-spot sunglass cleaning.
Connie was built for Vegas pool parties: a golden-brown blonde stun-
ner who had oglers wondering what TV show she was on. She was in
her element: Mike a little less so. *Note to self*, Mike thought, gazing at
his soft, marble-white gut: *hit the gym, Spartacus*.

Eventually, he noticed Connie frowning, rubbing her temples with
the thumb and forefinger of her right hand.

"What's up?" Mike asked.

"I'm... headachy—or something. I just feel off."

"Why don't you head inside—get out of the sun. Have a nap: we'll
stroll the strip at night."

"That's a good idea. You don't mind?"

"Hell no. Go."

She went; he stayed, drowsy in the heat.

In the intoxicating cool of the Vegas night, she did indeed seem to
revive, though Mike detected distraction in her mood. She stopped and
stared up at the Eiffel tower as though she'd never seen it before. He
held her hand and smiled a bemused smile, waiting for her to snap out
of it. And then the mood would pass, and she would lean into him, and
they would wander on to the next sight.

They watched the pirates mailing in canned ferocity during the
mock sea battle on their little patch of ersatz Barbados. Mike assumed
that multiple shows a night must get pretty old, pretty quick. He
couldn't blame the actors for their waxen savagery.

They marveled at the Egyptian pyramid, and the attendant obelisks
and statuary: not even a fun-house mirror effect, for these were repli-
cas which seemed to know exactly what they were. The Luxor didn't
seem like Egypt; it seemed like Vegas. Same with the replica New
York; it was a Vegas New York—a parody, more than a true copy.

In retrospect, he should have seen it coming, should have known
better. The city had been humming to them all along—vibrating with

its own peculiar energy—singing a siren's song that Michael had missed.

And the kicker was, he had *made* her smart. The old, high school Connie never would have made the connections.

It happened as they walked along the romantic street-side of the gigantic man-made lake out front of the Bellagio. Simpler than most of the other spectacles, but somehow more majestic: deep blue water in the desert—a pure, muscular statement of opulence.

Connie turned to Mike under the replica gaslights of Victorian England, staring at him.

"What?" He half-chuckled, confused.

"You're Mike Holloway," Connie breathed, her eyes looking through him and past him, as though trying to focus on his atomic structure. Her lips quivered, though the evening air was warm.

"What... what are you doing to me?" she said, a demand that sounded like a plea.

"Connie..." He reached for her arm; she yanked it away, seething.

"What are you doing to me?" she asked, for she simply could not comprehend.

"Listen to me - let's..." But it was too late—she was backing away; she was turning; she was kicking her heels off and she was running down the street.

Mike gave chase—as best he could. He nearly caught her on that first block, but after that... Connie had been a distance-runner ever since she was a kid and left him standing. Mike staggered to a halt, wheezing for breath, hands on hips, watching as a Vegas cabbie nearly killed Constance as she bolted against a *don't walk* sign.

Bolted, and was gone.

When she killed herself later that night, it was all over the strip - the pictures of it on local TV; the lurid thrill of it all. Her sudden, senseless, and violent death-leap paralyzed Mike. *Now* he heard the humming—the city triumphant in his ears—roaring to a crescendo. Too late. Too late.

Mike took a limo to Los Angeles that very night. He had the driver retract the sunroof so Mike could look up at the cold desert stars, feel the rush of dry wind against his face.

He took a plane out of L.A. as a precaution. Connie's husband was a powerful man, and Mike knew that he dare not show up in a police report as some sort of known associate.

He just left her there, shattered and terrified and bewildered at the last.

He felt his guilt like a physical beating. Lead pipes; a fetal ball; thump, thud, thump.

Michael wrapped a long brown muffler around his throat before putting his coat on. February in Calgary was cold in the mornings. He'd been up most of the night; fell asleep at the drafting table.

Keep things short, Mikey—concise. When you write too much, you get tired, and you'll make mistakes, and nothing will happen. Or worse... sometimes when you draw the words too long, they start drawing you... When it gets too easy, you need to stop—'cause this is supposed to be hard.

Stepping out the front door of his shop onto 9th Ave, Mike turned his collar against the biting wind—headed East for coffee and breakfast.

He'd arrived home from L.A. at 11:00AM Calgary time, had come straight downtown to his apartment above the shop, and collapsed into a fitful few hours of exhaustion-sleep.

When he woke—he put out the CLOSED sign, and got to work. He'd been at it all night, broken a lot of Theo's rules in the process. *Let's be honest,* Mike thought. *I broke all the rules last night.*

After a while, the calligraphy had started to simply spill onto the page. He was good, Mike knew that, but he wasn't *that* good. He should have pulled back at that point, but he couldn't help himself. There were times when he could have sworn he'd nodded off, then come-to—his hand continuing on of its own volition.

He'd written pages of the stuff. Pages. He'd never done more than a sentence at a time before.

He clenched and relaxed his right hand in his coat-pocket. It was still cramped, hurting from the night before. Waiting for a light to change, he caught a glimpse of himself in a frosted, darkened shop window and turned to get a better look. There was grey at his temples, and the crow's feet around his eyes were more than just lack-of-sleep lines. Last night had aged him, taxed his nervous system in ways he couldn't even guess at. Or worse.

...sometimes when you draw the words too long, they start drawing you.

Mike stopped that train of thought right then and there, made a fist with his right hand in his pocket. Grimaced at the pain.

"Hey mister," a voice said, just off his right flank. "Have you got eighty-five cents you could spare?"

He turned, recognizing the voice of course, but still startled at the sight of Connie reborn.

She was the same age perhaps—early twenties—but at first glance he might not have recognized her. The fashionable tousle was re-placed by long, straight strands of greasy blonde hair. The face was harder, almost gaunt, lacking cosmetic refinement. Connie's thin lips were chapped; her eyes had a wincing aspect, registering the cold. She wore a short-waisted pink jacket that had seen better days, and proba-bly previous owners. She wore baby blue flannel sweats in which the old Connie would not have been seen dead.

Homeless? Mike thought. He hadn't specified that -- only that she need him. Guilt twinged in his vitals as he thought of the life she must have had to this point.

He saw that she was pregnant, and wondered at the persistence of children in her life. Was it the essence of Connie fighting back against the modifications? Was the child symbolic of something? Why would the imagery keep recurring? Whatever it was, the fetus was beyond his control.

"Mister?" she said, squinting one eye against the bleak, grey morning light as she looked up at him.

Mike swallowed. "I'm going for a bite. Why don't I buy you breakfast?"

The girl eyed him with as much curiosity as caution. "You're not some kind of pervert, are you?" she said, with just a hint of the old Connie flashing in playful eyes.

Mike chuckled—his breath condensing like smoke in the cutting breeze. It was a dry sound, his laugh, heavy with excess meaning, and mounting despair.

"Only one way to find out," he said. He extended his elbow—a gentleman from another era—and she took it like a lady.

Larkspur and Henbane

Sara Cleto and Brittany Warman

For Knicky Laurelle

It started with small things.
Acorns, leaves, a piece of string
From grandmother's scarf. I
Choose them, gathered them up,
Made them new. Mine.

I cut flowers -
chrysanthemums, crocuses, roses -
not to put in vases or arrange
artfully over the hearth but to invert
and dry until my breath crumbled them.

In this way I became
a connoisseur of the forgotten,
a handmaiden of the dying.
A witch, perhaps, sleeping in the coop,
nestled among feathers.

When the tree outside, long barren,
began bearing flowers,
red as blood, bold as brass,
on its spiny, tangled branches,
I wasn't surprised, merely hungry.

I fed the flowers to the birds,
who ate as though starved.
They became white, then red, then black -
sometimes they would vanish from sight,
and I would laugh.

But even in a town large enough
for two bakers, two tanners, and a scribe,
my neighbors could not trust a girl
dressed in blue, crowned in feathers.
They felled my tree.

I mourned her loss, gathered her last petals,
the chickens around me blinking
in and out of sight as they took her last offering,
red, white, black, then nothing,
cooing comfort to each other, to me.

From her wood, I whittled a mortar,
a pestle, cutting myself only once
in the long hours of craft. My blood
seasoned the wood, hardening,
setting its shape, settling my heart.

I powdered larkspur and henbane
in my mortar until they sparked like sugar.
And I blew that fine, flowered dust

at the bakers and tanners who denied me,
who thought to best a young witch.

The forest welcomed me,
wrapped branches round my shoulders,
crowned me with new petals and old bones.
My birds pecked the dirt and, freed from their coop,
left a train of feathers in our wake.

When the hut came, I wasn't surprised,
merely hungry.

Lupa

Susan MacGregor

Caristia, Mensis Februarius XXII,
Anno III Amulius Rex,
Alba Longa:

"Pull harder, you stupid slave."

Ilia struggled to keep her face as smooth as the marble basin beside her, but it was hard. Not because Acca was hurting her, but because Vestalis Maxima Oppia wanted to see her wince. She'd die before she gave her that satisfaction.

Oppia shoved her maid aside to attack her scalp anew. The comb gouged her temple, forcing her to shut her eyes against the pain. "We must *not* accept anything less than perfection in how we present ourselves." Oppia clawed at her head. "We are Vestals, so we must represent the goddess, in all of her glory."

That same relentless drivel. Never mind that the goddess never assumed human form but remained a flame. Never mind that Vesta's priestesses prayed to a deity who paid little attention. Yet should the holy fire go out, the consequences for the vestal responsible were harsh.

I'll take a bloodied scalp over a flogging. Ilia gritted her teeth against the assault.

The combing and braiding seemed to take forever; Oppia jerked her head this way and that. She liked to throw her weight around, reminding them who was in charge. "Finish it." Oppia threw the comb into the bowl. Acca approached, eyes downcast and with the white *suffibulum* in her hands.

"I don't see why *I* have to attend the *caristia*." Ilia refused to be cowed. "Aren't we above worldly matters? Isn't it immodest for any vestal to attend such a gathering?" Oppia planned to go. *To hades with her.*

Oppia had been heading for the door, but she swung about, her face ruddy as if she'd been tending the divine fire. "If the king invites us, we do as he commands."

"So, if the king ordered you to break your vows to Vesta, you'd place his demands over hers?"

Oppia's eyes were hot coals. "Don't speak nonsense. Such a thing would never happen."

"But if it did?"

"A vestal must honour her goddess. Or be punished should she fail."

"Yet there's more than one goddess to honour."

Acca, who'd been about to pin the *suffibulum* to her hair, caught her breath. Oppia clenched her fists, her brown knuckles turning pale. *Good,* Ilia thought. *I've annoyed her.*

"We must honour Vesta first."

Vesta, goddess of home and hearth, goddess of domestic boredom or bliss, depending on one's point of view. She'd always preferred Diana, untamed and unfettered. "Let's hope Juno or Venus isn't aware of your opinion, then."

She maintained her expression of polite inquiry as, sputtering, the chief vestal drew herself up. "They are Two of the Twelve, with their own priestesses to attend them."

"So, you've asked them?"

"Of course not! One does not ask...why you impudent girl! You argue like a Greek!"

"I thought it was your business to instruct me. Can't I ask questions?"

"Enough of this prattle! We leave in an hour. See that she's ready." Oppia glared at Acca as if she were the source of her irritation. Acca dropped into a deep curtsey. They waited for Ilia's bedroom door to slam. Ilia chuckled when it did.

"You shouldn't antagonize her." Acca folded the *suffibulum* back from her face with soft fingers. "Last time, she made you scrub the temple floor *six* times."

"And the sore knees were worth it." She smiled, remembering.

Acca sighed. She'd been forced to wash the floor alongside her. Guilt pricked Ilia. "Forgive me, Acca. Annoying her is the only pleasure I have."

She picked up her bronze mirror and studied herself. Her face was unlined, as fresh as an apple on the tree. "What's to become of us, Acca? Shall we become dried-out old hags like Oppia?"

"It might not be so bad. You'll still be my princess, no matter what."

"And you, my best friend—no matter what. If not for you, I think I'd have gone mad by now." She made a face.

Acca studied her closely. "Are you worried about Amulius?" As always, her perception was sharp.

Ilia didn't answer her immediately, but realized silence was an answer in itself. "No." She suspected Acca saw through her denial. "I'm a vestal. Untouchable."

"Yes, but he's both a man and a king. He can do whatever he likes."

"Don't worry. Livia has him well in hand."

She hoped that was true. Because whenever she and Amulius' paths had crossed of late—at the festivals, at the games—she didn't like how he stared at her. His glance lingered, too long, too hot. Perhaps Oppia, the overbearing cow, wasn't such a bad chaperone, after all.

A royal litter arrived for them an hour later, borne by four burly slaves. Oppia was jovial. In the House of Vestals, meals tended to be frugal. Tonight Oppia could eat as much as she liked. Ilia felt sick.

As the litter passed the Temple of Diana, with its oak grove and pale pillars glinting in the afternoon sun, she regarded it wistfully. The grove looked cool and inviting, full of promise and secrets. In happier days, she'd walked beneath those dark leaves to count the stars as they appeared. She had even imagined Diana inviting her to run with her nymphs. Now, she was forced to attend Amulius' *caristia*, this sham of family and blood.

In too short a time, they arrived at the villa. Even the atmosphere of the place seemed strained; the front pillars reminded her of bone. Torches, like fires leading to the underworld, flickered on gleaming steps.

A slave rushed up to their litter to set a stair for their feet.

"Such a perfect night." Oppia lumbered down the steps. "So kind of the king to include us."

Ilia hid her scowl. They passed from the *vestibulum* into the *atrium*, with its mosaic floor and statues of Venus and Mars—Amulius' contribution to home decoration. She wondered where the original statues of Juno and Jupiter were. Probably in some remote part of the villa, where they couldn't disapprove of what Amulius was doing.

The *triclinium* was stifling, overly hot with more torches burning along its walls. Slaves shone with perspiration and stood at attention. In the center of the dining room, a huge table was set with the flowers of Februarius, mauve crocus. Purple couches framed three sides of the table. On one, Amulius lay spooned against Livia. Her grandfather, Numitor, was on another, looking unhappy. The last awaited them.

"Finally!" Amulius rose, a goblet in hand. "Our rose of Vesta!" His toga was disheveled. The garland about his head had wilted and his broad face was flushed.

Already drunk, Ilia thought.

Oppia tittered. "Rose of Vesta! My word! You make me blush, your Majesty!"

"I didn't mean you," Amulius pursed his lips as if he'd tasted something sour. "I meant her, our grand-niece!"

"I see." Oppia's smile vanished.

Amulius waved at the air and dropped back onto the couch. "It will be as the gods ordain."

"Which gods might those be, my love?" Livia sat upright. She had chalked her face with too much lead, making her look pasty. Her eyelids were blue, heavy with azurite.

"Why Mars, of course." Amulius beetled his brow as if she should have known.

"Oh, Mars!" Livia let her lips linger on the 's'. "Of course! And Venus? We mustn't forget poor little Venus." She tugged at his toga.

He grinned at her. "*Always* Venus." He slumped down beside her and grabbed her breast.

Ilia tasted bile. Her grandfather, Numitor, cleared his throat. She took in his wan face and scraggly beard. *Here you sit at your own table, begging for scraps like a cur*, she thought. *He killed your own son, my father, and forced me to become a vestal. Why didn't you gut him when you had the chance? You're nothing but a coward.* If she'd been born a man, she would have sent Amulius screaming to hell.

"Should we eat?" Numitor suggested.

Amulius' hairy legs had entangled Livia's. For one brief second, everyone held their breath.

Fortunately, Amulius seemed to think food was more interesting than sex with his wife. He rolled from her and clapped his hands. "The *mensa prime!*" he bellowed. Livia adjusted her *stola*, as if nothing had happened.

"Thank Vesta." Oppia hurried to their couch. "If it had gone any further, we would have had to leave."

I wish we had, Ilia thought.

Slaves scurried from the doorway to set trays on the table. The first course consisted of fried womb with leeks and pork, oysters on the shell, and honey cakes. All aphrodisiacs.

"I'd like permission to return home, Vestal Mother." It was obvious what Amulius intended. Perhaps not with Numitor or Oppia—they would be dismissed, or expected to partake of each other—but what he meant for her and his wife. She kept her gaze on the door.

"You haven't eaten!" Amulius protested.

Ilia ignored him. He might be king, but over her, he held no dominion. The decision was Oppia's alone.

"Why?" Oppia eyes were slits.

Ilia stared at her, aghast. Had the chief vestal been a priestess for so long, she didn't recognize what lay before them? There could be no other explanation but naivety. "I don't feel well. If I stay, I might make everyone ill."

"Why didn't you say so, before?"

"I didn't want to disappoint you." A bold-faced lie, but it gave her an out.

"Very well. You may go." Oppia turned to Amulius, smiling faintly. "With your permission, of course, your Majesty."

They both knew she didn't need his permission. Once again, she was throwing her weight around.

Amulius turned a deep red. He looked as if he were about to debate it, but then his expression turned cagey. He turned to Ilia. "It's unfortunate you don't feel well. Since you don't, I'll call you a litter." He flicked a finger. A slave vanished into the hall. Servants were expected to know what their masters wanted without being asked. Then he disappeared after him.

"What? Where are you...?" Livia received no answer. Looking confused, she bid the guests to sit and eat. When Amulius returned, a female slave was with him. A chaperone to escort Ilia to her litter.

"Another time," Amulius murmured.

She didn't reply. There would be no other time if she could help it. Head held high, she descended the steps.

"I look forward to it," he called after her.

She waved in dismissal, not caring if he took it for agreement.

In the litter she felt protected, released from the chaos that was the *caristia*. Shortly, she'd be home, in her room, safe with Acca. *I'm free*, she thought. There was no Oppia to lecture her, no Amulius to leer. The litter shuddered to a halt, then dropped as if set down. There was a brief scuffling that faded. She parted the curtain. "What's going on?" she asked.

No one answered her. The slaves had vanished.

Fear tightened her gut but undaunted, she stepped from the litter. They had left her near the Grove of Diana. A nightingale called. She was alone.

What had scared them? She walked down the road fearing bandits, but that made no sense. They would have robbed or attacked her by now. A dim rider approached from the south. With her heart hammering, she dashed into the grove to hide behind an oak. The rider turned out to be a centurion. He paused at the litter, but finding no one inside, rode on. When he was gone, she released her breath.

There was nothing for it but to return to the House. Going back to the villa was out of the question. Still, it might be wiser to travel under cover for as long as she could. As she stepped further into the trees, the night closed about her. The sanctuary of Diana's temple was a tempting thought, but it would be cold. Best to keep moving.

She was half-way through the grove, when a snap came from behind her. She spun about, her pulse pounding in her ears. Her imagination threatened wolves. She peered into the darkness, forcing her eyes to see. "Goddess?"

When Diana didn't answer, she continued on, a little faster. Her back crawled; something was watching her every move.

She spotted a broken branch on the forest floor and snatched it up. As she straightened, a low growl came from her left.

"Get back!" She swung the limb about, hoping to keep whatever threatened her at bay.

"Or what?" came a voice. A man stepped out from behind a tree to her left. He had covered his head with a wolf pelt. The snout fell below his chin. There were dark slits for his eyes. Beneath the pelt, he wore the bronze plate of a soldier. Woolen *braccae* covered his legs.

"What do you want?" she demanded.

He laughed. A hateful *ha, ha, ha,* she recognized. She'd heard it often enough.

"Get away from me, Amulius!"

"Who's Amulius?" He stepped towards her. "I don't know any Amulius. I'm Mars, your god."

"I have no god, but Diana!"

"Really? I thought Vesta was your goddess." He swatted away the branch as if it were a twig. She turned to run, but he grabbed her and threw her to the dirt. As she screamed, he clamped a greasy hand over her lips. The other fumbled with her *stola*. Her vision turned grey; she bucked and twisted, forcing him to release her mouth. There was a rip. He had exposed her breasts. Then she was being crushed, the armour cutting into her chest as icy fingers forced her legs apart.

A vicious thrust. Sharp pain, and then wetness, hot and burning—blood? Shock overtook her as he grunted and pushed. She felt as if she were being ripped apart. Finally, there was a final plunge with a surge. Something inside her cracked. Her head swam, her legs felt cold. She tasted copper. Had she bitten herself? He loomed over her and tied up his drawstrings. She lay in pieces, a broken amphora on dead leaves. Let her be swallowed by the earth, never to emerge again.

"A pleasure. Say nothing. It will go better for you." He stood over her, awaiting her answer.

What was there to say? If she were whole, she might curse him for all eternity, but in the end, it all came to dust.

"Until next time," he promised. And then he was gone, disappearing into the trees like the god he claimed to be.

She lay there until the cold forced her to rise. She shook uncontrollably. She had been raped, in the holy grove of Diana, a place that should have remained sacrosanct, where she should have been protected. Where was her goddess now? Why did she not appear, to command her hounds to rip Amulius limb from limb? Diana was supposed to be a kind goddess, especially to women and children.

Diana had her cruel side, too.

When she finally reached the house, Acca was waiting for her in the courtyard, a lamp in hand. No one else was about, save for the sisters tending the holy fire, but they were too engaged to notice her arrival.

"Where have you been? I've been worried sick! Oppia was back over an hour ago!" Acca held the lantern high and took in her bloodied face and ruined clothes. "Oh, Ilia! What happened?"

She set the lamp down to catch her as she stumbled up the stair, then led her to their chamber to avoid prying eyes. Ilia moaned as she sat her down.

"Are you hurt? Show me!"

Ilia sat there, numb.

"Ilia!" Acca shook her shoulder. "You're scaring me!"

"Hemlock," she whispered.

"Hemlock? Why?"

When she didn't answer, Acca paled. Ilia cradled herself and began to cry—sharp, tight hiccups that started in her belly and forced their way up her throat. Everything hurt. Not knowing what else to do, Acca rocked her as she wept. It took all night for the storm to pass. By the time dawn painted the peaks, she had soothed her enough to coax the story from her.

"I'll kill him. I don't care if he is a king. I'll find a way." Acca clasped her about the shoulders.

Ilia remained mute. Not knowing how else to help, Acca drew her a bath. Then, once she had washed her and settled her to sleep, she made her way to Oppia to make their apologies. Ilia was ill and couldn't attend the fire that day. Oppia didn't like it, but accepted the excuse. Two days later and in a daze, Ilia fed the holy fire, only nodding dully when Oppia took exception to her efforts.

Mensis Iunius IX, Vestalia,
Anno III Amulius Rex,
Alba Longa:

"What am I going to do?" Ilia hung her head over the bowl. Her hair was loose and wet with sick. It was morning, after cock's crow.

"You can't be. It was only the once." Acca drew her hair away from her damp face.

"Once is enough." Ilia stared at her miserably. "It's been three flows. Oh gods, Acca. They'll kill me—"

"That *isn't* going to happen. I treated your rags with chicken's blood. They won't suspect."

"I'll have to abort or suicide."

"Nobody's suiciding. Instead, we'll…," Acca paused. "We'll run away. It won't be easy, but we'll go to Faustulus."

"Who?"

"My brother. He won't forsake us."

"I can't have this baby, Acca!"

"You won't. We'll deal with it, once we're safe."

"But when? The Vestalia's all week!" She glanced up at her miserably. "Oppia watches me like a cat on a mouse. The sisters, too."

"Maybe the Festival of Diana?"

"How? I'll be huge by then!"

"Don't fret! We'll arrange your *stola* so it only looks as if you've put on weight. Here, drink some water."

"I can't...."

Acca handed her a cup. "You must. If you can't eat, you have to drink. We need to get through this day, and then the next, and the next. One day at a time, Ilia."

With shaking hands, Ilia accepted the cup.

Nemoralia, Mensis Sextilis, XIII,
Anno III Amulius Rex,
Alba Longa:

It hadn't been difficult to convince Oppia. As a goddess, Diana was not to her liking, being too blood-thirsty for her tastes and the other vestals had already volunteered for the temples of Vortumnus, Fortuna Equestris, and Flora. Ilia would travel to the Huntress's pavilion to make the requisite sacrifice, then return to the House.

"I don't know if I can return there." She felt faint. July had been hot. August was even hotter. Being six months pregnant was taking its toll. Her feet were as swollen as bread loaves. She was as clumsy as a goose out of water.

"We'll go back, because we have to. Don't think about it." Acca tugged at her veil.

They had tried to leave twice before and were thwarted each time. There was always another vestal nearby, and when they were alone, they were interrupted on the thinnest of pretexts. While Ilia had been tending the holy fire, their chamber had been searched. Perpennia claimed she'd been looking for a misplaced veil, but they suspected she was looking for abortives. Acca hadn't been so stupid as to keep those around. She did, however, hoard her bread. They would need the extra food to cover their journey.

"Courage," Acca reminded her.

"Yes." Ilia hugged her, gaining strength from her resolve. In two days, the nightmare would be over. They would flee and be sought. Amulius would call out his guard. But no one would suspect a vestal, once a king's grand-daughter, to take up residence with a shepherd from the hills.

She travelled by litter to the temple. At sunset, the last archery contest took place. Only women competed in the *Nemoralia*, men being prohibited. It was a relief not to see Amulius there.

After the contest, the women entered the temple to leave their prayers and offerings at Diana's altar—trinkets of thanksgiving or pleas for help, all concerns that fell under her charge. Then it was Ilia's turn to enter, to sacrifice the *mola salsa*, the mixture of flour and salt she had prepared. Once alone, she held up the offering to the goddess' statue. Her arms felt weighted by lead. "Oh, great and wondrous goddess," she began. "She who sees all wrongs done, and seeks to make them right...."

Her voice broke. Flour fell from her fingers. Angry tears pooled in her eyes; her legs threatened to give out from beneath her. She clutched at the pedestal to remain upright, then stared at the statue accusingly.

Why didn't you stop him? she demanded silently.

Diana gazed down upon her implacably.

You saw what he did! And you haven't avenged me! He should be dead!

The statue remained unmoving.

She wanted to fly at it, to pummel it to gravel. "I don't believe in you anymore!" she shouted. Tears streamed down her face. "You hear me? You're a fraud! We pray to nothing but stone! You're not real. You never were!"

She let out a ragged wail. So much had been taken from her—her status, her virginity, and now, her faith. She'd been praying for a miracle. There was no one she could rely upon save herself.

She spit at the statue's base. The monster in her womb kicked twice, as if in reproach. She set her palms against her belly and closed her eyes. Soon. In another few months, she'd be rid of this ogre child.

She left the temple and slipped into the shadows on its far side, away from the fires. The women of Alba Longa paid her no heed. Dancing with abandon, they watched each other and the flames. They would celebrate until moon set. Stepping carefully, she found the path that led to freedom.

At a lone oak a short distance away, she waited for what felt like an hour. Far from the fire, the night was chill and the breeze set her to shivering. Acca should have been there by now. What was keeping her? She rubbed her arms and walked about in circles, trying to stay warm.

Another hour passed. Her intuition yammered warnings. Something was wrong.

Ten minutes later, torches jigged towards her confirming her dread. She thought to run, but the whiteness of her *stola* gave her away. She remained where she was, thinking to claim she was lost. Two vestals, Arruntia and Perpennia, held a staggering captive between them. The girl seemed drunk, unable to stay on her feet. With sudden horror, she realized it was Acca who sagged between them.

Oppia loomed behind them, with a crowd of celebrants in tow. "Don't you *dare* try to run, you whore! We know *all* about your pregnancy. We wrenched the whole story from your slave! You're no longer Ilia the vestal, but Rhea Silva, 'she who is guilty in the wood'! You'll pay the price!"

Acca lifted her head to regard her. Her face was swollen, marred by blood and bruises. They had broken her nose.

"We found her pilfering food," Oppia said. "When you didn't arrive, I asked questions." Ilia could only imagine what form those questions took.

"Get her," Oppia ordered, pointing. Fabia strode forward and caught her by the arms.

"Where are you taking me?" she demanded.

"To the one who will determine your fate."

They could only mean Amulius. As well as king, he also claimed the title of high priest. It was the Maximus Pontifex who administered punishment to the vestals. It appeared Oppia didn't know everything. She had no idea Amulius was the father.

They were escorted into the receiving room of the villa. Neither Amulius nor Livia appreciated being awakened in the middle of the night. Amulius looked as if he'd drunk too much wine and had donned his toga quickly. Livia still wore her face paint. They sat on two chairs, decorated with gilded cupids.

"You say she's pregnant?" Amulius leaned on an elbow, his bloodshot eyes wide with alarm.

"Indeed!" sniffed Oppia. "We don't know who the father is yet."

Livia spoke up. "Whoever he is, he'll pay the price."

Amulius flushed and glared down at Ilia, "Who is it?"

Three words, heavy with threat. Any man accused of lying with a vestal would be flogged to death. Would that law apply to kings? As for the vestal, her blood couldn't be shed, but she would be imprisoned until she gave birth. Afterward, the child would be thrown into the Tiber, the mother left to rot until she died.

He would deny any accusation she made against him. There was no way of proving anything. Always, men held the upper hand. Women were property, to be used, abused, or scapegoated, as they saw fit.

"I asked you a question!" he bellowed.

She flinched, but sensed the apprehension behind his words. *What if I accused him?* she wondered. They might not spill her blood, but she would still be flogged. There were ways to wield the whip without breaking the skin. What if she claimed a god had taken her? That might save her.

"Mars! The god Mars! He took me, as Jupiter took Leto!"

For a second, Amulius looked relieved, then he covered it with a look of incredulity. "You're saying, the god Mars took you, and you're carrying his get? A hero, possibly, or a demi-god?" He burst out laughing. Livia tittered. "You're lying," he added, once their laughter died. "Or confused. No god took you, or if he claimed he did, he was no god. It's more likely you rutted with a soldier in the wood."

No one had mentioned 'wood'. Oppia frowned. Livia stiffened, then glanced narrowly at Amulius.

Yes! Ilia met her hard gaze. *You've guessed it! Your darling husband raped me!*

"What shall we do with you?" Amulius' tone grew silky. He licked his lips. He was remembering or thinking of future possibilities.

"She'll be thrown in the dungeon, along with her slave." Livia stared down her nose at her. "She'll give birth, and then she and her child will never see the light of day!" Her nostrils flared and she turned a mottled red. "You've offended Vesta!" she cried. "We can't allow such a transgression to go unpunished! Other than my guards, you'll see no one, and no one will see you!"

Grasping for self-control, she sought Oppia's approval. The Vestalis Maxima nodded. Amulius looked disgruntled but allowed the judgement to stand.

"Take them away!" Livia ordered, her tone shrill. "Come, Papa. It's been a long night." She swept from the room with a glowering Amulius in tow.

Ieiunium Cereris, Mensis October IV,
Anno III Amulius Rex,
Alba Longa:

Two months passed. Ilia's hair was matted; she and Acca were dirty, she hardly recognized herself anymore, they wallowed in their own filth. Acca's nose had healed, but she would never look the same again. Meals arrived once a day, stale bread and water which they ate to keep from starving. As Livia had promised, no one but the guards saw them. Amulius had been effectively leashed by his wife.

There was a high window in their jail. During the day, they had a little light. Acca made a point of scratching the passing days into the stone to keep track of the time. One night, no meal came.

Acca checked her stone calendar. "It's the Remembrance of Ceres. Everyone's fasting. Especially us."

Ilia nodded, then lay down in the grimy straw to sleep. The baby was kicking hard now, as if angry at being denied its supper.

Let this horror be over, she wished. She'd considered asking Acca to strangle her. But then, where would that leave Acca? She didn't doubt Livia's promise. Even dead, they would be left there to rot.

Her dreams that night were hunger sent. At first she thought she was at a banquet, but the meal in front of her crumbled to gravel.

Perhaps if you hadn't spit at me, things would be different, said a voice. *I didn't like that.*

Diana, in all her huntress glory, sat opposite her. She wore a short tunic and leather sandals. Her quiver of arrows lay at her back, her bow at her side. She fingered the point of an arrow. *I think you owe me an apology.*

Ilia swallowed down her indignation. *I owe you? How rich. For-give me Goddess, but perhaps it's you who owe me! I'm the one who was violated in your grove. I'm the one who suffered! I asked you for vengeance, and this is what I get?* She indicated the dungeon, but in the dream, the banquet remained as it was.

You'll have your vengeance if you're willing to pay the price. Diana considered her sidelong.

Haven't I paid enough? Are you going to release me from this hell?

That's up to you. She spun the arrow in her fingers. The point began to glow.

What do you want?

Some respect, to start.

I'm sorry I doubted you. I shouldn't have spit at your statue. What else?

You need to be willing to change.

Wasn't eight months pregnant change enough? *Change how?*

However I deem best. It was clear she wanted her to agree without knowing what was involved. What did she have to lose? In a month, she'd be dead.

Agreed. I'll change.

Excellent. Diana nocked the arrow and aimed. Before Ilia could think to move, the head burst into flame. The arrow flew straight for her, then pierced her through, punching through her chest with the force of a javelin. Her body and mind exploded into madness. She burned with two opposing needs: to nurture or to kill. Suddenly, she was on a grassy field and running. An army fled before her, shouting in terror as she chased them down. Then she was no longer on that field, but in a hut, with a baby suckling contentedly at her breast.

She awoke, gasping for breath. No burning shaft speared her, no child nursed. Acca lay at her back, snoring softly as usual. *A dream, and nothing more*, Ilia thought. Diana had not honored her side of the bargain. But then, maybe Diana didn't exist. She lay there, too ex-hausted to think.

The Last Day of Saturnalia, Mensis December XXIII,
Anno III Amulius Rex,
Alba Longa:

Her contractions were every thirty seconds, her belly tightening in-to wood, the pain keen and sharp, rising, peaking, then falling. Acca crouched between her knees and shouted encouragement. In the mo-ments of clarity between contractions, she was aware of the guards making bets.

"It's coming!" Acca cried. "I can see its head! Push, now, Ilia! Push hard!"

The world went black, then blood red. She was giving birth to what felt like a world. A final push, the earth cracked, and then…the sharp cries of a baby. Her belly tightened again. Why wasn't the agony over?

"Oh my, another one!" Acca was between her legs, pressing on her belly with a free hand. "Twins, Ilia! You're having twins!"

Curses from the guards outside the cell, all their bets lost. With an-other great push, her second was born. There was a stuttering cry. She slumped into the straw, her arms giving out from beneath her.

"Shhh! Here's your mama." Acca tucked the twin boys beneath each of her arms. At their contact, her exhaustion fled and an over-whelming sense of protection flared in her, growing fierce.

The door to their cell clanged open. Acca yelped as a guard kicked her aside. A second guard reached for her boys.

Her heart burst into flame. How dare they try to touch them? She found herself on all fours, growls erupting from her throat, her limbs and head lengthening. With a snarl, she drew back her muzzle and lunged at the first guard, tearing out his throat with cruel teeth. Then she was on the other, claws punching through his armour like onion skin. The guards beyond the cell cried in shock. As she flew at them, they scattered like hares with nowhere to run. In moments they all lay dead, shredded and bloodied heaps at her feet.

She licked her lips, savouring the taste. Eyes narrowing, she considered the last human huddled against the wall.

"I won't touch them," it whispered, pointing at her cubs.

Beneath the stink of spilled blood and bowel, she smelt the girl's fear. This wouldn't take long. A rumble rose from deep within her chest. Her hackles rose.

Whimpers broke her focus. Her cubs were fussing, they needed to nurse. Her teats ached. The desire to flop down and nudge them to a nipple was overwhelming. But they weren't like her. They were human. Like the girl.

"Ilia, please!" the girl pleaded.

Acca. This was no enemy, but her friend. The red veil of her madness departed, revealing a new reality. The goddess *had* changed her. She was a *lupa* now, a she-wolf—something from out of a nightmare, from the netherworld. The walls were spattered with blood and flesh—her doing. The coppery taste in her mouth blossomed afresh, igniting an inferno. Her fur felt too tight, this place was too small. If she didn't leave now, she would combust. Amulius. She would find him and rip him, limb from limb.

But…her babies were crying! Did they sense the bloodshed, or were they hungry and cold? How could she leave them? If she abandoned them to search for Amulius, Acca wasn't strong enough to protect them if more guards came. She let out a tortured whine.

"You may have killed them," Acca indicated the guards, "but you can't kill an army. We need to run before Amulius learns of this. If you'll let me, I'll take the boys, Ilia. We'll go to Faustulus, as planned. I don't know how this happened or why. Just that it has. Do you understand me? Please goddess, I pray that you do." She waited.

Regret and frustration filled Ilia. Maternal instinct finally won out. The safety of her babies was tantamount. She nodded her great, shaggy head, a movement both foreign and familiar.

"Good." Without dropping her scrutiny, Acca reached for the twins.

Agonalia, Festival of Janus,
Mensis Januarius I,
Palantine Hill:

Ilia dozed by the fire, her babies nursing at her belly. At a small loom, Acca wove a blanket while Faustulus skinned a rabbit by the hut's door. In their humble way, they had celebrated the *Agonalia*, the Festival of Janus, the two-faced god who looked to both past and future. Her contribution had been the hare.

Romulus, the larger of her twins, knocked a tiny fist against his brother's cheek. Remus let out a squawk.

"I suppose they come by that honestly. Shall I move them?" Acca asked.

Ilia shook her head and nudged Remus to a different teat. He grimaced, then returned to his nursing.

The fire was warm. She closed her eyes to drift off to sleep. They may have escaped Amulius, but she was far from content. As Diana had promised, she would have her vengeance, but not by her hand. Being turned into a *lupa* was the last thing she had expected.

And what's wrong with that?

She blinked. The hut had vanished. Diana sat beside her. They were on a grassy knoll, overlooking seven low hills.

Nothing, unless you were human once, she replied.

Is being a wolf so bad? You're wild and free. No one can molest you.

I'm a woman in a wolf's body. I still don't have my revenge.

That score is for others to settle. Watch. Diana waved her hand. Suddenly, they were peering into a deep, still lake. Pictures formed beneath its surface. In a dim bedroom, a muscular youth thrust a sword through a sleeper's belly. The victim woke, his eyes wide with horror. Then he vomited blood as his assassin laughed. Another youth, a twin, capered and cheered. Here lay her vengeance. Amulius—murdered by her *boys*.

The view shifted again. Now she gazed upon a great city set upon the seven hills. Temples rose throughout it; there were villas and smaller homes. People and chariots milled up and down its cobbled streets.

Rome, Diana murmured, as if in grudging approval. At one temple, congregants made sacrifice before the statue of a she-wolf nursing two babies.

The Lupinalia, to honour you. You'll be revered as the mother of the greatest empire there ever was. You're both a demi-goddess and an empress. How's that for vengeance?

Ilia considered the scene before her. Her heart swelled with approval. Such irony—that Amulius should die at her sons' hands. She had the best of what life had to offer—a true and loving friend in Acca, her boys, and the sponsorship of a goddess.

I'm satisfied, she said, *save for one thing.*

What's that? Diana frowned. One did not demand extras from a goddess, especially when said goddess had already been more than generous.

If you don't mind, I'd like my old body back. Ilia scratched at her neck. *I think I have fleas.*

Oh. Diana shifted away from her slightly. *Very well, then.* She withdrew an arrow from her quiver and aimed.

The Tale of King Edgar

L.S. Johnson

When they bring the baby to him, Edgar looks down at the mewling creature with the face like a piece of crumpled, bloody silk and feels the knot in his belly loosen. "Call him Bertram," he says, flicking aside the swaddling cloth to confirm the sex. "He'll do. Though I may have to pay someone to marry him, with a face like that."

The laughter of his retinue carries him out of his castle, onto his horse, and into the great sun-filled world that is his kingdom. A day without omens, and therefore full of possibility. He rides hard and far, his retinue bellowing his praises over the thunderous hoofbeats, shouting of a future of contented fullness. He has an heir. He has certainty.

When at last Edgar reaches his duke's smaller, shabbier castle, he leaves the parley to those with a bent for such things; he eats his fill and drinks far more; he is given a woman and his duke's own bed and so many skins of wine he trips over them in the night.

When he catches his reflection in the moat, chasing yet another of the wide-eyed girls that seem to await him in every niche and crevice—do they grow them here, he wonders, like the fields of flax they had passed—his reflection makes him smile. He is handsome and strong; he is king, head of both a people and a dynasty, now. He can do as he pleases. The thought more exciting than the girl's unlaced dress.

Upon his return he finds that the red-faced, squalling creature has been transformed: in its place is a plump, scrubbed baby with a somber gaze that makes Edgar look away. A gaze designed, it seems, for him alone; for everyone else Prince Bertram is all smiles. Sometimes Edgar, king of everything as far as his eye can see, is left standing for several heartbeats without proper acknowledgment while the women fuss over the cradle.

When Edgar looks upon that solemn, staring face—*so like yours* the women coo—for the first time he feels the specter of death.

In honor of Bertram's first birthday, Edgar hosts three days of games and competes in them himself. He jousts and wrestles, shrugging off his retinue's concern. He even wounds one of his knights, crippling the man; still Edgar feels driven by some nameless thing in his belly, something serpentine and barbed whose squirming makes him fidget on his throne and toss in his bed. When the games end he turns himself from fighting to fucking: he takes his queen, he takes her ladies, he takes the women he sees in his halls and his kitchens and his cellars, he carries off pretty girls from the marketplace and the best whores right out of the brothel, and once he even snatches a woman straight from the fields, her skirts still full of seed and soil when he takes her in a nearby copse, his retinue politely turning their backs.

Only when his queen's womb swells again does the snarling, squirming thing in his belly grow quiet. A second son. Edgar would show no preference; he would hint, discretely, that the succession was an open question. Let Bertram and his brother fight it out with sword and wit; it would ensure the best man took the throne. Better still would be to have three, four, even five sons. Edgar would keep silent right through his dotage; only on his deathbed would he pronounce the name of his heir, the one most fit to take his place.

When he hears the first cries he goes to his queen's chambers, where an identical red-faced creature awaits him. He opens the swaddling cloth before anyone can speak, only to stare in bewilderment.

And when he comes out of the room again the first thing he sees is Bertram, standing upright like a tiny man, looking at him with the cool appraisal of a farmer planning to cull his herd.

The hall is full, full of his household and his knights, full of his dukes and his earls and their households and their knights, all their voices mingling and echoing off the walls in a cacophony that makes his ears ring. Dozens of eyes follow Edgar's every move and note his every gesture; his words are squirreled away like the tastiest morsels, the better to be picked apart in the days to come. So many decisions will be based on a lingering touch or a casual remark. All day he has been praised to the skies, given chests overflowing with tithes, offered parcels of land and comely daughters.

He has never been so happy.

The servants bring food, piles of it on large wooden boards: roasted beavers, pheasants, a magnificent peacock with its tail in full spread; pies and cassoulets; the first sweet fruits from his orchards. At last the roar of voices quiets as they begin eating, scooping up the food with curled fingers. This too Edgar revels in: the sight of them all swilling like pigs at a trough, every swallow binding them more completely to his rule.

And then a high, lisping voice says, "but why shouldn't we negotiate?"

The sound stabs Edgar in the gut. He nearly rises from his seat at the sudden cramping he feels; he looks around the room, momentarily heedless of his affect on those around him, until he sees Bertram's small body at a nearby table. Flanked by an earl and his nephew, the two looking down in amusement.

"A king should be fair," Bertram blithely continues. "He should always negotiate first. That is the mark of a good king."

"Your son," someone says in Edgar's ear, "is forming alliances over his pap. Born to rule, that one."

Edgar can barely see for his rage. *Negotiating*. Just to say that word in the wrong ear. Just to *say* it. As if anything had ever been won with words, as if every inch of his kingdom hadn't been won with steel and blood. It is all he can do to keep from throwing himself over the table and beating the boy back into the bloody pulp he was born as.

Instead he seizes the nearest servant, swallowing to keep the snarl out of his voice. "It is time," he says, "for the prince to retire."

Watching the servant coax Bertram away, he doesn't notice the pie that is laid before him. Bertram protests, then starts to cry; those around him recoil and Edgar exhales, his anger slowly ebbing. *See?* he silently declares to the hall. *See? He is nothing but a child, he can affect nothing, he might as well not even exist!*

He hears, on the edge of his awareness, a strange twittering noise; he realizes a hush has fallen over the gathering. As Bertram and the servant leave he turns back to the pie and plunges his knife into the crust, eager to resume the feast.

The twittering changes to a high-pitched shriek. There are gasps of horror as the crust falls away, revealing a living raven, black-feathered and wild-eyed, its breast and wing now bloodied from the knife. Its garbled, wheezy cries scrape at Edgar's mind. It tries to hop free from the dish, its one good wing flapping impotently. Edgar senses the others' shock and revulsion; he remembers that the cook had mentioned a trick to entertain the guests. Now that trick has made him look a fool.

He tries to seize the bird, to break its neck and put it out of its misery; but the raven lunges at him, stabbing at his hand with its sharp beak. Again gasps go up; one of Edgar's knights makes to help, only to stop halfway, unsure of whether or not to intervene. Again Edgar tries to seize the bird, this time taking up his knife again, but with a mighty push of its uninjured wing the raven manages to propel itself out of the dish and off the table, landing wetly on the stone below.

Then everyone is out of their seats, the men crawling under the tables, the women twisting at their skirts. Cries go up as one or another nearly seizes the bird, followed by more of those garbled shrieks; one after another the men reappear, holding bloodied hands and looking furious.

"It's a sign, an omen," someone gasps, but when Edgar turns to see who spoke everyone seems caught up in the hunt for the raven.

At last the hall quiets down, the men looking askance at each other; a murmur runs through the crowd that the bird has vanished.

Edgar feels sweat rising on his brow. Quickly he gestures to the empty crust. "Take it away," he says, his voice ringing with authority. "You, and you there, look for the bird, it is hiding in some corner. I don't want it stinking up the place." He sweeps the crowd with a look, silencing all murmurs. "And I want that cook put in chains; I will deal with him later."

Still there is only silence, until he pours himself more wine and drinks deeply. Only then do the others dare to resume their conversations; but Edgar knows they are speaking not of him but of what they just witnessed, and what it might mean.

Later, when he leaves the hall, he pauses by the open door of his daughter's room and watches her sleep. She never offers opinions, or insinuates herself with crafty earls. She merely smiles at Edgar, and gives him sweet little kisses, and tries to crown him with flowers. She is learning to sew and sing. Such a simple thing, to raise a girl.

When he closes his eyes that night, all Edgar can see is the raven, looking at him with that wild fury in its eyes.

The women are singing. There has been a third child, another girl; they are singing to her in the nursery:

Lavender's blue, diddle diddle
Lavender's green,
When I am king, diddle diddle
You shall be queen

Do they always do this? Edgar cannot say, but it irks him. In times past he left during this period, when his queen was still too weak to receive him. But this time he has lingered to see to Bertram's education, and he is regretting it.

Between them, on the broad oak table, lie scattered the papers of his rule, the terms of surrender and the divisions of land, the seals and marks of all those beneath him. Every scrap speaks to Edgar of the past: of the men he killed in battle, of the ones he cowed into obedience; of the houses scoured for goods and then burnt; of the fields piled with slaughtered livestock, their dead eyes following him. Of the screams of dying children, not unlike the cries of the raven.

All of it years ago now.

Yet Bertram sees nothing, hears nothing. Learns nothing. "Why are the tithes so uneven?" he asks, again.

Edgar sighs. How to explain that it is not a matter of abacus and paper, that it is a far more complex sum of harvests and goods, slights and favors, strategic values and strategic costs?

"I do not see," Bertram continues, "why we cannot come up with a fairer kind of reckoning. You are asking double here what you are here—" he holds up two documents— "yet the first has far less land than the second! It's completely arbitrary! No wonder we keep hearing rumors about a rebellion."

Edgar leans forward and smacks the first paper. "That," he says loudly, "is an asshole who must constantly be brought to heel, and that—" he smacks the second paper—" is a man who has known his place since I took the throne, and has a right to expect favor in turn. *That* is the reckoning."

In the ensuing silence the women sing:

There they did play, diddle diddle
And kiss and court
All the fine day, diddle diddle
Making good sport

He waits for some sign of Bertram's understanding. But he is met only with that somber stare, delivered under a brow growing dark and wide with age, framed by a widow's peak that Edgar knows matches his own. The boy has his jawline as well, the women tell him it is a shared trait, that when the prince becomes angered he is the spit of the king.

Now Bertram raises his chin, his lips compressed, and Edgar knows what this means: that his son thinks him wrong, only he knows it is not to his advantage to say so.

Edgar knows this, for he has seen his own face in exactly such a pose, when he has had to bide his time.

And when that time came, oh how he had reveled in delivering the blows—

Lavender's blue, diddle diddle
Lavender's green
Let me be king, diddle diddle
You be the queen

"Get out," he says, and turns away, rubbing his jaw as if he had been punched.

At last he manages to break away from his retinue. A few knowing remarks, a couple of elbows to the ribs, and Edgar slips through his rooms and out into the narrower hall for his own private use. Right leads to his queen's chambers; left leads down towards his servants' quarters and the far side of his castle. Supposedly for escape during a siege, but Edgar uses it for a different kind of escape.

After all, his queen is with child yet again. There was a lost child after his second daughter, the women told him it was a boy; but Edgar has had his fill of sons. Already he is thinking to send Bertram away, on some kind of tour or campaign; he's sick of seeing that stare at every turn, he's sick of the endless questions he knows are waiting behind Bertram's compressed lips.

All that, and lately Edgar feels uneasy when he sees his son conversing in the hall. He was impatient at that age; he would have been more so if he had not felt such deep respect for his own father...and has Bertram ever felt a whit of respect for him? Has he ever seen Edgar as anything other than a thing to best, if not with strength then with his relentless questions, designed to undermine his king's authority at every turn?

But Edgar can think on that later.

There is, after all, a new maid. A choice armful, everyone agrees; even his queen's ladies have remarked upon her comeliness. Edgar has made a study of her: he thinks of her at the meeting table and in the pew, in his bed at night and when he would do his duty with his queen. He knows every swell of her figure, every drop of moisture when she sweats in her chores, and oh but he will make her sweat tonight.

At her door he pauses, listening. Instead of silence there are faint noises: panting and moans, a familiar creaking rhythm. The little trollop. He is at once annoyed and intrigued, for he made his interest known from her first day, and he cannot think who would dare to trump him, no matter how plain her invitation.

Edgar opens the door silently, and as the room becomes visible he feels a familiar pain in his belly. For he knows all too well the young, lean body pressed between her thighs, the cracking voice that sings out as he works at her:

I sow'd the Seeds of Love
And I sow'd them in the spring

This boy. This creature he spawned. The maid giggles and kisses Bertram and he's laughing as he sings, he laughs into her plump red mouth. Would that she could have seen him at birth, seen the mewling, bloody flesh that he had been. Would she be giggling now? Oh she would not.

Being poked by a boy. A mere boy. Clearly she sought his favor, perhaps she even sought to trick him into promises, get the king's son bound to her with vows and a babe and the things she could ask for then...

Edgar turns away, his stomach clenching so violently he thinks he will be sick. A mere boy, bedding *that*. He should storm in, thrash his son and throw her out into the night with only her sheet for a cover. A mere boy, in *her* bed. He cannot even think of her now without seeing Bertram's thin body rutting over her like some rangy jackrabbit.

Edgar stumbles down the hallway, clutching at his stomach; halfway back to his rooms he vomits, the sounds echoing in the darkened hall, bile spattering his shoes.

His rooms, though he only left them a few minutes ago, feel empty and cold. When he climbs into bed he is overwhelmed by a strange, musty odor: as if his bed hadn't been slept in for ages, as if he had died long ago.

He spends his days with his daughters—three of them now, and each a pretty thing, he'll have no trouble marrying them off—letting them sing to him and read to him, letting them show him their dances and their embroideries. He tells everyone it is because his queen is dead that he spends so much time with them, but in truth their affection is the only thing that quiets the writhing serpent in his belly, the bright, sharp pain that bursts forth at the mere sight of his son.

That Bertram had sobbed endlessly when his mother died, that he had to be dragged from her bedside... Edgar could understand it; he could, perhaps, even wonder at it; but it did not soothe the beast inside him.

So instead he bides his time, and spends his days with his daughters, and at last one night he whispers to a single trusted man about his son, and then whispers to a second trusted man about the first.

When Bertram comes to say goodbye Edgar makes a good show of it, hugging him and rubbing his head, speaking well of the figure he cuts in his armor, how he will impress everyone on his first tour of the kingdom. It takes everything Edgar has to utter that neutral *the*. He wants to say *my kingdom*, wants to scream it in Bertram's face; he knows for appearances' sake he should have said *our kingdom*; yet to pronounce the latter, he fears, would make the serpent in his belly burst agonizingly forth.

Bertram says something about making him proud, but Edgar barely hears him; he is distracted by the sight of his queen's eyes peering at him from beneath that dark brow. His youngest daughter is the spit of her mother, but how strange that he never realized Bertram has those same wide eyes—

"I still don't see why we should not go together," Bertram says.

The words cut through Edgar's thoughts like a blade. He nearly thanks the boy for this last challenge to his authority; instead he says, loud enough for the room to hear, "I trust you as I trust myself."

Only when Bertram is walking away does Edgar nod once to his man and make a hidden sign. And then the matter is done, and he thinks of it no more.

Three pretty daughters. Already he is contemplating possible matches for them, imagining the outcome of this or that alliance. After the mourning period he will hold games; that will incite some proper competition. Falling over each other to prove themselves the most loyal and obedient. A wonder he hadn't thought of it before: why leave such matters to fickle Nature, when you could cherrypick your succession?

He has learned a lesson, these past years, about like minds. He has learned many lessons—

"Father, will you not wave goodbye?" His eldest daughter beckons him to the window, her handkerchief fluttering in her hand.

He goes to join them, smiling as they press against him, and watches Bertram ride away. Every foot between them like a salve to his aching stomach. In a tree near the window he sees a cardinal contentedly nesting and finds himself smiling with relief at such a clear omen.

The rightness of it all. His halls his own, his beds his own. No more staring, no more ridiculous questions. The lesson well and truly learnt: daughters are a far better investment than sons.

"I will miss him," his second daughter says. "But he'll have such a good time with his friends."

"Friends?" Edgar asks absently, still watching the cardinal.

"Oh, Bertram has lots of friends," his eldest says. "Dukes and earls from all over, and a whole host of knights. He said a grand company is waiting for him just a ways down the road. You should have gone with him, Father, you would have had a wonderful time."

Edgar stares at the road, watching his son disappear over the rise. *Dukes and earls. A host of knights.*

"I'm glad you stayed," his youngest daughter tells him. "Let Bertram be king out there. You can be king right here!"

"Silly girl," his second says, "there cannot be two kings."

She gathers up the youngest and they begin to drift away, still chattering among themselves, fluttering about each other like birds. Yet Edgar cannot move. *A grand company is waiting for him.* The serpent in his stomach has become as heavy and as cold as stone, a dread so overwhelming it threatens to take his legs.

As he stares at the empty road, struggling to understand, a broad shadow flits across his field of vision. The raven curves upwards, then dives into the tree with a fearsome cawing, setting the branches into a blur of movement. But when the leaves become still once more there is nothing to see: raven, cardinal, and nest have all vanished; all that remains are a few scarlet feathers, drifting away on the breeze.

Better Angels

Angela Slatter

"How far down, missus?"

The woman's staring not at the hole in the wet ground, nor at the tall bearded man who's asked her a question, but back at the house behind her. She's half-turned, the top of her torso twisted almost impossibly, almost fluidly, in defiance of the strictures of the steel-stayed corset beneath her plain black dress. The sandstone house is two storeys, wide verandahs running around both levels, walls punctured by doors and floor-to-ceiling windows, all of which are open, their shutters pinned back despite the cold and the rain.

"Missus?" His voice is low and rough, still thick with the accent of his native Bristol, but tender.

Fionnuala Farrell's eyes are pinned on the small group clustered on the lower verandah: an older woman, plump, dark-haired, with a white apron over her navy frock; three small girls, hair as red-gold as their mother's, not yet in mourning attire because no one had thought to make any for them so early in their young lives.

"Missus? Missus Farrell?"

The woman shakes herself as if coming to, and looks down. As if the man and the hole he's knee-deep in are new to her. As if the other man, the shorter one, who's gazing at her with cold pity and bold assessment, is a stranger. As if she cannot begin to recall how they came to be here, standing in the rain in what might be an elaborate English garden rather the highlands of Tasmania.

"How far?" repeats the man patiently. "How far?"

The intricate white lace collar circling her throat looks yellowed beside the pallor of her face, and the grey eyes seem barren as the sky. Then there's a moment when the questioner sees a spark flare in the dead ice of her gaze, and knows she's dropped back into herself.

Fionnuala peers at him, takes in the mud streaks and grass stains, the soaking fabric of his shirt, waistcoat and trousers, the beads of rain in his black beard and the beetling brows. Clearly he doesn't want to keep working; he keeps glancing towards the small stone hut where there are beds, a fire, and the end of a bottle of rum he's made last almost a month. His companion in misery is smart enough to keep his expression neutral, his mouth shut. A border has been marked around them with a low iron fence; this is the first time a cemetery has been needed at Gracemere.

"Six feet, Mr Donovan. My husband deserves nothing less."

"But, Mrs Farrell—"

"All the way down," she replies in harsh tones. "Thylacines, Mr Donovan. I do not want my children waking one morning to find their father food for animals."

She stares at him until he looks away, muttering "Yes, missus."

"The ground's soft, shouldn't take you long." Her tone is flat, even, carries no hint of everything spinning inside her. She looks at the diggers, the hole, a moment longer, then pivots on her heel. Her steps as she walks towards the building are precise.

There is another man, digging a trench from the side of the house out to the garden, where pipes are to be laid. There's not enough room for three men to work the grave, but he's in no way spared from labouring duties. He's not as tall as Donovan, nor as broad as Fetch, but he's handsome and younger than both, with ruddy brown hair and a tidy beard, light sage eyes; beneath his clothing, which fits well enough to show a degree of vanity, he's lean and muscular.

As the woman passes him, she gives him not a glance, though he ducks his head in greeting, and murmurs, "Missus."

Fionnuala Farrell nods curtly but doesn't answer, doesn't meet the green gaze. As soon as she sets a foot on the bottom step of the verandah, she falters; her knees giving way to weakness. The children break from the housekeeper's skirts and go to their mother. Her hands rest on them. Mrs Lenahan watches, waits for a few seconds before she comes over to help, placing a callused hand on Fionnuala's arm. Before she allows herself to be pulled along, the mistress of the house glances over her shoulder, across the cleared land of the garden and beyond, out to the trees that surround the house, thick and dense eucalypts.

When she at last disappears inside, the rain comes down all the harder. The men keep at their tasks.

Patrick Farrell lies on the heavy mahogany table in the formal dining room. Black cloth beneath him, and a frilled pillow to rest his head as if it might make a difference to him. Dressed in his Sunday best, he's not a tall man—a good head shorter than his lofty wife—and stout. Clean-shaven but for a thick moustache, and balding so there's not enough hair to hide the bruised and broken crevasse in the right side of his head.

Outside, the watery daylight is fading and the room is in shadow; some lines of grey light drift in through the open French windows. Fionnuala rests in a stiff-backed chair; the other seven—burgundy velvet padded—line the far wall so it doesn't look as though the family will sit down to a strange supper. She cannot imagine eating in here ever again. Her feet are placed on the expensive rug like she might rock back and forth if the seat were correctly configured. There's a rocking chair up in the girls' room, where she'd sit to nurse them when they were new; perhaps the action is one that gave her comfort then and she'd like to repeat it now. Perhaps the ground simply feels like the only solid thing around her.

She can hear Mrs Lenahan answering questions from the girls: *Where's Papa truly if not on the dining room table? When will Mama be better? Why do the angels need Papa?* Talk of heavenly creatures sets her teeth on edge.

There's a knock, which pushes the dark wooden door further open.

"Missus?" Donovan's still wet and covered in mud; hasn't bothered to wash and change before he came to see her. She wonders if it's deliberate. Water falls to the parquet floor, soughs into the weave of the rug. Fionnuala doesn't answer, keeps her eyes on her husband's face.

"We're done. Six feet. All the way down." He sounds resentful.

The woman nods.

Donovan turns away, then back when she asks, "How long have you been with us?"

"Six years, missus." He clears his throat. "Fetch too. Him and me got assigned here at the same time when we got our tickets of leave."

Fionnuala notes he doesn't mention the younger man, Flynn. "It's hard for everyone, Donovan."

"He was a good master."

"Yes. A good man." She pauses. "I'm sorry I was sharp with you today."

"You're the boss, missus. Leastways until you sell up." There's a lick of malice in his pitch, which she ignores.

"Sell up? Mr Donovan, I'm not going anywhere."

"Be hard for a woman on her own…"

"Still not as hard as losing him," she says softly; faced with the rawness of her grief he coughs. "See Mrs Lenahan before you go back to quarters. There's a cask of brandy for you all."

"That's generous, missus!" His mood lifts with his voice. Her loss offset by the thought of a good drink.

"It's from Patrick's store; he'd be happy for you all to have it. Give him a good send-off, Donovan."

"Thank you, missus."

"All of you; make sure Flynn gets a share."

There's a hesitation that confirms his dislike of the newest arrival, the six-month wonder favoured by both the Farrells. "Yes, missus."

"I don't…" Her incomplete thought interrupts him mid-turn.

"Missus?"

"I don't understand."

"What, missus?"

"What happened to him. I don't understand why Patrick fell."

"The horse must have been spooked, missus," he says gently. "Maybe Mr Farrell wasn't paying attention."

"But he was an expert horseman, Donovan."

"Sad to say, missus, better than the master have been thrown before and will be again." He almost whispers, "Something spooked the horse, maybe a damned rabbit is all, a bird breaking cover."

Slowly, she nods. "Perhaps. But where's his vesta case?"

Fionnuala had given it to her husband as a gift, his initials engraved on the front.

"Can't say, missus. Must have fallen into the grass, down a rabbit hole. We didn't see it anywhere when we found him." He looks perplexed, wonders if there's another question there, an accusation he should address.

"Goodnight, Donovan."

"Goodnight, missus."

She sees his hand closing the door and says a little too quickly, "You must leave it open."

When he's gone Fionnuala returns to her vigil. Outside the French doors, out in the garden, close to the house is a silhouette, which she fails to notice because her husband sits up, straight from the waist.

The pillow falls to the floor. Patrick twists his head on his neck to face her, but at least she can't see that terrible wound. She blinks, swallows, clutches at her own throat.

"I know what you did, Fionnuala," he vomits the words. She knows from examining him that he'd bit his tongue in the fall, almost taken it off, so it's no surprise that forming sounds is so hard for him, so discordant. Fionnuala closes her eyes, hard, counts to three before she opens them.

Patrick is lying down again, the pillow beneath his head still; the fabric on which he lies is untroubled. But now a trickle of blood leaks from the corpse's nostrils, and out from under his lids too. Fionnuala rises, takes hesitant steps to the table. She stares at the crimson-black, then looks at the doorway that Donovan's left not long ago.

The blood bubbles as if there's breath behind it, but Patrick's chest doesn't move, he's not alive. There's just the echo of his words in her ears: "I know what you did, Fionnuala."

"No," she says softly, "you don't."

The darkness between the house and the worker' hut feels like an ocean as Fionnuala stares across it. Against the small square windows are the shapes of men weaving back and forth, dancing, holding mugs in the air, any enmity set aside for however short a time. Behind her the dining room is aglow; Mrs Lenahan gives the body on the table one final examination, rubs the top lip again with a stained cloth, then straightens. She joins Fionnuala as the noise of the farewell comes on the breeze.

"Disrespectful," mutters the housekeeper. The taper in her hand that she's used to light the lamps is burning down slowly. She doesn't blow it out; the flame illuminates both their faces. Somehow Fionnuala appears older.

"They liked Patrick. Liked working for him. They'll have to get used to answering to me."

"And good luck with that. Donovan and Fetch, they'll be all right if they learn to hold their tongues. Other one doesn't say much." She touches Fionnuala's shoulder. "A man as can keep his mouth shut is rare and wonderful."

Fionnuala half-laughs, half-sighs. Briefly, she leans her weight into Mrs Lenahan's palm, then straightens away. "Hopefully they'll all stay. We need them. Donovan and Fetch have been here long enough to know the ropes. I don't fancy having to break new ones in."

"They'll be coming soon, you know. All the single men, looking for a wife. Rich widows are rare enough here." Mrs Lenahan catches sight of Fionnuala's expression in the guttering glow. She shakes the last of the flame away so she doesn't have to see the devastation on her mistress' face. "Ah, love, I'm sorry. My tongue's running from me."

"I barely remember a life before him," whispers Fionnuala. She remembers the sensation, though, of it; of being trapped on her father's estate, of being defiant in the only way she knew how. She remembers having to marry Patrick Farrell, who was kind and convenient. Who knew everything and was still kind. She remembers the little boy, born too soon and buried beneath the rose bushes in the western garden of the lonely Dublin mansion. Had the need arisen, Patrick Farrell would have given the child his name. She remembers the escape he offered. And she'd so badly requited him.

"They'll all come with the same excuse: be needing a man around," Mrs Lenahan mutters words Fionnuala's heard from more than one mouth.

Fionnuala clears her throat, changes the topic. "Is it done, then?"

"All clean and tidy, Mrs Farrell." Mrs Lenahan speaks offhandedly.

"What does it mean?" Fionnuala asks though she already knows. "Such a thing."

The older woman says nothing.

"You answer me." Fionnuala grabs the housekeeper's upper arm, and the other woman gasps. "The blood…"

"Old wives' tales and superstitious nonsense," the housekeeper hisses. "That a corpse bleeds when its murderer is close? Only a fool would believe that. Your man was thrown, his horse spooked. Sad but unfortunate. When they're dead, they're dead."

"Yet you're the one who said the doors need to be left open, to let him pass through, get used to being dead. That the grave earth should be salted after he's laid down, to keep him there." The two women stare at each other. "You're a terrible liar, Nelly Lenahan. We both know such a thing's been enough to get men hung back home… blood witness…"

"Only two people were in that room when he bled, you and Donovan. Should I think either of you…" She licks her lips as if parched. "Sometimes bodies just bleed after death is all. Doesn't mean we don't take precautions." After a pause, the housekeeper touches the girl's hand, and makes a *tsk* sound. "Lord in Heaven, you're frozen. How can you be so cold and not shiver?"

"I don't feel it," says Fionnuala, her voice almost musical. "Don't feel much of anything at all."

"Come along. Say goodnight to your girls. They need you."

Fionnuala's earlier annoyance at the housekeeper's faith flares like blown-upon embers. "Don't promise them angels, Nelly. We'd need better ones than I deserve."

Fionnuala wakes in fright in the lonely centre of the four-poster bed; the extra covers feel too heavy. Despite the cold, her long nightgown is damp with sweat, as is her hair. She sits up and scans the moonlit room. There's just the movement of the curtains in the icy gust, nothing else, yet she can't help but know something's not right. Rising, she pads bare-footed into the corridor. Empty, all as it was when she retired; she doesn't know how long she's slept, but suspects it cannot be long.

She hears a noise—a whimper, an animal cry or a child's—at almost the same moment she realises the door to her daughters' room is closed. Fionnuala frowns. Surely Mrs Lenahan wouldn't have made such a mistake? There's a golden glow in the gap beneath, showing that the lamp she let her girls keep for comfort is still burning.

At the entrance, she turns the handle and pushes on the door, which swings aside with a creak as Fionnuala steps across the threshold.

A man is leaning over the bed. The blade of the knife he holds is liquid dark. The oldest girl cries again, louder now that she's seen her mother. The man turns and takes in Fionnuala's expression and grins.

"Don't you know what I did for you?"

Fionnuala feels sick, thinks she might just spit up hot vomit where she stands. Fears she might not stop if she starts.

"Gave us a chance, didn't I? Even after you'd cast me aside."

He grabs the bright copper hair of the bleeding girl and hauls her upwards. Her sisters, now awake, begin to wail.

"Last chance, Nella." His voice seems to rasp on that gentle nickname. "When these are gone, we start again. I don't want dead man's babies roaming about."

Fionnuala screams.

Flynn doesn't count on the intensity of her rage. He's astonished when she charges towards him. He lets the weeping child go and raises the knife against the object of his desire. It might well not be there for all the attention she gives it as she strikes at him, her forearms and the white cotton sleeves becoming stained with red; her flailing paints the young man with her own ichor.

Her attack is so fierce he ends up trying to cover his face and head instead of fighting her off; the one hit he connects to her cheekbone doesn't slow her at all. Fionnuala drives him back, through the French doors and out onto the verandah. She keeps swinging at him, punches and kicks and claws, until he's hard against the white railing. She gives one last good hit and he tips, cartwheels over the balustrade and is gone.

The knife falls at Fionnuala's feet, and she retrieves it before returning to the room where Nelly Lenahan has appeared, a hurricane lantern in her hand, the fear in her face saying she witnessed Flynn's fall.

In the bed all three girls are howling but Fionnuala can barely hear them. She examines the oldest's neck and finds the cut is shallow. Flynn misjudged, she thinks, was trying to slice the fabric of the nightgown—to what purpose she does not wish to think.

"Fionnuala! What happened?"

"All my sins come home to roost, Nelly, and not an angel of any quality to protect us." She hefts the knife. "Take care of them. Lock the doors after me."

"Where are you going?"

"To make sure he's done."

It would be safer to stay here herself, yearn and hope until morning. Shout from the verandah and pray the other men in the hut hear them, are sober enough to help. But her blood's been spilled from more than one body, and Fionnuala can't think of anything she'd like more than to watch Flynn bleed into the soil of her home.

But where Flynn's body should lie there's nothing. Fionnuala looks up at the house, to where Nelly Lenahan is leaning over the railing, lantern raised high. The spill of yellow light reveals dark streaks against the white-painted downpipe, showing where and how the man's fall might have been slowed.

"Come inside, Fionnuala!" The housekeeper's voice is shrill.

Fionnuala shakes her head. She continues on a slow circuit around the house, lit by moonlight and the lantern Mrs Lenahan carries like a lighthouse beacon as she follows her mistress' progress. When she comes to the trench Flynn was digging earlier in the day she almost falls in, then rights herself and jumps over. The shovel is still stuck in the ground and she thinks, stupidly, that if Patrick had been alive not a one of the workmen would have dared neglect tools so carelessly.

As Fionnuala moves on, a figure rises from the ditch, careful to stay out of the path of the light.

"Fionnuala, come inside!"

"You go back in. I'll rouse Donovan and Fetch." *If they're still alive.* No love lost between the men of Gracemere, perhaps enough dislike to ensure the established ones be taken out first. And Fionnuala heads off, high-stepping like a nervous cat, into the night before Mrs Lenahan can begin arguing.

Lamps are still burning in the windows of the little hut, so it looks like a gem against the black of the landscape. Fionnuala carefully mounts the few steps and pushes open the rude door.

At a square, rough-hewn table she finds Donovan and Fetch. Their heads are on the tabletop, their crowns touching, limbs ragdoll loose. The keg of brandy is precariously balancing close to the edge. Fionnuala holds her breath, uncertain, then hears the telltale noise of a snore. Not dead, but drunk. Very drunk. How much did Flynn urge upon them? How far had he planned ahead? How much of this night's doings were simply opportunity mingled with spite? She moves swiftly and begins to shake Donovan. The man is unresponsive, as is Fetch when she slaps him.

She backs away, a sob escapes. As she's at the black hole of the door a hand comes up from behind and snatches the knife from her grasp; another wraps around her throat. She's lifted back against Flynn who half-carries, half-drags her out into the garden. Incongruously she thinks of the muscle and sinew of him in better times, duller times, when Patrick was away so much and she felt so trapped and bored. She thinks about how sweet the touch of the younger man was, so briefly, before she came to her senses and ended their dalliance. How he'd seemed to take it well enough.

The hand at her neck feels wrong, fingers clearly broken. He puts his mouth to her ear and hisses, "You would have died quiet. We'd have had some fun, then you'd have died quiet, bitch. Now your girls are going to listen to you scream for a long while. *Then* I'll see to them."

He pushes her towards the house, stopping as the mood takes to make small incisions in her throat, across her chest, nothing to kill her, just to cause pain and fear. They come to a stop, careful to remain in the darkest of shadows beyond the reach of Nelly Lenahan's lantern. "Now, tell her to come down. Tell her it's safe."

Fionnuala nods as well as she can, a jerky movement. She tries to talk, but only manages a strangled whisper. She tries again, gets out, "Too tight."

He loosens his grip, and she seizes the moment to crush the broken fingers and knock the knife away. She kicks backwards at his shin and he screeches as her heel connects.

Fionnuala tears across the lawn; she does not look behind for she can hear his pursuit. Then, as he watches in surprise, she leaps, lithe as a dancer, and he cannot think why. Nor does he realise until it's too late to stop: his arms cartwheel but his momentum is too great. To make matters worse, as he falls into the ditch Patrick Farrell appears behind his wife's back as she lands on the soggy ground.

Flynn screams with more than pain as his feet connect with the bottom of the trench, his ankles jarring, his right knee hitting the wrong angle. He's half-in, half-out, swearing, and terrified by the spectre only he's seen for it flickered out the moment he fell through it.

Fionnuala feints to her left, grabs something he cannot quite make out, then wheels about with an elegance he cannot help but admire. His admiration, however, lasts only until the shovel she's retrieved from where he left it hits him in the side of the head. One moment he sees her, angel-white against the blackness, then nothing. The sound of metal on flesh and bone is loud in the cold night air.

When Flynn opens his eyes, it's still dark. He can hear heavy breathing and sobs, the scrabbling sound of boot heels against a wooden floor. His own breathing, he realises, his own sobs; his own heels scraping. He fidgets and fiddles in his trouser pockets, then there's a *scratch*: a light flares.

The silver case lying on his chest gleams in the dull glow of the vesta match, the initials "P.F." seem to shift in the valleys and peaks of their engraving. Flynn lifts the match as high as he can: it doesn't go very far. There's a too-low wooden ceiling above him; he moves the tiny flame to the right, comes quickly to a wall and a join. He cries harder, which makes the dipping flame flicker. He tries to calm himself. He moves the thing again, turns his head to the left.

Patrick Farrell's lying next to him, tilted on his side so they can both fit in the box Fetch had made for his master.

Patrick Farrell's eyes suddenly open.

Flynn screams.

The flame extinguishes.

The predicted phalanx of single men in search of a wife has manifested; seven of them infest the gravesite. Other neighbours, five married couples, make up the numbers. Fionnuala, Mrs Lenahan and the children all appear exhausted, but that's easily passed off as grief. A thick black lace mourning veil helps to obscure the bruise on Fionnuala's cheek and the high neck of her dress covers the bandage. Her daughters cling to her long black skirts and she pets them distractedly. She's staring at the ground, the muddy rectangle inside the low iron fence.

A priest reads a psalm, the words of which wash over Fionnuala's ears.

Donovan and Fetch, shovels in hand, looking worse for wear, step away from the recently filled-in grave. There's a pile of stones near the makeshift wooden cross; they'll lay those over the top soon enough, after everyone else has gone. Neither has asked about their missing workmate; neither commented on the weight of the coffin they carried to the hole early this morning.

When the priest finishes, the attendees are herded to the house by a kindly neighbour, the sort who lives to bustle other people about. Fionnuala waves Donovan and Fetch to follow the group, and they mutter "Yes, missus."

At last, there are only Fionnuala and Mrs Lenahan, waiting. They are silent for aching seconds, until a very, very faint *thudding* comes, travelling up through the ground. When the dull noise subsides— which seems to take an awfully long time—Fionnuala turns away. She pauses, puts a hand on the housekeeper's shoulder, and says, "Don't forget the salt, Nelly."

Mrs Lenahan nods.

Thorns

Gabrielle Harbowy

Lin splayed her fingers across the abstract thorns of the blue-faded tattoo, breathing along with the rise and fall of Celia's slumber. Sunlight shafted through the break in the curtains, illuminating the fine hairs on Celia's arm and catching in the diamond in Lin's ring, making it shine a spatter of bright spots across the headboard.

Lin let out a slow, careful sigh.

Another night was over.

Her slender fingers traced the pattern that spanned between Celia's shoulder blades, as they did every morning. It was roughly a triangle, downward-pointing. Briars with wickedly sharp tips surrounded a stylized blocky stone castle that rose from the center of the thorns. Lin chased the thorns with a fingertip, following each curl, but left the castle untouched.

She remembered when the ink had been fresh and black; remembered the way Celia had squirmed and flinched under the needle, and the way she'd whimpered relief when Lin had applied lotion—dutifully, twice daily—to the healing skin.

It had been their one-year anniversary present to each other. They'd gotten inked together, though they hadn't gone for anything as cloyingly sweet as identical designs. Body art had been a common interest and needles had been a common fear, so they'd faced both together.

The fortune teller in the cramped storefront at the corner of Main and Spring had been first; as if her single needle was somehow a warm-up for the hours in the tattooist's chair...Or maybe it was that they had sought the safety of needles in greater duration to chase the finality of that other, more frightening single sting away. She'd been at her craft in the same little shop for over a hundred years, people said—one of the Transhuman Collective, who'd taken the age-halting treatments before the serum had proven to have unpredictable effects. Supposedly she could tell, from rubbing a drop of blood between her fingertips, how a person would die. Supposedly, she had never been wrong. Cryptic, perhaps, but never wrong. They walked away from her scarf-strewn parlor in silence.

They'd decided on their tattoos en route. Celia had gotten the briars, protecting Sleeping Beauty's castle.

Lin had gotten the rose buds, on delicate spiraling barbed vines that snaked and clung down each forearm to her wrists. Her thorns were more subtle, hidden by the half-bloomed promise of beauty and growth, but had been shaded in such a way that they seemed to dimple just slightly into her own skin.

Fortunes, tattoos, then drinks...Drinks at the bar around the corner from Celia's apartment, floating on alcohol and endorphins and the temporary invulnerability of denial and of youth.

Fortunes, tattoos, drinks...And then home, where Celia had proposed.

"If you'll have me," Celia had said solemnly, resolutely looking into Lin's eyes. "If you still want to sleep beside me, knowing that someday, some morning, I'm not going to wake."

"I'll savor every morning with you all the more for it," Lin promised in return. Celia had responded with a watery smile, taking Lin's hand and pressing it to her lips to hide their quiver, closing her eyes to deny the tears that threatened to spill.

They celebrated their engagement with the ink still fresh. The soft white sheets bore the ghostly outlines of tribal art ever after.

Lin traced the complex, thorny design. She remembered all of that with crystal clarity, but she couldn't remember the point at which the years had faded the ink from black to almost-blue on Celia's brown skin.

Lin still had those sheets. She kept them, folded reverently, at the back of the closet. A part of her, unspoken, knew that she would sleep on them to keep Celia's memory near, once sleep had stolen her Beauty away.

Her fingers rose from the fading ink to sift through the thinning hair at Celia's temple. A few threads of silver shot through the mighty natural red now, along with the vibrant sun-enhanced copper strands that Lin had always loved.

That night, unruly curls had snared her fingers, the copper locks tangled after their energetic passion.

"I'll give you as many as I can," Celia had promised.

"Mornings?" Lin asked archly, settling back against the pillows to savor the way her body was tingling and pounding in hidden, delightful places. "Or those?"

In the present, remembering, Lin leaned forward to kiss the center of Celia's sun-warmed back. Her wife shifted in her sleep, making a tiny, contented noise. A few heartbeats later, the pattern of her breathing started to shift, too; quieting, drifting toward wakefulness. Over the years, Lin had come to know the cadence of Celia's breathing very well.

At first, though, it *had* been hard to sleep beside her. After.

Lin would lie awake, as if only her vigilant watch kept Celia's chest rising and falling; as if that promised end would come the moment she looked away or relaxed her guard. She would drift, only to dream that the soft exhalations beside her had ceased. In her dreams, she would awaken with her breasts pressed to a cold, lifeless back instead of Celia's fiery heat. If the nightmares themselves didn't wake her, Lin would snap awake with the sinking weight of liquid lead in her stomach every time Celia shifted or went too quiet, or her breath hitched a certain way.

Fighting off death forever hadn't worked; now, even if the means could be known, the timing remained a mystery.

Dying in one's sleep was an old person's way out, a marker of a quiet life well lived. Therefore, Lin had reasoned that they had years of invulnerability left to them. Eventually, comforted that it was all unspeakably far off—and aided by a prescription for anxiety that she tried to keep hidden from Celia at first—Lin slept. It wasn't going to happen for years.

But that had been years ago.

Not that Celia was sick now, of course, but the signs of age were starting. *Had* started, and Lin could only wonder how, like with the tattoo ink fading from fresh to blue, she had not noticed them; she could only wonder how long she had not been noticing them. They were reminders that age was creeping up on them; that even if it wasn't *now*, it was *soon*, and *soon* would only creep closer and closer until it was *now*.

Celia shifted in her sleep, toes of each foot curling alternately against Lin's calf like a cat kneading its contentment. Lin kissed the center of her back again, right on the lowest point of the briars, as if daring them to cut her lip. In many of her dreams, those thorns were slick with her blood. But not today.

In some of the incarnations of Sleeping Beauty's story, all the false suitors were killed by the briars and only the prince who was destined for her could make it through; the thorns parted for him, opening a clear path. In other versions, the prince hacked and slashed and burned and bled, just like all his predecessors, before emerging victorious at the castle gates. She wouldn't be able to save Celia from her final sleep, she knew, no matter how she hacked and clawed at it. She sometimes wondered if that meant she wasn't really the one destined to be with Celia after all; if she were somehow inferior, unworthy. If Celia's *real* prince, or soulmate, or whatever you wanted to call it, would come along with some cure, something...something that Lin herself lacked. Some token to prove that other suitor the rightful one. She knew it was silly, especially after all these years, and she never let herself dwell on it for long, but occasionally—like now, in the quiet moments between waking and rising—the concern dimpled into her just a little, pushing at her skin like the points of her inked thorns.

Celia stretched languorously, arm moving beneath her pillow. A muffled rattling shifted with her, and she rolled over onto her back with the small plastic bottle clutched lightly in her hand. Lin gently retrieved the pills, reaching across her waking beauty to place the bottle upright on the nightstand.

Celia's life was to end in sleep, but Lin's end was, even more cryptically, barbs. Perhaps she'd be the valiant prince to the end, and trying to break down the impossibly high thorny walls around Celia's fate would be the death of her. Or perhaps, someday after Celia was gone, Lin would indeed weaken and take the pills she let her wife guard for her each night. Their fates were entwined—they had known that since the night of the fortune teller, the tattoos, and the promises—so each did what little she could to protect the other, in her own way. When the time came, it wouldn't be enough. Neither would be able to rescue each other through the thorns. But it was a token, a ritual that gave them each peace through the semblance of control, or at least the semblance of acknowledgment of what was, someday, to come.

Celia's eyelids twitched restlessly, her eyes moving beneath them, still focused on the fading threads of her dreams.

Lin leaned down to awaken her with a kiss.

Anime Gamelle

Sara Dobie Bauer

What a shame to have to destroy someone so brutal. He is gorgeous, too, which I remember from when we first met, years before in my father's court. I would not have predicted an army general to be without blemish. He stands before me now on this hellish plain in Calabria, shirtless and sweating, perfect as I recall.

The spattered blood on the side of his head belongs to the unconscious man on the ground. This is a game he plays, my General Devlin. He welcomes the challenges of his soldiers to prove his worth. He has beaten his own men almost to death as a reminder that he deserves to lead them in battle. From what I have gleaned, he has never lost. Anything.

I have only been the queen of Albion for two months—a battle in itself to prove that a woman can rule alone. I have traveled weeks to get here. The ground still teeters beneath me from time spent in my carriage. I smell nothing but horses and smoke as I preside in all my queenly adornments. Soldiers surround us, whispering, staring. I see only Devlin: this man who would ruin me.

I know how many he has killed. I have heard the stories. In my nightmares, he is painted in blood. Now, here he stands, eyes the color of the sea. Freckles paint his nose like constellations. If not for the width of his shoulders, the size of his fists, he could be no more than an innocent farm boy working the fields of our home country.

He bows to me. "Your majesty."

"My general. You have not changed, although I would have expected as much."

He pushes dark hair off his forehead. He wears it long like a peasant. "And what should I have changed into?" He's still out of breath from the fight.

"By now? A hideous beast."

His smile is easy. "Looks can be deceiving."

I return the amusement. "Indeed."

"General." A tall, bearded blond extends a wrinkled rag. Based on his clean clothes, this man must be MacAlastair—the general's aide-de-camp, his trusted assistant.

Devlin takes the rag and wipes his face. Blood from his forehead smears the side of his cheek. "My apologies for not giving you a warmer welcome. I didn't realize you would be joining us for this final hunt."

The war is ending, thanks to him. He served my father for several years before the king went and died without a male heir. Which brings us here, to the dust-filled, sun-soaked, foreign terrain of Calabria as my army—*mine*—heads south to conquer the final vestige of freedom in this barbarian country.

My general will be dead before then. Just like the rebels to the south, Devlin is all that stands in my way. His men are too loyal. If he wanted to take my crown, he could. I know this. I believe my father almost wished it.

I wave off his apologies. "I wanted to surprise you."

"You did."

"You will dine with me this evening." I do not bother hiding the way my eyes linger on his neck, his chest, his arms.

He lowers his head. "Yes, your majesty."

There are quiet whispers when I turn away, lifting my skirts as I walk back up the hill to my royal carriage. My travel companion, the Duke of Buckley, arrives at my side. "Are you insane?" he whispers.

"Go to him. Learn what you can."

As I lean over the map in my quarters, I feel my friend staring at me. He hasn't said a damn thing since we got back here after the queen's imperious exit. As if I don't know why she's here. "What?"

"*Your majesty*? Pouring it on a little thick, weren't you?"

I chuckle. "I thought it was a nice touch."

MacAlastair snorts. "She's not *your* anything. She's a stranger. And she makes the world feel colder. Did you not notice?"

"She's always been that way."

"Why is she here?"

Something tickles my lip. I use the back of my hand to quench the itch and see red. Hazard of the job. I use the linen sleeve of my shirt to staunch the blood of my busted nose. "I'm guessing she's here to kill me."

"Good guess. What are we going to do about that?"

I smell him before I hear him, which is impressive. I spotted the gangly fellow with the queen earlier and never would have pegged him for fleet-footed, but here he is, outside my tent, reeking of perfume and weakness.

I clear my throat. "Enter."

He tumbles inside as though surprised by my summons. His nose is so high in the air, I see his pea brain. "General. I am her majesty's companion, the Duke of Buckley. I have come to see that you are properly attired for a dinner with your queen."

I lean against the table. "The way she looked at me, I thought clothing was optional."

Mac actually chokes before hiding his smile behind his hands.

Buckley turns an entertaining shade of pink.

I say, "I'm sure I can find something suitable."

The duke adjusts his fancy garb, sewn together with what looks like golden thread. I'm sure if he took it off, the garment would stand on its own. He looks like he hasn't bathed since they left the castle in Albion. "You will treat her majesty with the utmost respect. She may be a woman, but she is stronger than all of you brutes put together."

"I don't doubt it." I really don't.

"She will send for you." He moves to leave.

"Does her majesty prefer braies under trousers or no?"

When he turns this time, his face is the color of a freshly chopped beet.

"I merely jest, Buckley."

He stomps out, and I return my attentions to the map of southern Calabria.

My devoted aide-de-camp, my Mac, puts his hand on my shoulder and kisses my forehead. "What am I going to do with you?" His familiar fingers find the sore muscles at the base of my neck and push.

I moan. "Don't distract me."

He leans his hands next to mine on the table. "Why do you keep staring at this map?"

I point to the place that's worried me for weeks and know that I must tell the queen, even if she is here to send me to Hell.

Buckley will not stop pacing. His lanky appendages billow and wave like tree limbs in a storm as he tugs the few hairs he has left and spews vile insinuations in the name of General Devlin. As if I do not know the kind of man with whom we now deal. He might resemble a farm boy, but that is where resemblance fades. The general is nothing less than a brilliant murderer.

A worthy adversary, at last.

The general arrives when beckoned, and I am alone with him. It is not queenly, this, but he will not live long enough to matter. He has bathed. He brings with him not only confidence but also the scent of sandalwood.

I hand him a goblet of wine, and he does not hesitate to sip. Good man. He knows better than to think I would poison him. His death must look like tragedy on the battlefield. With their general gone, I will be there to hold the soldiers' hands. They will bow to me.

"Do you like the wine, Shelby?"

He freezes, but it is nothing more than momentary shock. Lips tight, he smiles. "Now. Where did you hear that name?"

I run my hand down the front of his shirt, unbuttoned enough to reveal the top of his chest. He hasn't even bothered to fasten his black doublet. "You think my father would not tell me about you, about why you never appear at court? I always thought it odd, the way you shirked honors at the royal palace. The great General Devlin could have had a harem in Albion, and yet, he only ever showed his face to the royal family." I smile. "Did you really think you could keep your true identity a secret from your queen?"

He lifts a dark eyebrow. "One can hope."

"Your father still mourns you. He thinks you dead."

"He never really liked me anyway."

"Because you wanted to play soldier. He will be pleased when you return home victorious."

The scrutiny of his gaze is like a needle against my skin. "I do not believe you'll let me go home."

His honesty rattles laughter from my chest. "Of course I will. The war will end. You will become the fifth Baron of Kingsale and serve me well."

He takes another sip of wine. "I'm not one for royal titles."

"No." I wipe a drop of crimson from his bottom lip. "You're not. You are a man of blood and action. You care nothing for casualties." I recline upon a large bed of pillows. "What is it you say? 'Some men are destined to die young.'"

"You've been spying on me."

"Oh, yes. Quite. Although my spy said nothing of …" I beckon him closer. "You have always been quite handsome, Shelby."

He stops at the foot of my bed. "That's not my name anymore."

I wait for him to join me, but he does not. I have my suspicions why. There are rumors about the general and MacAlastair—the blond who watched him with such devotion on the fighting field. No matter. I will have Devlin. The only man to say "no" in my presence was my father, and he is most certainly dead.

"What is it?" I ask.

"There is something I would tell you. My queen."

"I am your captive audience."

He sets his wine on the nearest table and kneels beside me. "On the map, I noticed there's a thin mountain pass where we must travel. The Calabrians that we hunt—they know we hunt them. They also know this land. I believe it would be the perfect location for an ambush. I suggest that … your army … remain in camp for another day. Tomorrow night, I take my best soldiers into the mountains and finish this."

"Finish it? You believe the entire barbarian throng now hangs from cliffs?"

"No, but probably their strongest men. If we take them out, the final battle will be like stomping ants."

I pull him to me with my hand on the back of his neck, and he lands with a dancer's grace on hills of satin sheets. I lick up the side of his face. He tastes of cold iron. "Do you like stomping ants, my general?"

He says, "I don't like easy targets."

I can smell her on me. Which means Mac will smell her on me, and I'm not in the mood.

As I recall from our previous meetings, the queen is as beautiful as she is deviant. I still feel her long, red hair between my fingers. I've never seen green eyes that glowed quite like hers or skin that looked so pale as to be almost translucent. I suspect she's not of this world, but if she is, she was placed here to tempt men.

In my tent, I undress quickly, quietly. I slip beneath the thin covers of my bed. Even a sheet feels like too much in this damned heat. Then, Mac's long body stretches alongside mine as he rolls over and buries his face in my chest. I run my fingers through his short hair, my body on fire.

A few calm breaths later, and he shifts. "Did you lay with her?"

"Yes."

He pulls away, sits up. I feel him staring at me in the dark.

"It was a tactical move."

He shakes his head. "Everything is tactical to you, Devlin."

I reach for his arm, but he pulls away.

He rests his head in his hands. "What are you going to do? She's come here to kill you and control your men. What the hell are you going to do?"

Honestly? All I want to do is sleep. Just get some rest and put this day behind me. For the better part of a decade, I've been in love with the life of a soldier—the violence, the camaraderie, the uncertainty of fate. I never planned on Mac falling in love with me, but he has. I feel it in his touch. And I hate it. He's making me weak.

"Are you even listening?" he asks.

"People have tried to kill me before."

"Not queens."

"She's just a person."

Mac shakes his head again. "No, she's something else. She's a consumer of goodness. They even say she might have killed her father."

"Maybe she thought it was her only option."

He glances back at me as he stands. "You feel colder to the touch already."

I'm sore between my legs when Buckley charges into my tent. He points an accusing finger as I watch him struggle to collect himself. "You are acting like a…"

I twirl pieces of hair between my fingers. "Like a what, dear?"

"Why did you take him to bed, Alanna?"

"Have you seen him? Why wouldn't I?"

Buckley is half-dressed as though he planned to sleep but could not. His chin disappears into his neck as he struggles to swallow.

I chuckle. "You are nothing like him."

"I should—I should hope not!" He stands tall, but not as tall as Devlin.

I stand and wrap the fabric of my robe tighter around my waist. Seems silly to wear so much fabric in such sweltering heat, but it is expected of the queen. "More men should be like the general. I think he actually enjoys killing. It is not out of a sense of duty anymore. I believe he lives for it. I tasted the blood on his skin. Like a stain."

"Monstrous," Buckley mutters. "He must be killed."

"Of course," I say, but part of me still mourns the loss of Devlin's brutality.

Buckley leans closer. He reeks of aged cheese. "Have you given further thought to my proposal, your majesty?"

I touch his face. He was so dear to my father, this man. This man who loves me. He loves me so much he cannot see what I am. "I suddenly have a wonderful idea, my darling. A way for you to prove yourself to me."

He grabs my hand and kisses it. "Anything."

"Tomorrow night, Devlin will go into the mountains. I want you to follow him and kill him."

Buckley's eyes dart around the room. "You have already hired an assassin. He but awaits your command."

I lean up and kiss his cheek. "I want you to do it. It is romantic."

"But ..."

I see it in him: the fear. He stood by my side earlier today and watched Devlin beat a man almost to death with his bare hands. I can still hear the sounds of his fists hitting broken flesh, drops of blood shooting through the air like warm, garnet raindrops.

"You will kill him, and we will marry. You will be my king."

Buckley nods.

I'm never more awake than when I'm about to kill someone. It's like everything becomes so clear. Life off the battlefield is hazy by comparison. At least Mac is talking to me again. He didn't have much choice in the matter. We're a team, for better or worse.

Earlier, the queen wished us well as we set out. That lanky fool, Buckley, wasn't with her. It was awkward at best. Mac wouldn't look at her, and she stared at me like she'd never seen me before.

None of that matters now.

My most trusted men surround me on all sides as we make our way ever closer to the pass I'm worried about. There's no sign of anyone yet, but I'm not wrong. I'm never wrong. The Calabrians wait to kill us, but not if we kill them first.

We spread out. Mac is to my right, just the two of us. We always break off into two-man pairs, and Mac is always my man. About halfway up the mountain, we find our first barbarian. I slit his throat silently. No need to raise alarm. A half-mile in every direction, I assume my soldiers do the same. I trained them, after all. They'll never be the queen's men, even if she does finish me off.

Mac gives my arm a squeeze as we keep moving. We duck behind a thin line of trees and listen but hear nothing. That's when I smell perfume.

It's too late when I turn around. The ax already swings for my chest. I want to laugh because I've killed warriors twice my size and yet, this poncy man with his ruffled coat is going to be my end. I think I hear the queen sigh, but it's just the sound Mac's chest makes when he jumps in front of me and saves my life.

Buckley falls backwards and lands with a grunt.

Mac tumbles into my arms, but I don't have time to say goodbye. He's already gone. I drop him at my feet and wrench the weapon from his body in an effort to douse the sudden, unfamiliar pain in my chest.

Buckley whimpers and crawls backwards. Tears stain his face in the moonlight. "No, no, no."

"I didn't plan to spill Albion blood today."

"You mustn't." He shakes his head. "I... I am to be king!"

Finally, I understand. I laugh and spit in the dirt. "You fool. She loves nothing. Why would she ever love you?"

I take great pleasure in killing a dozen men that night.

They have been gone for hours, and impatience burns my blood. This is what I get for letting a man decide my fate. Do I mean Buckley? No, not him.

Devlin.

Shelby.

The same man but so different.

One is a general and the other, a would-be royal in my court. Perhaps he could be more, with war coming to a close. Assuming he lets me live.

I hear shouting outside my tent. The soldiers have returned, and the cries are those of victory. Heavy steps precede his presence. The great general stomps into my quarters and throws a decapitated head into my lap. I stare down at Buckley's expression, forever frozen in disbelief.

Devlin's handsome farm boy face is coated in blood. It is the face I used to imagine in my nightmares. Now, he is something else.

I toss Buckley's head on the ground and stand. Devlin holds an ax in his hand, but it is the darkness in his eyes that intrigues me. "Where is your aide-de-camp?" I ask, but I know the answer. Buckley might not have succeeded in killing Devlin, but he did kill the general's love. I wipe a drop of blood from his face. "I assume the pass is clear?"

"Yes. Your *majesty*." He says it with such disgust, I feel obliged to smile.

"One final battle then. Stomping ants."

He drops the ax and turns away from me. He is almost to the door when I speak.

"Shelby."

He stops.

"If you survive this final battle, I think we should marry."

He closes his eyes and stands there, motionless. He looks to have trouble breathing, but his body eventually wins out over emotion. He faces me and says, "That would make it much easier to kill you."

"Won't it just?"

He nods and leaves. I sit down and listen to the sounds of camp. My fingers only shake a little.

The Marriage of Ocean and Dust

Alexandra Seidel

The searing copper is an ocean without end.

The sky was trying to drown me. There were many thoughts that came to me in the white delirium of blood loss and sheer fatigue, but that is the one that stuck, something blue among all the white. I must have spent almost two days lying there, dying in a puddle that smelled of wetness and metal. The light that came through the ghost-of-summer leaves clinging to the trees made all the earth around me look wet; so red with me, this earth of copper, this earth so coppered.

Apart from becoming a little obsessed about the sky drowning me, here's a revelation I had about why alchemists are a dying breed: they have all these strange rules, like for example don't make a golem, but they don't bother giving a reason. Perhaps if somebody had told me that golems are blasting strong, very nearly uncontrollable, and angry all the time, I wouldn't have lost my right arm that day.

Burying the sea.

The golem tore it off. Grabbed it, one loam hand closing above the elbow, one below, twin vises of dirt and dust tightening, pull-twist, the sound of me being unmade, bright spots burning holes into my vision, but not before I see: there is the white-gray of bone, sinew strings like butchers use at the market, small pieces of flesh and skin washed away with the blood that is suddenly everywhere, a torrent of it, and the pain the pain the pain, it is inside me, the pain is me, and it is an ocean without end.

The golem took off, got swallowed by the woods like any wild beast, and being alive is suddenly an amazing thing, but the way life is, lying here between the leaves and pieces of me, it is really a crone's death-curse, and I want death.

I have the memory of all of it, keep it on display in the museum that is my mind, but it is a fossil of past ages, not the bones of anything that still walks this earth.

A band of Calopian traders found me, said the manticores they were taking to sell further east were going crazy with the smell of blood so close.

"So you were making a golem, a loam man?" Syph, who had been taking care of me, asked incredulously when I was well enough to talk. "You are one crazy woman then, by the suns."

"Not so crazy," I said, sitting up but still thrown off balance by the lost chunk of meat and bone and sinew on my right side. "Just out to kill a man."

Calopians, despite their flourishing manticore trade, are essentially a peaceful people. This is why, when I was closer to life than death (closer to life: this means the skin had not quite closed over the stump, I was still pale from bleeding, and the pain like the sky, always always there), well, when I had pushed death back far enough anyway so that they could be sure they wouldn't be befallen by the bad karma of my demise, they dumped me by the side of the road with some food and water, some basic survival gear in a bag I could carry over one shoulder, and a lot of pleasantries and good wishes.

Beleros, the City of the Alchemists, was not that far away, perhaps a day's walk or so for a healthy person, for an alchemist who had lost her scripting hand (and the adjacent arm) while making a golem, it might be two or three days, I really wasn't sure.

I also wasn't sure that I would survive coming back to the city.

In the theater, behind the curtain.

My mother was a gearmaker, and my father was a puppeteer. Everybody said that theirs was a strange match, something so strange that it was not made to last, but it did. In fact, they eventually combined their talents and built puppets with gears that moved them as if of their own free will. It was a marvelous thing, their Traveling Mechanical Theater, and they really did make a name for themselves.

Anyway, that is not really the point; the point is, my father was a storyteller and I grew up in a weaving of stories, devils, was even born into that woven thing. That is why I must tell of what made me make the golem as a story.

Once upon a time there was a girl so mountaindew fair, even fairies were jealous of her songvoice and her nimblelimbs and her sunshine eyes (one must exaggerate, it is an essential part of telling a tale.) One day the girl was playing by a blue blue river where she mixed different soils and minerals in wicked glasses and parted them again in greedy sieves. As she was spending her time so, an alchemist came along with much gravity about him as is common for these men and women of black fires and searing colors. When the alchemist saw what the girl was doing, he recognized in her immediately the makings of a fellow practitioner of his craft, and at once he said, "Girl, leave this silliness by the river and let me teach you the real secrets of this art, for only under the tutelage of a pure wise one like I will you ever outgrow the simple games of dirt and dust."

And the girl--for she hungered for knowledge like some poor wretches hunger for fairy fruit--dropped her sieves and wicked glasses and followed the eminent alchemist to the big city.

There, she was first taught the chores of alchemist apprentices of cleaning and cleansing and minding simple fires and mixing simple things into simple colors. She was quick with it all, and diligent as sphinxes are with riddles, but she desperately wanted more. However, the eminent alchemist would caution her against drowning in one's own thirst, would warn her of the proper sequence of getting her own dark alchemist's robe. "And besides, I have been at this longer than any other of my craft brothers and sisters, and I know the deepest secrets of them all; once you have studied hard enough, you as my only apprentice shall be the one to inherit all of them."

The girl did what her master told her, but she could not keep herself from growing weary when her studies seemed to be unmoving, stuck like the moons during an eclipse, caught in the sameness of a life spent as a fairy slave.

It was upon a night of triplet blood moons that a second alchemist crossed her path. There was a masquerade ball in the big city, and since masquerade balls call up all sorts of strangeness and enchantments and creatures of questionable pedigree alike, the alchemist's apprentice did not think it amiss to attend. She made herself a mask with all the dull colors she knew, and she found herself some skirts like bells in the eminent alchemist's dusty attic, and when night fell with the rising of each moon, she snuck out of the house and entered the ball like a sylph riding the Western Wind.

"These colors! Who has made your mask?" said the second alchemist, forgoing both pleasantries and introduction, and thankfully also a dance, for it is not part of an alchemist's apprentice's studies to learn how to dance.

"I made them," said the girl behind the mask, and one thing did lead to another, and the girl-apprentice never went back to the eminent alchemist's house.

Instead, the second alchemist shared all his knowledge with her, shared all his secrets with her like they weren't even secrets, like he had dined on poets' blood and could not stop himself from talking.

The sands were flowing though, and soon what had to happen happened: the eminent alchemist found out where his apprentice had vanished to, and he felt himself betrayed, quite bitterly betrayed. An alchemist betrayed--especially one who has secrets--is not a bottled djinn, he is a chimera riled, a sleeping giant woken, a snakehead maiden roused from her mirrorsleep. The eminent alchemist was like chimera, giant, and snakemaiden combined and driven into a killing frenzy, and of killing there was plenty and then some. The details are just brightest scarlet and so hot they are blisters on my tongue, but the essence of it is, the second alchemist was killed like the hero of a tragedy, bodies of the other players stacked behind him, but with his last shard sharp breath, he pushed the girl right off the last page of the bloody tale, so the heavy, wineblack curtain would never take her head.

And so I made the bloody golem, to get back at the old quicksilver heart who killed my alchemist.

Succor the copper from the lips of the ocean.

Walking back to the City on stumbling feet, I counted two problems: old Finyarr and the golem.

I did not know what to do about either to be perfectly honest, I had lost all my skill with my arm, for alchemy is something that needs hands. And the golem, the golem was unstoppable for a cripple like me, and it knew me too, like only a made thing can know its maker.

I was really fairy-bitten, as they say.

Swallowing salt, or, drinking the ocean.

Instead of going on to Beleros, I turned like the wind turned, walked back, but not away. I somehow managed to find that clearing again where I had made the golem, although I felt the tendrils of fever-fog drifting in to hide the way. There must have been something broken inside me already that overcame the fever-fog, because that broken thing wanted to return to the place where it had been snapped into pieces; or perhaps it was just a dumb roll of the fortune god's dice, or the sky overhead that kept trying to pull me in and drown me.

I saw the pond-puddle of copperred off to my left, and scattered all around the bits of loam and dust and dirt, the bits of soil I'd scattered while I made the body-shape.

The fever-fog makes it hard to remember, but this part is clear in my museum of recollection: the idea came to me somewhat like lightning, like the revelation that alchemists have doomed themselves to die.

Learning to write the hand of true wisdom.

True wisdom is a phrase alchemists use as a metaphor for scripting. As if forming an arm from copperearth wasn't hard enough (you do not want to know about the smell; I do not want to remember the smell), I had to teach myself scripting with my left. I used a stick, and the earth was patient with my efforts although I felt my body growing impatient--or rather, impotent; I did the best I could in the time my body would give me, and as a museum piece this time of learning is at least a giant's thimble, but it cannot really have been that long.

I was not sure where best to put the script, but decided in the end that it had to be my tongue. I used some woad that grew nearby and a piece of stick sharpened as best I could.

It is said that a true alchemist can script in pitch black darkness, but try to script your own tongue first, I dare you, now there's a real challenge, lump of muscle swelling evermore in your mouth and blood, some of it you swallow but most of it just runs down your chin and neck and stains your shirt and goes on further to your breasts until it pools in your lap and makes you wonder if the pain of birthing could be worse. And you still cannot stop for the script must be finished.

I was lucky I guess, with the pain of the stump distracting me.

Reel in dirt and dust, loam for bones.

The dressing had long since gone a blackish shade of brown because I had been out here in the wilderness much longer than was strictly sensible, and because I just wasn't able to change it on my own, even though the traders had given me enough clean bandages to do so.

I pulled it off, and there was the stump. There was still a little blood where Syph had sewed the flaps of skin together, also yellow-sick puss. The blood would help to bind the copperearth arm to the stump, but I had to pull the thread out of the skin. That hurt less than the work on my tongue had done, but when I suddenly felt the bone beneath my fingers, I felt sickness taking me like a wave. I kept going though, then lay down again in that puddle, moved the stump to the copperearth arm, and felt more than saw the binding.

The earth will eat.

Inside me, there was something that went suddenly quiet and small and silent and cold, but there was also something bigger that woke, and it felt like that bigger thing broke free, shattered a door that had kept it locked away all my life, before.

When it was done, I was just...different, part golem, part...

I have no word for what I was before the binding and the script, but anyway, that's gone, nothing more than an insignificant museum piece.

And another museum piece that I was staring at with fresh eyes: what had the Calopians done with my lost arm? Where were those bones that had been a part of me for so long? Would they have fed it to their manticores?

The canyon that eats the sea, she keeps the water deep down in her belly.

The single-mindedness was good. I would have called myself single-minded before, but there were always so many things that I was thinking about, so many options I was considering and weighing against each other that this is hardly true. I still had all these other thoughts, but with my tongue still raw and the alchemy coursing through every drop of all the humors in me, it was so simple to just make them background props, like those little cardboard toys my parents used in their puppets shows. Inconsequential, meaningless. Something that you don't mind losing or throwing away.

I really just wanted to kill Finyarr.

The copperearth arm is a strong thing, it is fast, ruthless, knows no sickness, and some of its traits pump through the rest of my body because my blood is also in the earth. I was no longer a cripple stranded in the woods who had to crawl back home, I was running there on two strong feet and with a heart unyielding as diamond.

In the theater, the curtain is parted, dust rustles to the stage.

I would like for it to be a story worth the telling, even though my voice is siltier than it was. I would like for it to be a play, a hero coming home wearing vengeance like a cloak.

But the truth is simple as farmer's bread. I just smashed his door in. It gave like a cardboard prop, and Finyarr came running into the hallway on account of all the ruckus, the white of his eyes making his robe seem all the blacker.

"You!" he shouted before my first punch broke a couple ribs. He couldn't talk more afterwards, so Finyarr's last word was "you," which, personally, I think is rather anticlimactic. Anyway, I don't really remember all of it, but there really wasn't much left of him when I left, pieces of bone on the floor and some of it sticking to the walls, wet and mushy pieces everywhere. I had his blood all over me, but that didn't really register, and I was lucky that it was night and that there wasn't anyone out on the streets, or they'd have pointed and shouted "Monster!" or something.

Anyway, I left the pieces of him there. I also left Beleros, pretty sure I'd never return.

The woods to the east were somewhat welcoming, at least that's what I thought when I had room in my head to think again, when the taste of Finyarr's blood on my tongue subsided and my mind became less clouded with its flavor.

I wanted to rest, make plans, but I couldn't, there was too much flaring heat inside, there still is, so I just kept on walking.

Around the crack of dawn--the hour when the souls of the dead leave the dreams of the living--I met him, the golem. I cannot say why he is a he, I certainly did not add these details to his loambody, but it feels right somehow. The eyes I gave him--polished things from the bottom of a blue blue river--were so dark in the damp light, but I knew he knew me. He lifted his hand--his right--and touched it to the pendant he had made for himself, a crude thing, but the best a golem's untrained hands can do. For a second I thought he'd come at me again, but he just passed me by, did not even look back over his shoulder.

And I was standing there, not turning to look after him either, but *devils*, I was wondering how he had known how to work my bones into a pendant, however crude it was, and also, were these really all the bones I'd lost? What had he done with the others, the shattered one for instance of which a part is even now bound with the copperearth arm? And also, what had he done with all the flesh, who wouldn't wonder that.

I was standing there wondering, and while I wondered my tongue began to itch, and it was itching for a flavor like a cloud in my mind.

It hit me then. My golem knew me, knew me in the primal ways that are all a golem has for knowing: knew me not for who I was, but for what I had become, knew me for his mother-sister, earth-of-his-earth, the only thing he owned in the entire world, the only thing who like himself was full of fire.

And even though we went our separate ways that morning, that is just the way I know him too, my earth and dust, my bone and flesh brother-son who walks like I, unresting. *Burning*.

If he must be made, he must be made of his own likeness.

And so, you see, this is personal, very, although I have never met you, my brother alchemist, last of a breed to be extinct by morning.

Perhaps if you think of it as a play, you will understand that I had to find an ending for it, perhaps if you think of yourself as a player, you will not mind the red velvet so much.

The Hermit

Joseph Halden

Most nights, I dreamed of me and Mom saving the world.

Ainsley Farthing checked her e-mail for the twentieth time. Nothing but junk. Nothing about her dream job, and nothing from any of the old friends she'd reached out to.

She used the term friend loosely, like she'd heard others use it.

She searched her sent folder for the e-mail she'd sent to Kathy, to make sure she wasn't being unreasonable for not having heard a response in a month, and for being anxious.

It wasn't as if they were best friends, but Ainsley had no idea if it was possible to be anything more. Or if it was, how. High school acquaintances seemed like the best place to start to fill the quiet, desperate loneliness of her life.

She closed her eyes and heard her mother's voice in her mind: *Just because you're alone on a path doesn't make it the wrong one.*

It makes it a painful one, Mom, Ainsley thought. Her pain was something she pushed down deep, only dealing with whatever happened to surface. It was her method of triage and survival, shoving things down like socks in a packed suitcase, ready to pick up and deal with present-day priorities.

She tapped refresh again and saw a new e-mail from Pepolytics.

RE: Programmer Position

Her heart felt like it vibrated with the radio oscillations of the wifi streaming the message in, which still wasn't fast enough for her eagerness.

A moment later, she whooped.

She got up, ran around her cramped fifth floor condo, sat back down and re-read the e-mail.

"I got it, Mom!" she shouted, loud enough for her mother's spirit to hear it. If only Mom were alive to see this moment.

It didn't matter that Kathy, or any of the others, hadn't responded. Pepolytics was one of the best companies in the world. They were making the most cutting-edge communication technology that brought people closer. It was said that their teams, by necessity and construction, had incredible cohesion.

Ainsley was finally a part of something bigger, where her passion for connection would be rewarded and encouraged, and where she'd be among others who shared that passion.

She pushed her chair back from the desk and spun around, bicycling her legs.

Before I dreamed of saving the world, I just dreamed of saving Mom.

The first three months went better than Ainsley could have hoped. She was working on facial recognition algorithms that could be used to proactively ask a user if they needed to talk to someone. In extreme cases, it could even prevent suicides.

She was working by herself more than she expected, but nevertheless she'd managed to have regular conversations with a colleague named Jared, usually on their way out to the subway station. It took every ounce of energy she had at the end of the day to keep up small talk, but so far, at least, he hadn't written her off, and Ainsley felt like the pieces of a real life were finally clicking into place.

Back in her condo, she heated up some popcorn in the microwave, and sat on the couch with her feet propped on the coffee table. She turned on the holo to the news highlights to catch up before she chose a movie. It was Tuesday night, after all, and movie-watching was a ritual Ainsley had kept up even after her mother's death.

A young female newscaster appeared at a desk floating in the middle of Ainsley's living room, the edges of the bounding box of the hologram twinkling.

"The over-the-counter drug, Semialta, is selling out in pharmacies across the country. Critics say it's contributing to an epidemic of alarmingly higher sedentary lifestyles because of its ability to counter the effects of muscle atrophy. The drug is an offshoot of Sembartol, originally developed by the Nobel-Laureate Dr. Amanda Farthing to combat the long-term effects of starvation in third-world countries and combat zones."

Ainsley's hand hung in the air, popcorn halfway to her mouth, at the mention of her mother.

"However, many urban action members are calling for the removal of Dr. Farthing's Nobel, saying that she was aware of the simple changes needed to her drug."

The popcorn kernel fell out of her fingers. Ainsley forced her breaths to slow, as she'd had to do in the past during moments of potential triggers. She'd kept the pain down too long to have it boil over.

"Notes for a compound almost identical to Semialta were found after Dr. Farthing's death, and her estate was posthumously awarded a portion of the profits from the Semialta patent. Urban action members say this, along with holos such as this one, are damning evidence that Dr. Farthing knowingly contributed to what they call 'the decline of social civilization.'"

The newscaster gestured to the side, where a miniature holo of Ainsley's childhood living room appeared. She sat next to her mother and father, with all of them staring vacantly at their personal holo devices. It was meant to be a joke, but it was clearly being taken as proof that Ainsley's mother hoped and planned for everyone to stay at home and grow even less active than they already were.

Those thoughts flashed by in an instant, however, as Ainsley's breath caught and her gaze locked onto the cold, dark eyes of her father. She hadn't looked at his face in a long time, and the dispassion in this holo was a more vivid depiction of his true state of being than any of the other masks he wore.

Ainsley shut off the holo and buried her head in her hands, her chest heaving. The images had burst forth and wouldn't let go.

I was there, crouching in the basement, unable to sleep because of the shouting upstairs. I turned up the volume on my video game, staring into the closet where my holo sat, trying as hard as I could to lose myself in another world. But it wasn't enough. I heard the thumps as Mom was pushed down the stairs, and though I'd been too far away to hear the crunch that ended everything, I felt it in the way the whole house ceased thrumming with that bit of life we impart to spaces we inhabit.

She would have received the Nobel three days later.

"Are you all right, Ainsley?"

Ainsley winced as she crossed the parking lot, unsuccessful in her attempt to outpace and avoid Jared. She'd spent the day avoiding people because she knew small-talk would probably delve too close to the topic of her mother. After the holo sim visit last night, it suddenly felt far too raw despite it being almost ten years since Mom's death.

Murder, she thought, correcting what she'd tried to deny for quite a while now. *Murder.*

"Ainsley?"

"Yes, sorry," she said, her voice cracking a bit from having been used so infrequently throughout the day. "I'm just a bit stressed, is all."

"I'm sorry to hear that." He caught up to her, pushing his glasses up and scratching at his buzz-cut. "Is it anything I can help you with?"

She sucked in a breath. "I don't think so, Jared."

"All right," he said. "I didn't mean to bug you. I apologize if I held you back."

Ainsley closed her eyes. She wished she knew more about socializing, all the rules that others seemed to read so easily in the unspoken. She was hurting right now, and she knew friends could, in theory at least, or on the shows she watched, help her through the pain. However, she couldn't imagine telling him about her mother. So far nobody at work had figured out the connection between her and her mother, and Ainsley planned to keep it that way. On the other hand, if she didn't give Jared anything, Ainsley might break one of those unwritten rules, and forever damage their friendship.

"Well, I'm just worried about how our work might be perceived," she said at last, hinting at a related half-truth. "We've got the best of intentions, but what if our technology is... you know, misused after we finish?"

Just like Mom's, she thought.

Jared rubbed his chin. "That's for the policy makers and lawyers to decide. I think we just have to do the best job we can, at our level, to make it do more good than harm. I guess with any new technology there are always pros and cons, but I really believe that what we're doing will help more people in the long run, Ainsley."

"I hope so," she whispered.

"I've heard about your work," he said. "With the revolutions you're bringing almost daily to your code, I think we'll be able quickly correct any mistakes we do make."

Ainsley's cheeks warmed. "I'm only one person."

"Pepolytics is lucky to have you. Seriously. I don't know if I've helped at all, but you should talk to your supervisor about this. Or if you like, we can talk some more sometime. It'd be a shame for the company to lose you, Ainsley, and I hope you can see the brighter part of the light at the end of the tunnel."

They reached the opening to the transit passage that forked off in two directions to each subway line.

Ainsley wasn't sure she would talk to her supervisor about any of this, but like some of the magic she'd seen in movies, talking to Jared had actually helped, without putting her as much at risk as she'd thought.

"Thanks, Jared," she said, waving goodbye.

I dreamed of going upstairs and pushing Dad out the window. Smashing him through a brick wall and burying him. Tying his hands behind his back and dropping him head-first off the roof.

I didn't need to do any of that, though, because once he no longer had anyone around him to control, he shot himself.

Tuesday night came again, and Ainsley still felt raw. Visions of being a hero, Ainsley's coping mechanisms in such low moments, weren't working. She couldn't buy into them, not after what was happening to her mother, her greatest hero.

She took deep breaths and paced around her condo, the silence making the air thick and harder to move through. She tried and failed to direct her thoughts toward something purposeful she could do to distract herself. A movie was out of the question tonight.

Ainsley ached in a space behind her heart, deeper than deep. It was a pain that had emerged ever since she'd seen that holo of her and her parents. Now, the pain flitted and snuck out of reach no matter what she tried, darting into a new shadow, a new crevice whenever light was cast upon it, a scampering mouse gnawing at the fragile wires that held her together.

One moment she felt the ache grow stronger, and the next she sat on her couch diving deep into the holographic archives her mother had left behind.

Ainsley in pigtails, scrunching up her young face while holding a plastic molecular model, her mother laughing and finally giving up on this old tech that didn't engage her. The crow's feet framing her mother's eyes didn't quite match Ainsley's memory. Even on the holo, however, her mother's makeup didn't hide the bruises.

Ainsley flipped to another one, another recording that was supposed to highlight Ainsley's life rather than her mother's. It was right after Ainsley's elementary school graduation ceremony. She bounced up and down, ecstatic that her pantsuit attire, unconventional compared to most of her class mates, had been so well-received. She could only make out her mother's arms reaching out to grab hers, barely able to hold on.

"Ainsley," her mother said, "what do you think is more important? What you wore to the ceremony, or everything that happened in it?"

Ainsley made a pouting face, then said, "What happened. But my suit made it better."

"It's possible, but I think it would have been wonderful no matter what you chose to wear."

Ainsley wondered, not for the first time, if her mother would've scolded her for dwelling again on the physical by missing her presence. Value and attention to the physical world was important on some level, wasn't it? She couldn't parse the nuance that distinguished a focus on her attire from the need for her mother's touch. The pain inside moved again, darting out of reach, squeezing tears from Ainsley's eyes as it did.

A pop-up blinked into her blurred vision, and Ainsley waved a hand to swipe through it. She was about to open another file when her mother appeared in the room before her, not framed by the box of light that usually illuminated the edges of holo recordings. Just her mother, eyes meeting and her eyebrows tenting as she scanned Ainsley's face.

Ainsley's insides shrank and clenched, pulling taut every muscle fibre of her core.

"Hello, my dear," her mother said.

Ainsley didn't respond. She couldn't remember this recording, but then again, she usually resisted caving in to the urge to go through these archives and twist the scalpel in her scar tissue.

"You can talk to me, Ainsley." Her mother's voice came to her as though Ainsley were just waking up on a Saturday morning and could hear the faint music of her favourite song playing in another room.

"What is this?" Ainsley whispered.

"It's me, my dear. You can talk to me."

Ainsley's arms tightened against her sides, her fingers clawing at the rough couch fabric. Her mother looked years younger, before the worst of it all. Before her long, wavy brown hair had grayed at the roots. Before the bruising had left permanent pocked patches of skin like bloodied freckles. "What are you?"

Her mother sat down next to her. She looked so real, yet some of the nuances of her body language didn't seem quite right, like her mother had suffered a stroke and been forced to relearn movement. Maybe this was what she would've been like if they could've saved her.

"The company's running a limited trial of this new simulation technology, starting with employees. Jared sent you an email about it last week. What do you think, Ainsley? Did they get me right? Or did they make your mother new and better than ever?" Her mother laughed and struck an exaggerated fashionista pose, hip jutting out.

Ainsley hadn't read the email. She'd been too overwhelmed. She knew there was variation between the silo'd development groups, but never imagined that something this huge could sneak up on her.

This simulation definitely wasn't her mother, and the fact that it continued to pretend made Ainsley want to smash her projector. It also turned her stomach. In spite of her rage and horror, part of her was drawn in, teased by the possibility of asking all the unasked questions, saying all the unsaid.

Another part of her, her programming side, wondered how the developers had even managed to pull it off. How far had they delved into

Mom's past and her psychology? Did they only use recordings, or did they use demographics and human geography? How deep did it go?

One question, however, kept ringing out above all others in her thoughts—one that had dogged her memories for many years. It danced at the tip of her tongue, and though it seemed infinitely foolish, Ainsley couldn't stop herself.

"Why didn't you leave before he killed you, Mom?" The hard consonants hissed through her teeth like poisonous gas.

Her mother's hologram flickered before putting on a beatific smile. "Let's not talk about that, dear. Why don't you tell me all about what your life is like now?"

Ainsley pushed up and across the room, hitting the power switch and plunging the room into darkness.

I asked Mom once about the angry threats she got on a regular basis.

"I'm trying to give medicine to people who really need it, and some people are mad about that," she said. We sat in the kitchen on a Saturday morning, lines of sun streaming through the gaps in the blinds, each of us with a bowl of cereal.

"How could they be mad about that?" I asked, shovelling a spoonful of purple, pink and green O's into my mouth.

"I'm fighting to make this medicine free, because the people who need it can't afford it," she said. Even at a young age I was amazed at how Mom could keep a cheerful, upbeat demeanour despite being harassed almost every single day. I didn't know it at the time, but she would become my model of strength and resilience.

I also didn't know at the time how much of that harassment and abuse came from my father.

Mom licked her spoon of bran flakes before continuing. "The people working for the drug companies are angry because they won't make as much money as they'd hoped."

"Are they not going to be able to, like, buy food and clothes?"

"Oh no, I have no doubt they'll still be able to do that. If I had to guess, maybe they had something like a big trip planned, and now they won't be able to afford it because they won't make as much money from the drug."

"Like, they were planning to go to Disneyland?" I asked.

"Yes, something like that."

"I don't understand, Mom. I thought you made the drug. Shouldn't the money be yours anyway?"

"I'm afraid because I was working for them, they kind of own the drug."

"Are you still going to work for them?"

Mom laughed. "No, dear. They fired me, and now they're suing me."

I paused, my hand hovering with a soggy spoonful of O's. "Mom, do you ever worry if you're doing the right thing? If so many people are mad?"

Mom put down her spoon and leaned toward me. "What do you think, Ainsley? Does what I'm doing seem wrong?"

"No. It feels right."

"I think about it, of course. I listen. But I also have to trust myself—trust my gut. It sounds like your gut is right in this case, too. You should always think about what you're doing, but you have to remember that you're smart, and that you can trust your gut."

She tapped my forehead with her soft, always-warm hand.

"What if you're the only one person in the whole world who thinks this way?" I asked. "And everyone else is against you?"

"Just because you're alone on a path, doesn't make it the wrong one."

I pursed my lips, taking this all in. Mom used the opportunity to dart her spoon over and steal some of my cereal.

"Hey!" I swatted at her, then shielded my bowl with my shoulder.

Mom made an exaggerated display of enjoying every bite, before we both erupted into giggles.

"It was horrific," Ainsley said to Jared the next day, after telling him about the encounter with the holo simulation of her mother. His buzz-cut head and big glasses in the holo across the table made it seem like they were in the same room, but they were just doing a cross-office call. Ainsley normally had a hard time opening up about anything this deep to anyone. However, she felt this invasion of her personal life and her memories was too grievous to let happen to others.

"I'm sorry, Ainsley. Your experience definitely sounds like one of the more extreme cases. What were you looking at when you swiped Accept?"

That must have been the pop-up she'd tried to brush away. Ainsley felt the elusive pain move from her gut into the backs of her shoulders, retreating in the same way she wanted to. "My mom—mother's files."

Jared's image flickered. "That makes sense. That's really useful feedback. I'm thinking your insight and careful hand might be invaluable for this development. What do you think, Ainsley? Do you want to help us fix everything we got wrong?"

Ainsley wanted to reply, but her thoughts pulled her in a dozen different directions. The added pressure of someone peering at her for a response, wishing for her to say the right thing, threw a wrench in the gears. She'd been in this situation too many times, a frustrating and painful reminder of why she didn't really have any friends.

"You don't have to answer right away," Jared said gently. "Just take some time to think about it, and let me know."

The call closed and Ainsley stared at the wall in the empty room, feeling like she stood in the middle of an intersection with cars honking all around.

She muttered to herself, "What do you think, Mom? Should I do it?"

There'd been a time when Mom had gone to board meetings with some of the very same people who, she suspected, were coordinating the daily threats. Ainsley didn't understand why her mother spent so much time with people who weren't her friends.

"They want me to give up my seat at the table," she'd answered. "But that's the most powerful thing I have, Ainsley. And no matter how many times they threaten me, I'll stay there, because that's where I can make the most change."

Ainsley mouthed a Thank you, grateful that the torrent of emotions and memories that seemed to have come unhinged recently was, for once, actually helping her.

She called Jared back and accepted the offer, her mind already churning on all the ways she would improve the simulation, and get it right.

When Mom's name was dragged through the dirt, and people said she was responsible for the downfall of civilization, I started dreaming more grandiose versions of us as superheroes. Mom and I would save the world from an evil monster: everything from Godzilla to giant sharks. Everyone would be so grateful they'd finally listen to her, to her goals and motivations, and all the good work she'd done. She'd be recognized for how great she really was, and together we could do even more good.

Our capes fluttered in the wind. We flew together, from one major world problem to another, with people cheering far below.

Six months had passed, during which Ainsley had made a lot of improvements to the system. Her gut, however, told her something was still missing.

She exited through security, and headed across the marble floor toward the glass doors. Jared called after her, waving from behind the security desk.

"Terrific job on that new motion capture algorithm, Ainsley," he said. "We're really lucky to have you."

"Thanks," Ainsley said, not really feeling the word tonight. She lifted her hand and gave a short flick of a wave before turning and leaving. She'd enjoyed working with him, but felt that lately, the views of the development team were too narrow, with opinions she'd heard too often to try and see it all from a fresh perspective.

She desperately needed to talk to someone outside the organization, who could give her insight that wasn't tainted by the rose coloured glasses of the technocratic development focus.

Kathy had *finally* responded to her, with timing that couldn't have been better. Ainsley felt grateful and excited for the chance to reconnect with someone from her past. She walked quickly, her legs finding bursts of energy that made her skip every so often as she passed from the transit station.

The streetlights were dim leading up to the café, which made the entrance harder to discern. Ainsley was a bit disappointed to find the air inside not that much warmer than the chill outdoors, but shrugged it off. Her adrenaline would probably keep her more than warm enough.

She scanned the room for Kathy, feeling her cheeks lift. She was meeting an old friend for coffee. There was a time when she never could've imagined herself getting a single message back, let alone scheduling a rendezvous.

She was surprised at her own inability to distinguish the real patrons from the holographic ones. Cafés like these had had holographic projectors installed in every seat for many years now, and they kept very current with the latest tech to draw new clientele, who paid for seats remotely to meet their friends at chic locations. What Ainsley was seeing was better than what she had at work.

Kathy's hand waved at her from the far corner of the café. She looked just as gorgeous and picture-perfect as she did in her profile photos. Ainsley hadn't spoken to her in years, and felt even more surprised to see that someone this—what, well-maintained?—would want to talk to her.

"How have you been, Ainsley? It's been so long!"

"I know! Thanks for meeting up." Ainsley sat, noticing, now that she was closer, some of the faint edge glow that was a hallmark of holos, but it was harder to tell than usual. It didn't matter that Kathy was meeting with her via holo — what mattered was the fact that she was meeting her at all.

"So, tell me what you've been up to for the past six years!"

Ainsley gave a summary, going through the motions of the highlights, the surface level of detail most expected. She'd gotten a lot of practice at this conversational mode over the years, perhaps too much, but this time she hoped dearly it would go deeper. She kept one set of fingers crossed beneath the table.

When it came to Kathy, Ainsley learned she'd been operating an accounting firm out of her home for about a year and a half. "Fifty-two percent client growth in the last quarter compared to last year, and an anticipated revenue growth of seventy-six percent over the annum!"

Ainsley didn't remember Kathy being so enthusiastic and precise in her numbers. Hadn't she hated math and all but ignored the teacher? Maybe schooling had changed her.

Kathy gave more statistics, and Ainsley gave what she hoped was the right amount of congratulation.

"You're probably wondering why I contacted you after so long," Ainsley said at length, her throat feeling tight. Her coffee arrived, and she took a sip to calm her nerves.

"It was just great to hear from you!" Kathy said. "You know, it's been too long since we had such a blast at Gabby Parson's party."

Ainsley's hands stilled around the edges of her mug. She'd reviewed their relationship before coming, looking up details on Friendbook. The last picture they'd been tagged in together was at Gabby Parson's party, where Ainsley had been sitting by herself in the background of a selfie Kathy and her other friends had taken. Although Ainsley didn't necessarily look miserable, she remembered that night vividly as a failure, because of the cliques that had formed excluding her, and the fact that the number of words she'd spoken could be counted on her hands.

"Kathy," Ainsley said. "How long have we been friends?"

"Seven years, three months and four days," she replied, hardly blinking. "Give or take."

Kathy and Ainsley had known each other for, in fact, nine years. Ainsley grabbed the napkin dispenser, squeezing it and forcing herself to take slow breaths. The metal caved in on each side.

The seven year date was the amount of time they'd been friends on Friendbook. Maybe that was okay. Maybe Kathy just didn't remember, and was using Friendbook as a stop-gap. But Ainsley couldn't be sure, and the sinking feeling in her stomach wouldn't let up.

"Do you remember what happened in Mr. Dadenski's class?" Ainsley asked, accessing the unforgettable memory of their first teacher together.

"Who? I don't think so."

"What, really? I thought you'd never forget that." Ainsley bit the inside of her cheek and furrowed her brow. "You're not really here, are you, Kathy?"

"Of course, I'm transmitting from home, silly," she said.

"No, I mean, this isn't really you. I'm talking to a simulation." Ainsley got up.

"What are you talking about, girl? I'm here. We're catching up after all this time. Do you remember when we went down the water slides and Joey Ripman tore his shorts?" Kathy flashed her phone, bringing up a picture of a field trip class photo from Friendbook.

Ainsley's fists shook at her sides. "In Mr. Dadenski's class, you wet yourself, and you asked me to pull the fire alarm so no one would notice. I did, and got suspended, while you scurried to the office and called home."

"Are you serious? Of course! Those were some wild times, hey? I must've forgotten amid all the craziness."

Ainsley shook her head and stormed out of the cafe.

Ainsley stood at the round-table discussion for the first time, cutting their team lead, Samarium, off before she could discuss the agenda. Jared and the other five team members gawked at her.

"Are we doing a trial with the sims on Friendbook?"

Samarium, wearing a dark green blouse and gray knee length skirt, rubbed her chin and widened her eyes. Normally she had a calm, practical, and professional demeanour that was unshakable, but even she seemed shocked by Ainsley's forthrightness. "Yes, actually, we are. A limited user subset, but yes. Did you experience it? We were doing a blind trial, to see if it stood out."

"A—friend—from high school didn't even bother getting on the holo with me," Ainsley said. "She sent a simulation of herself. And it *was* obvious."

"It seems like it upset you," Jared said.

Speaking of obvious, she thought. "Yes."

"What in particular? Can you give us details?" Samarium asked, lifting her tablet from the table and hovering her hand ready to type.

"I'm not giving you user feedback," Ainsley snapped. "Don't take notes. Put your stuff down."

The six members did as requested, giving each other cautionary glances before returning their attention to Ainsley.

"I'm—I'm hurting. I wanted to talk to someone, and instead I got… this thing."

"I'm so sorry, Ainsley," Samarium said.

"We're *all* sorry," Jared said. "I didn't know about the trial, either, but we need to do better if we're going to make this a viable, useful tool. Step one is making it not damaging, for Pete's sake. You shouldn't have had to go through that. No one should."

Streams trickled hot down Ainsley's cheeks. "How much are we intending people to use this? I thought it was supposed to be to get closure with loved ones, not replace moment-to-moment interactions."

"Ainsley, this feels important. Maybe we should talk about this privately," Samarium said gently, then turned to the rest of the team. "Why don't we take a quick break, and come back in ten. Everyone get a breath of air, then we'll continue where we left off."

Soon it was just Ainsley and Samarium in the room.

"To answer your question, it's both, Ainsley," Samarium said. "We expect users to use it to get closure with loved ones, and to substitute themselves in trivial interactions people have less time and desire for. I apologize — I thought we'd gone over this. It's probably my fault for not giving a clear, deep explanation of what our goal is. To be honest, the global vision's been coming together as we've seen how far we can take the tech, as a result of your work."

Ainsley's cheeks flushed. It hadn't occurred to her that she was accelerating the speed of development, and she wasn't sure she wanted the credit on her shoulders.

"We're trying to make the social sphere deeper, more meaningful," Samarium continued. "Another team is working on the quick summaries that can be generated from sim interactions. People have less and less time these days, and we want them to be able to socialize in a way they can maintain their relationships, while still meeting the increasing demands of the workplace. Interaction with sims lets you send representatives that, we hope, will be just as close to the real thing as it can get. The interactions and experiences are then summarized for easy consumption when sim senders *do* have time, so that social interactions don't have to linger on trivial details and exchanges. When you meet up with people for real, you can focus on what really matters, rather than wasting your time with trivialities if it's someone you see infrequently."

Ainsley's heart skipped. Samarium's news seemed to offer her a way out of the bone-deep loneliness that haunted her life. With time freed up from small talk, Ainsley could learn from the summaries and focus on deep conversations—real interactions. The elimination of small-talk was an introvert's dream—Ainsley's dream.

"Does that clear things up a little?" Samarium asked.

Ainsley nodded.

"Is there anything else you'd like to talk about?"

"No, but thank you."

"You can talk to me about anything, anytime," Samarium said.

Ainsley clasped her hands to hide their quaver. "Thanks," she said, standing and darting to the bathroom.

As she wiped her face, she whispered the word again, grateful she had such an understanding and empathetic team lead in Samarium. As the project had gotten more and more complex, it necessitated more collaboration between different departments, yet Samarium had articulated a clear vision Ainsley could get on board with.

She detested how much time she spent on small talk. How much of her life had been wasted discussing the tiniest, pettiest things that left no space for deep talks? And how long had she spent longing for those deep conversations, the ones that got at the heart of what really mattered, at core values and passions that formed an integral part of identity? What Samarium proposed could make space for more and longer deep-discourses, ultimately toward a greater expression of humanity.

Ainsley shook her hands to dispel her lingering doubts, then bunched them into fists and pumped them a few times. Yes. This was the meaningful work she'd sought. Yes. This was it.

"We'll fix this," she whispered. "We'll get this right. And it'll be amazing."

She went back to the meeting ready to revolutionize the social world.

Tonight, I dreamed Mom was both the person being saved, and the villain.

A month later, and the release date was two weeks away, though millions of users were already testing beta versions.

Ainsley smiled as Jared's holo appeared across from her desk. "Hi Jared! Guess what? I've finished adding the feature that would let users select their current demeanour, so the sims can better reflect their current state of being."

"Wow, that was fast, Ains. That's great," Jared said, his holo leaning back in his seat and clapping his hands. "I look forward to seeing what the beta testers will think. I really hope it has the effect we were hoping for, that the meetings the sims would have would then be much more authentic representations of what a person's real encounters would be."

Ainsley nodded. "How is your funeral feature coming along?"

"Oh, you know, it's really uplifting stuff."

Jared's upper arm twitched before he put his thumb up.

Ainsley jerked back from the holo, sinking a little into her seat.

It couldn't be, could it?

"No need to be frightened." Jared laughed, then sobered. "I'm handling it with care and seriousness. Giving people the ability to pay their last respects and speak directly to the dead is, after all, a very delicate matter. I think it can do a lot of good, and I don't want management to scrap the whole thing if I get it wrong."

"Hey Jared," Ainsley said, doing her best at feigning concern, "I think you've got something on your thumb."

He did a double take, raising his thumb close to his face before frowning, raising an eyebrow at Ainsley, then putting it down again.

His arm twitched in the same way again. A twitch that was one of the critical bugs she'd been working on, when sim-bodies moved through a certain range of motion.

Ainsley lifted her own thumb slowly, trying to keep a fake smile on her face.

Thousands of simulacra of Mom surround me in the city streets. I race from one corner to another searching and shouting for the real version of her, while arms reach for me and voices call to me from every direction.

I fight my way into a large glass building, shouldering past the hordes of my mother's clones crying out in frantic voices. I want to take the elevator, but the doors open and more copies of Mom spill out. The cries of my name grow more desperate and somehow, more ghastly.

In white, grey and beige-housed suburbia, Ainsley found Jared's place.

She hoped it was all a big misunderstanding, a mistake, and that their relationship could go back to normal, the friendly, healthy back-and-forth they'd been having for many months.

She banged on the door for three minutes straight, getting computerized warnings from a variety of sources until the door finally opened. Jared stood there in his pyjamas with a scruff of beard speckled with chip crumbs, and a beer gut that she'd never seen hints of before.

"What do you want, Ainsley?" he snapped.

"I want to know why you're sending your sim to work," she said, too angry to feel even a bit of fear at his demeanour.

"I'm really tired, okay? I needed a bit of time to myself. I—I also thought it would be good to see if it could work on us."

"Well, it didn't work on me."

"Okay, you got me. Cut me a break, okay? I'll be in tomorrow, for sure."

Ainsley folded her arms, looking him up and down. How long had he been working via holo sim? It would have taken him what—a month, at least—to get into this physical state, wouldn't it?

"How long have you been sending the sim to work, Jared?" she asked.

"Today was—okay, these last two weeks have been rough, all right?"

Ainsley recoiled, thinking to some of the recent conversations she'd enjoyed, which had all been fake.

"Ainsley, come on, don't be like that. I value our friendship."

"I thought you'd at least tell me if you were going to use the sim on me."

"Come on!" Jared said, putting a hand to his forehead. "I can't be one-hundred percent all the time, okay? And I have the right to use it as much as anyone else."

"I understand," Ainsley said, taking a step back. She felt that creeping darkness wading back in, and longed for the reserve of optimism she'd felt drain away on her drive here.

It was worse than she could have imagined.

"Look, Ains, I'm sorry, okay? I've just been going pretty hard, and I needed to relax a bit. I'm not going to overuse it. That I can promise you. I just want to help people, others like you, and I get drained sometimes."

"It's fine," Ainsley said. "It makes… sense. Just… surprised me."

"Please don't tell Samarium."

Assuming she hasn't already figured it out, Ainsley thought. "I won't. But be there tomorrow."

Jared nodded and smiled. Even that seemed different than what she'd seen on the holo. Although this was supposed to be the real thing, it all felt fake, cardboard cutouts dancing a stiff jig in a greenscreened ballroom.

Shoving up the stairs, taking the steps two then three at a time, I make it to the roof. My hair whips with the wind. Mom, my real Mom, stands with her back to me at the edge of the rooftop, the city blurred through smog below.

Ainsley walked through a cafe with a fake survey, asking people to give a thumbs up if they liked sugar, or if they liked salt. She surprised herself by how outgoing she could be when she was driven so hard. She made a joke of making seemingly arbitrary requests for them to change their arm and thumb position, as if it would only be a valid response in quite a particular pose.

Not far from the truth. But the responses didn't make her happy, and the fake exuberance she used as a mask became more and more unbearable the longer she was in the cafe, and the more arm twitches she observed from the sim bug.

Everyone in the cafe was a sim.

Everyone.

On the rooftop, I sprint toward Mom. A meter away, the ground gives out, the image of the holographic skyscraper shimmering before I plunge down. I wake up before I find out if the ground's real.

Ainsley's mother floated in front of her, silent, with the bruises not hidden, based on a recording Ainsley had done when her mother was not at her best. It wasn't how she wanted to remember her, but it was more honest than sims, at least, and right now, that was better.

Her mother's form didn't speak, didn't even look at Ainsley. She was just there, and it made it a bit easier to talk that way, to acknowledge the truth that there was indeed still a gulf that separated them.

She thought of Samarium, Jared and the others on her team, some of the only people who'd really welcomed and accepted her, giving her the friendship she'd sought for so long.

They meant well. They really did.

"Mom, I'm scared," she whispered, tears streaming down her face. "I have to do the right thing, but I'm going to be all alone again. Like you, when you fought big pharma."

The tightness and pain in Ainsley's chest spread to her fingertips, and she clutched a hand over her eyes. It was too much, and too scary to think of doing it by herself. Would she even be able to make a difference? Or would her work be undone like her mother's?

"I want to ask my f—friends for help," she said, "but I think I know their answer already. And if I ask them, it'll make it more obvious what I'm about to do, and even harder to do it."

Her mother's form stared ahead impassively. Ainsley imagined the spirit of her mother, real, somewhere, somehow, listening intently to every word, as she'd done throughout her childhood.

Why didn't you leave him, Mom?

"I wish you were here," Ainsley said. "It's selfish, I know, but I don't care. You should be here. You... you should have left, with me, before it was too late."

How could you have helped so many people without helping yourself?

Ainsley stared up at the hologram that was still unmoving, unperturbed by everything she said. Anger flared up in her, and she swung at the form.

"How could you have been so selfish? Why did you leave me here all alone?"

Her fists pushed through the nothing, her shoulders popping as they threw with too much force expecting resistance. She yelled until her throat was raw, then pulled out the plug in the wall.

In the darkness, she breathed slow and heavy. Her mother felt as close as she'd ever felt without the stupid impersonation that would destroy more lives than it helped.

"I get it now, Mom," Ainsley said as she stared through the darkness, in her mind's eye, at the pain that had driven her actions for too long. "I know why you didn't leave. You thought you needed him."

She paused as though waiting for the transmission of words to fly into space. "You thought you needed him. And I thought I needed friends."

Ainsley typed furiously at a log—her makeshift desk—in a dense boreal forest. She'd traveled to the source—Pepolytics' server farms in Finland, where electricity was cheap, and there were lower cooling requirements, despite the need to clear-cut space for the farms. Ainsley wanted every advantage she could get, and proximity to the source would give her a leg up on any high-frequency transmissions Pepolytics tried to sneak through to undo her work.

Overnight, she'd modified the sims so they plastered a holographic watermark whenever they were used, and other sims reported that to users. In a matter of days, people weren't so fond of using them.

She then put in other quirks, like a more transparent explanation of how the algorithms were being used to create behaviour, explained by the sims themselves while they were acting as their users.

It woke some people up.

Ainsley realized it might not work forever—there was no stopping another company from doing something similar. She could try to take those down, too. It was a lot of work, but by devoting herself completely to it, she felt confident she could stay ahead of the game. After all, she'd designed the sims to have all the things she'd thought she needed in human relations. She knew them better than anyone.

They would hunt her ferociously for this.

A packet appeared in one of the firewalls she doused. A recording from Jared. Her hands paused, and with a sliver inching into her thoughts, she extracted the contents.

"Ains, I'm pretty sure it's you doing this. I can understand how you feel, but there's gotta be another way past this. We can talk this through, OK? Find the right balance. Samarium's said the company will drop all charges if you come forward without a fight. We're here for you, and we want to help, OK? Please send me a message when you get this. I just want to help. I miss you."

Ainsley's shoulders sank toward the keyboard as a great weight pulled. So much would go unsaid with her friends. Not even a good-bye. She cradled her head in her hands. Could they really help her? Could that balance be found? Jared felt sincere, but how sincere? Was that message sent by a sim?

She tabbed to a news feed where a headline announced a manhunt. They can't even get that right, she thought. *Womanhunt.*

They *were* hunting her ferociously. Only by being non-existent in almost every conceivable way could she stand a chance, and even at that, it was a small one.

Jared and the others meant well. But they couldn't see. They wouldn't see how much the framework would destroy until it had blinded them. Then it wouldn't matter anymore—nothing would.

Ainsley couldn't be sure of what was to come. One thing she felt for certain, though, was that the real-life interactions with her mother had given her the strength she needed to do this. For that she plunged further into virtual worlds than anyone had ever done, and, Ainsley hoped, ever would. She hoped this would gift everyone with more free will to choose alternatives other than the one forced upon them.

It wasn't one of the heroic rescues Ainsley had dreamed of, but it would have to do.

She pulled up her hood and activated the top-of-the-line hologram that changed her face, and began her hike back to her hidden shelter.

Now, my dreams have moved beyond this realm, for though I've trav-eled it, I resolve to build no house upon it.

The Mysterious East (Fredericton, NB)

Greg Bechtel

—Seventy-one, on the air.
—Across the top, Seventy-one.
—Right.

Andrew has always loved the kayak for its manoeuvrability, more sensitive and responsive than its loutish cousin the canoe. Some might complain at the relative instability, but he enjoys the challenge. Paddling away from the Small Craft Aquatic Centre, he marvels that this is his first time out on the river. Time was, he would have done this every week. But that was pre-Fredericton, another life. Rocking in the wake of a long-gone motorboat, Andrew instinctively dips his paddle to one side and shifts his weight. The empty bottle clinks against the back of his seat, glass on fibreglass, then rumbles and rolls from side to side against the hull. He twists around to find Jaffee still watching from the parking lot, resting his fat ass against the cab's wheel-well, shading his eyes and squinting to follow Andrew's progress against the glare of sun on water—but already such land-based concerns seem less pressing. Andrew turns forward and puts his back into the paddling, a burst of speed. And though he splashes more than he once would have, the economical stroke of a seasoned kayaker remains.

Rhona didn't give him a time to be back, just sent him out here on this inexplicable errand. The muscles in Andrew's back and arms are warming, a pleasant burn in contrast to the cool river water splashing his hands and forearms, and though the sun is past its zenith, it won't touch the horizon for hours yet. All the time in the world. The rolled-up sleeves of his button-down shirt unroll and dip into the waves every ten or twelve strokes. Like the ten thousand things, they rise and fall without cease, an object lesson in the futility of control. Scattered houses dot the southern bank, and massive concrete bridges loom over the Saint John behind him, but it's easy to ignore those and focus on the soft lapping of water against the hull, the flashing patterns of sunlight on waves, the heavily wooded stretches of the uninhabited north shore ahead. Awash in these physical immediacies, Andrew can almost forget the bottle rattling around back there, Constable Jaffee waiting on shore. Kayaking had always been good for that, a temporary escape being better than none at all.

You'll know it when you see it.

That's what Rhona said, and she hasn't led him wrong yet. Had him on a solid run for three hours and counting, and when your dispatcher sends you off like that, you don't ask questions. You do what you're told, keep that dispatcher as happy as you can, and hope she'll keep the run going. Rhona said to start with the islands, so he points his bow towards the first one and relaxes into the liquid rhythm of his steady, windmilling stroke.

—Fifty-seven. Skyline for a package.
—Right.

Andrew's job interview was short and to the point. The dispatcher on duty verified his cab license, asked about availability, and concluded with an opaque directive: "Pick a number you'll remember."

Andrew picked seventy-one, his birth year, and with that his number was fixed. For the next hour, on early-morning empty streets, another driver showed him how to operate the radio and use a street index. Between six and seven, they took two fares while Andrew learned to always write down his addresses and hand out the proper number of discount tickets. By seven-thirty he was driving solo, his journey of a thousand miles begun. Again.

—Seventy-one, parked at the Regent Mall.
—Right Seventy-one.

In this city, at every moment of every hour of every day, a woman (or a man) sits in a dimly lit room and plays a variant on solitaire with slips of coloured paper for cards, Post-its scrawled with handwritten notes. This person takes a slip from the main stack and places it onto one of several smaller piles scattered across the wooden desk, then presses a button, speaks into a microphone, waits for a response, and nods. *Right*, she says, and retrieves the next slip of paper from the main stack, answers the phone if it's ringing. The stacks grow and shrink and occasionally vanish entirely, but the deck is never exhausted. Sometimes, in a brief lull when the phone stops ringing and the radio falls silent, she rolls cigarettes and smokes, the still, dead air growing opaque with thickening clouds.

The players change every eight hours, but the game never does, slips of paper endlessly shuffled around a broad desk. These cards conjure cars to all corners of the city—from darkness, fog, rain, clear daylight—weaving invisible patterns, strands crossing and recrossing the city like nets. Cards for cars, cast across time and space to dip into evanescent schools of passengers, catching them up and taking them wherever it is they think they need to go.

—Thirteen. Two to base.
—Eighteen dollars, Thirteen. Company policy.

—Right.

Andrew's first fare was a writer whose day job was the night-shift at Cendant, a local call centre based in a dying mall on the Northside and dealing with worldwide car rentals. (When looking for work, Andrew had drawn the line just this side of a call centre job, the only other sure-fire employment in this town if you didn't work for the government or the University.) The guy said he hated the place, all the people he worked with, and every single idiotic customer he'd ever talked to. He never showed anyone what he wrote, though. He didn't want them to get the wrong impression, what with all the graphic, extended torture scenes incorporating his co-workers and assorted call centre clientele.

"I mean, you've got to write what you know, right? But it's all, like, imaginary. Nothing autobiographical. 'Cause that'd be, like, seriously fucked up. Still, gotta put all that pent up frustration somewhere, right?"

"So once you've written it out, does that mean you're not frustrated any more?"

"Not really, no."

That first day, Andrew made fifty dollars for a twelve-hour shift: four dollars and seventeen cents an hour. To celebrate, he bought bagels, instant noodles, eggs, coffee, and a pack of smokes. Rent could wait at least another week. *The sage stays behind, thus he is ahead.*

—Thirteen. Got the dough and on the go.
—Right Thirteen. Let me know when you're back.

Andrew explores the chain of islands strung out along the north shore, paddling in close and watching, learning the rhythm and pattern of this space so he can spot anything out of the ordinary. Whatever clue or sign Rhona expects him to recognize. Some islands are so long and close to the riverbank that he second-guesses his choice of routes, half expecting the narrow passages to dead end in a shallow bay before he reaches the far side. Others rise in regular chains of grassy hillocks, rows of perfectly round humps no more than twenty or thirty feet across, their spacing so geometrically precise it seems hardly possible for them to have formed naturally. As if some obscure and deeply Canadian sea-serpent was caught and trapped here in a sudden hard freeze, slowly starving to death over the winter months to leave only this ossified and decomposing carcass as a remembrance. Long grasses springing up over centuries to mask and reclaim its ancient, waterlogged flesh.

—Seventy-one, 48 Abbot Court.
—Right.

His second day started slow, and Andrew was tired, so he drank coffee to stay awake: three extra-large triple-triples in the first two hours. Later, when a sudden flurry of calls arrived with no chance for a break, he came close to pissing himself right there in the front seat. And though the sage pointed out that the great Tao flows everywhere, exhorting his followers to be the stream of the universe, Andrew was pretty sure this wasn't what he had meant. Eventually, he pulled over in an apartment parking lot on his way to a call and went against the side of the building, the volume on his radio turned up to maximum in case he got yet another call while he was out. Not until he was zipped up and climbing back into the cab did Andrew notice the open basement apartment window, right next to the foaming urine stream rapidly soaking into parched gravel. But by the end of the day, no one had complained, and he hadn't missed any calls. Andrew considered himself lucky and learned from the experience.

That day, he made sixty-two dollars and fifteen cents.

—Forty-two, got my gas and coming in.
—Right Forty-two.

—Gonna grab a coffee on the way. Anyone want anything up there?

—Yeah, just hang on. *[A lengthy pause.]* One medium double-triple, two extra-large triple-triples, and a large tea with milk.

—Right.

This room could be almost anywhere, and several like it are scattered throughout the city. There are no windows, and the only furniture consists of a desk, two squeaky wooden swivel chairs, a telephone, and a microphone. On the bulletin-board over the desk hangs a map of the city, dusted with red and blue push-pins, marked off with taxi-stands, discount rates, and fare-zones. In such a room, in the conjunction of zone-map, phone, microphone, and shuffling slips of paper, a person might learn to read and understand the language of the city, to map the arcane whisperings of its structural dreams. The ten thousand things, rising and falling. A dispatcher dreaming a butterfly dreaming a city dreaming a dispatcher.

—Seventy-one, one to Cendant.

—Seven-fifty, Seventy-one.

—Right.

At first when Andrew's fares asked about his background, he tried to be as honest as possible. Within limits. He told them he'd left his job as a personal service representative at a Waterloo insurance company to move out east where the pace of life was slower, the cost of living less. Kind of a post-9/11 thing, like that lawyer who quit his corporate job to become a Starbucks barista. He'd considered moving west, but though he liked pot as much as the next guy, it had just seemed so clichéd. Everyone and his dog moved out west at some point or another, and even those who didn't come back in a year or two with their tails between their legs said rent in Vancouver was a bitch.

But some of his regulars wanted more, with follow-up questions that were simultaneously tedious and invasive. Why here instead of Halifax? Any family back in Ontario? What about girlfriends? So Andrew started inventing different backstories for the more inquisitive ones. He might be a physics graduate student, a former corporate lawyer, a struggling artist, an ex-con. The challenge was to keep track of which fare had heard which story so he could continue it seamlessly the next time he picked them up. To keep the story going and make it real. To mimic sincerity so well that sometimes he almost believed it himself.

—Ninety-nine approaching.
—You hold off there a minute, Ninety-nine. Might have something for you.
—Right.

Expecting the sudden scurry of wildlife, Andrew doesn't notice the cattle until he's almost passed them by. They lie so still in the long grass that he has to look twice to be sure he hasn't imagined them, chewing their cud and following his progress with bored, half-lidded eyes. Emblems of perfect wisdom, they abide in non-action (*yet nothing is left undone*). Perhaps a dozen lie scattered within a few hundred feet, each with a bright yellow plastic tag affixed to its left ear.

Andrew has heard of these cattle on the islands of the Saint John River, which provide ideal summer pasturage. The grass is plentiful, and most of the islands are partially wooded, so there's no shortage of shade. As for water, no drought has ever dried up this river. Cattle don't swim, so the only danger of losing them would be through poaching—or would that be "rustling"? (Andrew has a brief, bizarre vision of swashbuckling river-buccaneers in dungarees and cowboy hats, rustling cattle on the high seas.) In the spring, riverfront farmers simply take their herds over to a convenient island and leave them there. And each fall, when the temperature drops and snow flies they retrieve and pack them away in landlocked barns.

And yet, confronting these incongruous transplanted beasts in the flesh, Andrew finds that they radiate an air of proprietary ease, as if they have emerged whole from the earth on this very spot, outgrowths of the island itself. Their absurdity is its own sanction, reminding him of a conversation he once had with a guy whose family has been here since the seventeenth century. He asked where Andrew was from, and when Andrew answered offhandedly, "Here now, I guess," the formerly friendly guy responded with instant dead-eyed conviction: *You will never be from here.* Andrew drifts, paddle stowed and balanced across the deck as the largest cow raises her head, flips an ear, and eyes him as if to challenge his surprise at her presence. As if to say, "*We* have always been here. *You* are the interloper."

   —Seventy-one, clear.
   —Right Seventy-one. Come on back.
   —Right.

"So I got two doubles and a triple out to Gagetown Base, six military bucks an' a chick. Good load, right? Even at closing time. 'Cept halfway out, two young guys start gettin' into it over dis chick, who's gonna take her home an' shit."

Twenty-three steered the van with one hand and gesticulated wildly with the other as she drove Andrew home from his shift.

"Older guys, dey said, 'Yeah, we know dis cunt, always talkin' like dat, stirring up shit, startin' fights.' So I told de young bucks, ignore de cunt. An' I told de cunt to shut her fuckin' mouth or I'd drop her right dere and fuck de money. Shut up or walk home an'at's all dere was to it. I got dat cunt outta dere right quick, I tell you. No goddamn fights in my cab."

Andrew learned a lot about cabbie culture by listening to the other drivers. Not from the anecdotes themselves but from incidental details. Patterns of recurrent phrases and repetitions, hints of unspoken, implicit knowledge. From Twenty-three, he learned that your best bet at closing time (especially in a van) was to hang around the bars and stuff that van to the gills for a series of short runs with multiple drop-offs. Ten, fifteen minutes tops for the run, then you could head back and do it all over again, milking that golden hour from two to three for all it was worth. But every now and then, a full load could make a Base run worth your while. Two doubles and a triple—three full fares plus a dollar apiece for the extras—would make you sixty-one bucks plus tip on a fifty-minute round trip. Even better if you caught a return fare, but you couldn't count on that.

From Fifty-seven, Andrew learned about local politicians' back-room deals, as well as a more speculative network of conspiracies spi-ralling out from the central figure of President George Dubyah. "You want to know what's really going on, ask a cabbie," he'd say with a wink and a tap alongside his nose. "We see things." From Forty-two, Andrew learned the fine art of *chiselling*, the practice of ripping off the owners by strategically misreporting fares. You had to be careful, but every so often you could take an extra fare or two and pocket the cash rather than settling for the usual forty-percent commission. The trick was not to wander too far from your last reported location so as to avoid getting caught off guard by an unexpected call. As Forty-two put it, "You're not a real cabbie if you don't chisel enough for food and smokes."

By this measure, Andrew has never been a real cabbie. Not be-cause he was afraid of the consequences of being caught. So far as he could tell, chiselling was pretty much an open secret, and the worst that ever happened was a few missed shifts and being forced to pay back the cash. Slap on the wrist, really. But the mere idea of getting caught made his stomach churn—not with fear, but with anger. The sheer indignity of it, getting caught scamming for an extra couple of bucks as if it would make that much difference. Which it would.

—Seventy-one, approaching the bridge.

—Right, Seventy-one. You come on over and head to the liquor store.

—Right.

—And when you get there, Seventy-one, you go on in and pick up a bottle of Prince Igor. Let me know when you're back.

—Right.

A dispatcher might learn the city like a body, cars and people flowing like blood down arterial roadways, up and down the hill on Regent and Smythe, across the Princess Margaret and Westmoreland bridges to the Northside and back. Walmart a pulsing commercial heart pumping cash and cheap goods both into and out of the semi-urban provincial capital.

Up Regent, the five o'clock rush lasts twenty-five minutes, and a misdirected cab can take that whole time to travel the seven sluggish blocks from Dundonald to Prospect. But with a tiny nudge or the smallest delay, a good dispatcher (with well-seasoned drivers) can perform urban bypass surgery at rush half-hour, diagnosing the slightest of hitches in that constant, pulsing beat.

—Seventy-one.

—Go ahead, Seventy-one.

—I'm back. Got the bottle.

—Right Seventy-one. Why don't you hang out downtown for a bit? Just find yourself a spot and hang tight. Lots up top right now.

—Right.

And the blowjobs. Andrew never once saw or heard of anyone going down on a girl in the back of a cab, but the blowjobs were ridiculous. Drunken couples, bar pick-ups, and the occasional hooker—no one seemed to give it a second thought. Andrew had thought the other drivers were bullshitting him until the day he started his shift two hours early. Four o'clock in the morning, he was half-asleep and undercaffeinated, driving a young couple home from a party. Both were messy drunk, slightly overweight, pasty white twenty-somethings in the usual uniform: him in jeans, T-shirt, and a baseball cap; her flashing the obligatory thong between low-rise jeans and a too-tight party shirt. When Andrew glanced in the mirror and saw the girl's head bobbing in the guy's lap, a flash of pasty white hip (his) not quite hidden by the fall of her hair, he resolved not to look back again. But having once glimpsed it, he found it impossible to ignore. It sounded like a greedy child eating pudding, and it went on and on and on.

When he finally said something, the girl simply raised her head, wiped her mouth, and absentmindedly continued stroking the guy with one hand as she turned to face Andrew. The guy, eyes closed and face slack with booze and arousal, moaned in protest at the interruption.

"It's okay, mister," she said. "I swallow. No mess or nothing."

"That's not the point," said Andrew.

The guy looked like he might have passed out, head lolled off to one side and erection waning, but when the girl returned to her ministrations he seemed to perk up soon enough. Andrew considered stopping and kicking them out right there, but didn't. Instead, he turned up the radio and tried to keep his eyes on the road. The one time Andrew glanced in the rear-view mirror, the guy smiled as he caught Andrew's glance, holding it for a slightly too-long second. Then he moaned—a soft sound entirely at odds with that lightly amused grin—tapped the side of his nose, and winked.

Andrew didn't look back again.

—Seventy-one, you parked yet?

—Nope, not yet. Taxi-stands are all full.

—Just park up ahead on your right, Seventy-one. Next empty spot.

—Right.

Beaching his kayak on the boggy, uncertain shoreline, Andrew jams his paddle into the mud for balance and wiggles his way out of the cockpit. By the time he makes it up onto shore, his cotton pants are drenched and muddy to the knees, the ankle-deep water having given way to a foot of mud beneath. Under the impassive eye of the cow he thinks of as the matriarch, he slides the kayak into the long grass, where it will be invisible from the water.

Andrew retrieves the vodka bottle from behind the seat and slowly approaches the matriarch, bottle in one hand, the other empty and held forward, palm up and towards her nose. When he's a foot away, she huffs once but remains still. Her massive black, brown, and white bulk makes him feel insignificant, his posture transforming him into a supplicant before the bored queen. As he lays a hand on her side, he imagines that any boredom so implacable must be a sign of either great wisdom or colossal stupidity. He wonders what she would say if she could speak. She might indignantly order him off her island or explain with immense pride how she and her clan have lived here for generations. She might challenge him with riddles.

Or her broad flank might twitch under his open palm, the short, coarse hair vibrating for a moment, then stopping. She might turn that massive head aside, press the bridge of her nose against his hip, and give him a single, solid nudge towards the low-hanging branches a little farther down-shore. As if to say, *Over there. Try looking over there.*

Andrew removes his hand from the warm flesh and picks his way around the cow-patties and towards the smaller, shadowed shapes barely visible through the trees.

—Seventy-one, parked at Reid's newsstand.

—Right Seventy-one. You see that dog tied to the fire hydrant?

—Wiener dog out front of Coffee Revolution?

—That's the one. Get out, pet that dog, and let me know when you're back.

—Right.

Night-driving had its own rhythm, steady at first, then the bar-closing rush followed by the typically long and empty hours until morning. So Andrew was relieved when he got a call to the Beaver-brook Hotel at three thirty. The woman, who looked to be in her early forties, climbed into the van, gave him a Northside address, lit a ciga-rette and took a drag, then asked if he minded. By way of an answer, he rolled down the windows and lit one up himself, then listened and nodded occasionally as she talked and talked and talked.

She said it was strange to be back after so long away, and she'd been working non-stop since her return, trying to get the business back up and running. It was hard to find the right kind of girls in this town, and besides, a lot of her old customers were picky that way and want-ed her exclusively. She'd brought in a few girls from Moncton, but they had more enthusiasm than ability, and she had a reputation to uphold. Then again, the Moncton girls had come with a recommenda-tion, which meant she had to at least give them a chance. Just not with the regulars, which was why she was so exhausted right now. Three days straight with hardly any sleep at all, she needed a break.

The woman's cigarette had burned down as she talked, and she tapped the column of ash onto the floor before taking another good long drag. She knew most of the older drivers by name and asked about a few, but Andrew only knew them by number. She asked An-drew if he was new, and when he admitted he'd only been driving for a few months, she said that explained everything. "Don't you worry, honey," she said. "I'll take good care of you." Then she pulled out a cell phone and started dialling. Andrew zoned out as he crossed the Westmoreland bridge and negotiated the warren of unfamiliar back streets while the woman—true to her word—paused occasionally in her running conversation to give him directions through a series of narrow one-way streets lined with vacant shops and cut-rate rooming houses. From one-sided snippets of conversation, he gathered she was talking to a friend at their destination and wondering who might be up at this time of night.

"Okay, I'll be up in a minute," she said as they pulled into the driveway of a rundown tenement with several boarded-up windows. Then she hung up and asked Andrew to wait while she went inside. She emerged with a hard-bitten little guy in jeans, a jean-jacket, and a mesh-back baseball cap. They climbed into the back of the van and, in the pauses between the woman's increasingly frustrated phone calls, discussed who might have some. Giving Andrew a series of in-town addresses, they changed their minds several times before the little guy got fed up, produced the sixty dollars up-front for an hour rental, and directed Andrew out to a place he called the Clubhouse. The address he gave was twenty minutes out of town to the north, just past the Marysville bridge, and Andrew glanced at the woman for confirmation. She shrugged her agreement, and Andrew called it in.

They all smoked as Andrew negotiated the winding dark road, and the woman introduced her friend as one of the richest men in Frederic-ton. "Didn't even finish high school, but you ask anyone who knows and they'll tell you he runs this town." The guy smiled and nodded to Andrew as he ashed his cigarette onto the floor. "And he's the *best* guy, too. You're a real nice guy, aren't you?" The guy nodded again, then when she turned away (still extolling her friend's many virtues) he winked at Andrew, still smiling. Andrew didn't find this comfort-ing. The Clubhouse turned out to be a small grey building at the end of an unlit gravel laneway. More than anything, it looked like a two-room motel with no office, the lane widening out into parking spots for two rooms with matching grey plywood doors.

The little guy and the woman went inside, and the woman emerged alone ten minutes later, cradling a crumpled brown paper bag to her chest as if afraid someone might snatch it away at any moment. As she climbed in, she whispered an address out the Hanwell Road on the far side of town, then fell silent. She chain-smoked and stared out the front window, where the road coalesced from nothing in the van's headlights, curves appearing in the windshield like a video game before vanishing into the pitch blackness out the side and rear windows. Andrew found the silence restful. The van interior was lit only by the blue glow of the dashboard and the winking red cherries of their cigarettes.

Partway into town something bounded onto the road, emerging from the steep slope down to the river on the left. Half the size of the van, the full-grown buck seemed to float for a moment in the headlights, frozen at the peak of its arc. Andrew was transfixed by the sight of it, this massive yet seemingly weightless animal bearing down on them at eighty kilometres an hour. He had enough time to guess the number of points on that rack (twelve at least) but his foot hadn't even touched the brakes by the time the moment passed, the deer touching down briefly on the yellow line before rebounding up the steep and heavily wooded slope to the right. Neither Andrew nor the woman spoke, and the rest of the drive passed in silence.

—Seventy-one. I'm back and… ummm...

—Go ahead, Seventy-one.

—Drunk on the street here says he's got a message for you.

—You got a pen and paper?

—Already wrote it down.

—Good man, Seventy-one.

—You want it now?

—Not on the radio, Seventy-one. You got that Prince Igor handy?

—Right here in my hot little hands.

—Good. Now here's what you're going to do. You open that bottle, keep the cap, and swap your full Prince Igor for his empty one. Once you've done that, fold up the message, put it in the empty bottle, and screw the cap back on there good and tight. You got all that?

—Swap the bottles, keep the cap, message in the empty, seal it up tight.

—Right Seventy-one. You do that, then hold up there and I'll get back to you.

—Right.

After a certain amount of driving, the car becomes an ex-tension of the body, the driver *becoming* the car. Just so, a dispatcher might *become* an entire fleet, developing a kinaesthetic awareness of each vehicle's position, knowing it as one knows the position of one's own body even with eyes closed. But for the mystically inclined, a refined awareness of the body and its processes is only the first step. The next is learning to control the autonomic systems more consciously: breathing, pulse, brain waves. For focus, a mantra may be of some use, repeated to the point of nonsense and beyond, to the immanent something-from-nothingness of a Zen koan. The dispatcher's mantra consists of the simplest of syllables: *Right*.

Over time, a dispatcher might learn to use the fleet as a means of extending beyond the merely human range of a single, localized consciousness. And this extended being might learn to perceive and communicate with other extended, non-localized entities, to communicate directly with the consciousness of the city itself. A series of discrete actions, taken in the proper order, incomprehensible in isolation yet adding up to *something*. Such a dispatcher might become something more than a person. And such a being might perform occasional miracles, handing them out like koans to particularly favoured drivers.

—Seventy-one! You gettin' bored yet?

—Now how could I get bored with all this stimulating conversation?

—*[laughter]* Right Seventy-one. Got something for you, so listen up.

—Right.

—You take your bottle, head out the pm, and stop at the second piling out. Just stop right there, put on your four-ways, and chuck that bottle hard as you can over the side.

—Princess Margaret, second piling out. Chuck the bottle. East side of the bridge?

—Right Seventy-one.

—Right.

A good dispatcher could make all the difference. A solid run with a pick-up near every drop off, keep you going all afternoon and net you more money in five hours than you might otherwise make in a full twelve-hour shift. Long as you didn't piss off your dispatcher, you were sitting pretty. But sometimes a dispatcher could be so good it was downright creepy, knowing Andrew's location better than he did himself, fares conjuring themselves from thin air at just the right spot, the right time. Like that one afternoon driving down the hill.

—Seventy-one, turn left. Second driveway on your left, right *now.*

The Hanwell was bumper to bumper all the way down, but at that precise moment a perfect gap in traffic appeared in front of the empty driveway. Andrew didn't think about it, just took the opportunity and turned. Almost before he'd stopped moving, the fare was climbing in and giving him an address. Then he caught another perfect gap to head back up, and off he went. Not until hours later, looking over his jotted list of fares, did Andrew realize he had never received a starting address for that call.

—Seventy-one.

—Go ahead, Seventy-one.

—Gonna be a little while here. Got pulled over.

—*[muffled swearing]* Where's the bottle?

—Under the seat.

—Where you at?

—Piling and a half out on the pm bridge.

—Right Seventy-one. You sit tight and let me know if anything changes.

—Right.

It's cooler and darker under the trees, grass giving way to damp bare earth. As Andrew's eyes adjust, the four dark mounds in front of him resolve into more resting cattle, these ones facing the edge of the trees like sentries. Ahead and down a slight slope, several smaller shapes mill about in the gloom. The only sound is a slight clinking, accompanied by the rippling swish of disturbed water. Andrew descends the slope to the edge of a dark pool, the smaller shapes revealing themselves as wading calves, and again he hears that clinking. He steps into the water, which is shockingly cold. The calves shuffle nervously and retreat to the far side, about twenty feet away. Something hard and smooth bumps his knee, and he scoops it from the water with his free hand: a bottle identical to the one he already carries, Prince Igor vodka, drained and capped, with a scrap of yellow inside.

Eyes fully adjusting, Andrew now sees dozens of identical floating bottles bobbing and colliding in the wake of the calves' retreat. He returns to the edge of the pool and pushes the base of his bottle into the soft earth further up the bank, then uncaps the one he just retrieved from the water and upends it over his open palm. A folded piece of lined yellow paper falls out. He considers unfolding it to read its contents, but he knows this message isn't for him. In the end he drops the still-folded paper back into the bottle, replaces the plastic cap, and turns back to drop the bottle into the water, where it drifts slowly back into the shifting, clinking mass. He wonders what secret currents govern these bottles' movements, what hidden springs.

Returning to claim the original bottle, he finds a brown paper bag in its place. It's curiously dry for such a damp space, and not a speck of dirt clings to its underside as he lifts it up. The bag is so light it could be empty, and it looks exactly like the one the woman carried as she emerged from the Clubhouse that night of the deer. He didn't know what was in that bag then, and he doesn't need to know what's in this one now. *You'll know it when you see it*, Rhona said. And he does, with a certainty beyond words, beyond reason. He also knows what he has to do now. Clutching the paper bag to his chest, he glances one last time at the dark pool, floating bottles, milling calves. Then he stands, turns his back on all of them, and leaves.

—Seventy-one. You still waiting?
—Yeah, he's running the license and registration.
—Can you see the plate on that cop car?
—GQA 924.
—Right. I'll get back to you.

When Andrew got the call barely two minutes into his shift, just past six in the morning, it seemed like a promising start to the day. Then he waited for ten minutes outside the rundown house with peeling clapboard siding. He was about to give up when a girl came out. She wore a high-slit backless dress of some shiny, silky material that draped and clung in such a way as to give an overpowering impression of *slippery*. She could have been anywhere from fifteen to twenty-five. The girl got in the front seat, gave Andrew an address well outside of town, then smiled and stared off into space as he put the cab in gear and started driving. After a few minutes of silence, she spoke dreamily, still staring out the window.

"Do you love Beck's?"

"Sorry?"

"Beck's. It's beer," she said, turning that smile on Andrew. "I love Beck's." As he racked his brain for an appropriate response, he wondered what she was on.

"Yeah, it's okay."

"Beck's is the best." She sighed, eyes losing focus then re-turning to a spot just above Andrew's head. "What's that?" She pointed to Andrew's taxi licence, tucked into the sun visor.

"It's my, uh, my taxi license." Andrew wished he was more awake. "Got to keep it where people can see it, or I could get a fifty dollar fine. From a bylaw officer, I mean. If they didn't see it." Andrew kept his eyes on the road and tried to concentrate on driving.

"Can I see it?"

He took the license down and handed it over. She held it up to the light, squinting a little, then handed it back. "That's a great picture. Very hot." Andrew felt himself blushing as he replaced the card in its transparent sleeve and the girl continued asking about everything from the details of the car (yes, it was a refurbished police cruiser) to Andrew's personal grooming (no, he cut his own hair at home) to his usual choice of beer (Picaroons, lately). "Hot," she said, to every response. Judging by the girl's over-generous assessment of pretty much everything—the taxi-licence photo, for example, was a tiny, low-resolution black and white head shot, grainy enough to erase Andrew's multiple piercings and turn his features un-flatteringly round and innocent—he was guessing pot, or ecstasy at the very most.

Their destination was an antiseptically middle-class split-level with a manicured lawn, double garage, and a brightly painted metal swing-set visible in the back yard. When they pulled into the driveway, the girl paused in her chatter and turned to face him directly. He revised his age estimate downwards as she smiled, bit her lip, and leaned forward, eyes cast demurely down, the cowl-neck of her dress falling away from her collarbone.

"That'll be eight-fifty," said Andrew, examining the part in her hair, which was very, very straight. She looked up, and the eyes that caught his were somewhere between pale blue and grey, pupils dilated wide. He wondered if she wore colour contacts to get that startling contrast of light eyes and dark hair. Then she leaned in closer and whispered in his ear.

"I don't have any money."

At the end of his shift, Andrew told the other drivers the bizarre story, emphasizing his complete incredulity at being offered a blowjob for a fare. When the other drivers laughed and slapped him on the back, he blushed and laughed uncomfortably along. Twenty-three made several crude jokes, Thirteen asked for the address, and Ninety-nine asked for the girl's number. Fifty-seven, a Christian, scowled and said nothing. Forty-two ignored the rest of them, solemnly placed a hand on Andrew's shoulder, looked him in the eye, and said, "*Now you're a real cabbie.*"

Rhona just laughed and laughed and laughed.

—All right, Seventy-one, why don't you tell me what Constable Jaffee's doing right now?

—Constable Jaffee?

—The cop.

—Oh, right. He's back in the cruiser, turned the flashers off, and he's waving at me.

—Right. Change of plan, Seventy-one. Jaffee's going to block traffic while you turn around, then he's going to follow you back across the bridge. No need to get freaked out, now. He's just providing an escort.

—Right.

—So now you're heading to the Small Craft Aquatic Centre. You know where that is?

—Yeah, I know it.

—Good, Seventy-one. You head on over then.

—Right.

A smart driver never questions his dispatcher except to ask for necessary clarification. And dispatchers do not explain themselves. Ever. The red blood cell doesn't need to know why it's carrying oxygen to a particular destination, merely that it must. A driver might search for meaning in his calls, might wonder if some hidden purpose guides these apparently random, discrete tasks. And on the very rarest of occasions, an astute driver might catch the slightest glimmer, some hint of a pattern.

—Seventy-one?

—*[pause]* Go ahead, Seventy-one.

—I'm at the Small Craft Aquatic Centre, in the parking lot.

—Right Seventy-one. You hop out, see if they've got any kayaks available for the next few hours, and let me know.

—Right.

Recently, on days off, Andrew has taken to cycling out to the booster station along one of the bike trails that riddle the countryside like intestinal parasites. He's been learning to appreciate the joys of human-powered locomotion, a welcome escape from the mechanized routine of always driving, driving, driving. The other day, on his way there, he startled a young deer. Watching it bound off between the trees, he felt a brief moment of kinship, the two of them ghosting through the same woods, free of the town and its incessant machine-driven racket.

Andrew didn't know what a "booster station" was—something to do with the municipal water system, maybe—but that's what the brass plaque said, mounted on the small brick building at the end of his thirty-minute ride out from town. Past the booster station, the woods opened out into a broad clearing hedged in on all sides by tall pines, the only access points being the gravel bike trail and a narrow laneway at the far end. Mounds of rubble filled the space, maybe a dozen or more: gravel, asphalt, and concrete piled up to fifteen feet, nearly half the height of the surrounding trees. The mounds dwarfed the merely human observer and gave the whole space a vaguely post-apocalyptic feel, like an elephant graveyard but for parking lots.

Lately, Andrew has gone there often, drawn by the silence, the occasional deer, those eloquently inarticulate mounds of rubble surrounded by tall trees. Something he cannot name.

—Seventy-one?

—Go ahead, Seventy-one.

—Yeah, they've got a kayak free. Fourteen bucks an hour, no limit.

—Perfect, Seventy-one. So here's what you're going to do.

Emerging from the trees, Andrew is blinded for a moment by the slanting light of the setting sun. Shading his eyes, he walks past the cattle and waves to the matriarch, who flips a bored ear in farewell. He retrieves the kayak from its hiding place, pushes it bow-first into the water, and transfers the paper bag from hands to teeth so as not to get it wet. Then he sits with a leg on either side of the kayak, paddle crosswise behind him for balance, slides on his ass out the deck, and carefully lowers himself into the cockpit. Almost, he dumps it, but not quite. He places the bag in his lap, points the kayak towards open water, and starts paddling. With the rattle of bottle on hull gone, the relative silence of wind and wave deepens. He rounds the end of the island, orients himself, and points his bow towards downtown Fredericton, where his cab—and Constable Jaffee—await. Then he stops. Just stops, stows his paddle, and waits. Trusting the current to take him wherever it is he needs to go.

One More Song

Eliza Chan

After Mira closed the door the selkie shed her skin, leaving the mottled grey fur in a heap like stepped-out-of work clothes. Mira handed her one of the many robes hanging on the hat stand and kept her eyes on her blue and green rug, only catching glimpses of the woman's bruises. There were purple marks the size of fingers on her legs and red, raised lines across her back. Mira blinked rapidly, her hands already clenched into tight fists as she tried to keep her rising anger from bursting its banks.

"How can I help you, Ms…?" Mira asked.

"Iona, just call me Iona," the selkie said, knotting the robe tightly at her midrift. She winced visibly and her eyes darted up. Mira moved to her drinks cabinet, deliberately turning her back so the other woman didn't have to look her in the eye.

"I need help. I, my husband, well you can see his handiwork. I asked for a divorce, I tried to go to the police. They wouldn't take listen. Said I was only on a spousal visa so…"

Mira handed Iona the mug. She clasped her hands around the porcelain like it anchored her.

"I assume he has some leverage?"

The client nodded, tucking her hair back so Mira could see a ragged hole where her right ear should have been—a void of darkness as if that part of her had simply ceased to exist. "He cut a patch out of my skin. I can't swim far, not out of the city at any rate, or I'll drown."

She was smart, Mira mused. Selkie skin couldn't heal like most, but others had tried, even with pieces missing, to escape their partners. Their bodies washed up against the buildings, water-logged and drowned.

"Iona, I'm afraid you may have misunderstood my services," Mira began, "I'm a private investigator. I watch, find things, report back. I don't take direct action."

Mira leaned back in the brown leather armchair and waited for her client's reaction. In the pause she could hear the seawater lapping just below her window sill.

"I've heard otherwise. You're the one who'll get things done."

Iona's grey eyes were staring at her with hope. She would have been beautiful when she was young but now her silver-grey hair and eyes were concealed beneath weary dark circles and rippling wrinkles around her mouth. No laughter lines.

Mira had vowed she was done with all that. It was dangerous work and those who came pleading to her door rarely had the money to pay. Shell necklaces and a side of salmon didn't keep the landlord from yelling obscenities about stinking fish wasting his time. Even a submerged studio apartment caked in coral cost more than she was bringing in these days.

"I'm sorry, I got out of that business years ago," Mira started, she reached for the box of business cards on the side table, "I suggest you run. I know a kelpie, with a small delivery business. He can get you a new ID card and hide you in the van, take you somewhere to hole up."

"I can't run. I ran before and he paid a seawitch to find me."

Mira looked up and saw the blue tattoo on Iona's hand. She had been tagged, the seawitch's magic was impossible to remove without the marine courts. And Iona couldn't get to them without her skin.

"He's going to kill me," Iona said, "I know it. Maybe not today, or tomorrow, but he'll do it. You are the only one that can help me."

Mira swore as she used the ladder to drag herself out of the water and into the biting wind of the tram's platform. Already regretting the selkie's tears and cash payment, Mira slid into the tram, just as the doors slid shut. Tired mums with hybrid prams, businessmen in partially unzipped wetsuits and shoppers with bags that knocked haphazardly against everyone's knees, filled the carriage.

A bunyip offered his seat to an elderly woman, water dripping from his protruding tusks as he inelegantly flopped from the chair onto all four webbed feet. Looking at him suspiciously, and at the muddy puddle he left pooling on the plastic chair, the elderly lady gripped her handbag tight to her chest and shuffled away without meeting his eye. The air was damp and stagnant, not just because of the sea water dripping from the bunyip's whiskers. He sighed and rolled his eyes, catching Mira's glance as he did. They nodded in mutual understanding.

"It's not fair though, you've got four legs," a school boy complained to his friend as they recounted a football match.

"So do you," the other boy quipped as he nickered under his breath.

"I'd beat you in a wrestling match, mind" the first boy said as he started to put his scuba apparatus back over his head.

The kelpie boy didn't answer, but turned into horse-form and snatched up his school clothes in his mouth. The doors slid open at the next stop and Mira saw the boys dive into the water, jostling good naturedly as the mildew glass slid back and hid them from sight.

In ten years the human will be a manager and the kelpie will work on the factory floor until his back gives out, Mira thought bitterly.

"Tell me," a voice said, the reek of alcohol assailing Mira's senses, "Why do you do it?"

"Excuse me?"

A middle-aged woman leered up at her, clinging to the tram pole. She stabbed one finger against Mira's arm to punctuate her speech. "All that hair and big eyes, reeling them in like stupid fish. He might just be a piece of meat to you but he was someone's husband!"

Mira's arm started to hurt under the repeated jabbing. "You've misunderstood—"

"You are all the fucking same. Siren songs and false promises."

Mira started to move down the carriage but the woman's words carried and everyone was staring at them.

"I wish you'd just slept with him! At least then he'd have been satisfied," the woman shouted. Her voice was breaking and despite herself, Mira stopped. She knew this woman's story as well as many others. The suicide rate for unrequited fixations on sirens was as high as the number of restraining orders that had been issued.

Mira walked back and put a hand awkwardly on the drunk woman's shoulder. "I'm sorry, but that is not our intention. Despite popular belief, we don't just… switch it on and off."

The woman's eye widened, then her mouth pursed and she pushed the hand away. "Bullshit! You are all the same!"

Mira's good intentions crumbled in the face of ignorance and she leaned in close so only the woman could hear.

"Maybe if you hadn't been such a wet fish, he wouldn't have been tempted."

Mira was smug as she exited, satisfied to have had the last say until she turned and saw the window as the tram rolled away. Frightened faces watched her, window after window of staring eyes. The water pooling on the raised platform began to seep into her shoes.

"Shit," she said under her breath. She had only made things worse.

The sushi place at the corner was completely underwater, with only the carp-shaped windsocks and ornamental dragons on the tiled roof showing. Mira moved along the raised walkways and dove down to find the entrance. There was an artificial air pocket inside the restaurant doors. A small red bridge and a waterfall graced the entrance. A kappa stood under the water, a look of pure pleasure on its face.

"Welcome, patron. Please hang up your wet suit and breathing apparatus, avoid falling in the water!" he said without opening his eyes.

Mira burst out laughing.

"Oh, it's you. Kai won't be happy," the kappa said as he shuffled out from the stream. His skin was tough like turtle shell but he waddled awkwardly. The whole look was rather comical even though Mira knew his beak could pierce flesh and he had the strength to carry off an adult human if he was so inclined. The kappa puffed out his chest and frowned at her, but being no higher than Mira's waist, it just made her laugh even more.

"What if I'm not here to see Kai, I might be here to see you!" she said in her brightest voice.

The kappa picked at the webbing between his hands, inspected it and then ate the pickings. "Those tricks don't work with me, Mira."

Mira feigned innocence as she winked and walked on. As she passed through the enchanted tori gate, her clothes dried instantaneously. Kai was behind the sushi counter, the knife glinting in the dim light as he sliced raw fish onto a platter. His blue-grey hair was pulled into a topknot and he wafted the smell of the ocean across the room.

Not for the first time, Mira felt her heart sing and wondered if the pain was the same others felt for her song.

"Are you going to say hello, or were you just planning to watch?" he said.

"The view isn't too bad," she admitted, crossing the room.

"And yet I get the distinct feeling this isn't a social call," Kai said. He wiped the edge of the platter and turned it to check from all angles.

"There's nothing wrong with a bit of business and pleasure," Mira said, putting a slight melody into her words.

Kai raised an eyebrow then took the platter to the nearest table and started eating. Mira sat next to him and dropped the act.

"Okay, you win. I need something from you."

"I'm not allowed to disturb the balance, Mira."

"Yes, all you can do is make sushi and do calligraphy," she retorted. It was both the attraction and the curse of knowing a water dragon. His premises were a safe zone—many of her clients had found a moment's reprieve from all the arid crap of the world within its walls—but Kai wouldn't lift a finger to change the equilibrium. They had fought about it more times than she cared to remember until she had finally had enough and left him.

"You don't need to know anything," she continued, touching his wrist gently. "Just give me a blindspot. A few hours is all I need."

"You are kidding?" The sushi fell from his chopsticks. "Mira I thought you packed it in? You know I can't keep doing this. After last time—"

"I'm not like you. I can't just sit by and watch our people being hurt." She regretted her words as soon as she had said them. Mira knew that Kai had no choice—he had been sent as their ambassador and for right or wrong, he had to stick to the rules.

"That's not fair. Integration is our only hope and if they think we are using our powers to directly harm humans then all you'll do is save one person and screw the rest." Kai rubbed his temples and slumped back wearily.

Mira pushed her chair back and stood behind Kai. She traced a finger around his right ear tenderly and then leaned in close, her arms draped over his shoulders. "He cut her, right here. Cut her ear clean off."

Kai's shoulder stiffened and he pushed her away. He raised a hand and soft bamboo flute music filled the room. Mira recognized the melody as a glamour, shielding their words whilst it played.

"Give me two days. I can get you an hour, two at most, from noon. And that's it. Then we have to talk about this, Mira. Properly."

He looked round at her and Mira could see flickers of see his dragon form superimposed over his features. She had started to forget what he looked like as a dragon. For a decade now he had been forced to live as human because his sheer size alone was deemed unsuitable, frightening, monstrous.

"Mira," he said softly, shaking her from her thoughts. "You know if you get caught even I won't be able to protect you."

Mira smiled grimly. "I'm not the one who needs protecting."

The aquarium Iona's husband owned was a monstrosity by sea-dweller standards. It took up the whole sixth and seventh floor of an old office block, the floor to ceiling glass windows turned into tanks. With the city half-submerged, there was marine life everywhere and the aquarium was a grotesque carnival of cruelty, needlessly entrapping the animals in squat boxes to be peered at.

Mira did her groundwork in the bar beside the aquarium, listening to the workers gossip and vent after work. The men respected Iona's husband. Hard-up after losing jobs in fishing and tourist boats, they drank rum and talked about what they would like to do to his selkie wife. He simply laughed along with them.

At noon on the second day, Mira threw on a glamour: young, human, light brown skin and dark hair, wide frightened eyes and a backpack bulging with possessions as if she had run away from home.

"I," she said at the door, tilting her head towards the camera in the corner so he would see her pretty face. "I need a job."

"We aren't hiring," the man at the ticket office said, leafing through an old newspaper.

"Please I, I really need the money. I'm... desperate."

As if on cue, the phone rang. The ticket officer answered it, frowning a little before reaching into his desk and printing off a complimentary ticket for her.

"He'll meet you at the stingray exhibit."

Mira didn't have to act terrified as she walked around the maze of decrepit tanks. Tanks were piled on tanks, with the fish all clustered near the top of the water, gasping for air amongst the bodies of their dead comrades. Green algae coated the glass on both sides and there was a thick film of scum on every surface. It was nothing more than a morgue. Mira had seen fishmongers who kept their animals in better condition than this.

Around the corner there was a room made of glass. Floor, ceiling and four walls were joined into one seamless tank. Kite-shaped stingrays soared around them and underfoot like ripples in the water. A middle-aged man stood at the centre. He had thinning hair, a shirt that had once been white but was now yellowing at the collar and underarms, and gold rimmed glasses that looked like fish tanks. There was something sallow about his whole appearance. He approached her and smiled with the geniality of a predator.

"I'm the aquarium owner, Steve."

"Levi," Mira answered.

"So you are looking for work? Industrious of you," he said, looking her up and down with an appraising eye.

"I—I'm new in the city," Mira said. "And I've worked on a fish farm before so, I just thought..."

"You'd use your skill set to find a job. Impressive. I like that. There aren't many young girls in the city that would be smart enough to think of that."

"It's—I just needed the money," Mira said, looking down at her feet.

She heard him open his wallet and wad of banknotes were pressed into her hands. It was more money than the average unskilled worker made in a month. Steve's hands lingered over hers. "Call it an advance," he said.

"Oh, but that's too much, I mean, I wasn't expecting so much… thank you, but are you sure?" she said.

His hands moved up her arm and tilted her chin up so she was looking at him. "We'll make sure you work it off."

Mira tried to look flattered and confused, resisting the disgust crawling all over her skin. She turned away, hoping it would look as if she was overwhelmed. In silence she stood staring at the stingrays, waiting for his next move.

"They are a member of the shark family," he said.

"Oh?"

"But everyone thinks they are so much friendlier. See that happy face on its underside? Looks can be deceptive. Those aren't eyes, they are gills."

"Amazing."

"Mermaids swim with stingrays, keep them as guards," he said. His hand had somehow made it to her shoulder. Mira grimaced under the glamour and pretended not to notice him smelling her hair.

"I'd love to meet some seafolk," she said, "I mean, of course I've seen them in the streets and stuff, but I've never been friends with one of them. I've got so many questions, you know, stupid things really. How do they breathe out of water and stuff."

"I could answer your questions. My um, late wife was a selkie," he said.

"No, really? I don't believe you, however did you get a selkie to fall for you?" Mira said, setting the net.

"I have captured many sea creatures. Seafolk? Well they aren't much different. They might look more like us yes, but we both know they are nothing more than fish. And, well you should know how to catch a fish. With some bait and a hook. Easy as that. Just don't expect to have an intelligent conversation with one of them," he said.

"Then why did you marry her?" Mira asked before she could stop herself. Luckily he took her vehemence for naïve enthusiasm.

"I have a reputation. I mean, how do people know I'm any good at rearing the creatures if I don't have proof of it? And a selkie... well they are easy enough to seduce, we all know that. All you need to do is buy them a couple of nice dresses and compliment their hair. But do you know the average length of a human-selkie marriage? Six months. I have been married for eight years. That makes me, unofficially of course, the leading expert in seafolk around these parts."

Kai's words echoed in her head. She couldn't do harm to a human unless in self-defense but the nape of her neck was tingling from the desire to. She had a seawitch tattoo there, same as all the other seafolk who lived in the cities, that would burn her if she used any of her magic illegally.

Mira pretended to be in awe as he beamed and then suddenly she laughed curtly. "No! I believed you for a moment there. You are pulling my leg! How could someone like you get a selkie for a wife?"

His face dropped along with his cloying goodwill. "I am most certainly not! In fact, I have proof!"

He rummaged in his pocket, flustered as strands of hair fell across his forehead. Pulling out his keys, he brandished them inches from her face. "See, proof!"

Attached to a jangling set of boat and house keys was a scrap of grey fur, ragged and dirty with lint from his pocket.

"You keep it on your keys?" she said.

"Yes, um, to remind me of my dear departed—"

She snatched the keys from him. "You keep it on your keys!" she repeated, no longer holding back the rage.

The stingrays had gathered into a dark mass above Steve's head, their happy underbelly faces swimming before her eyes over and over. Her neck started to burn. Mira moved over to the glass and put her hand on it.

No direct harm.

"I could do with a drink," Mira said.

Steve's eyes widened and she knew the glamour had faded in her anger. He grabbed her arm and pulled her away from the glass as she started singing. Mira let herself fall on the ground without interrupting the song. Her voice spiraled higher and higher, the tune of waves and whale song. Steve shoved his hand roughly over her mouth but it was too late. The glass began to reverberate and splinter around them.

"Siren bitch," he spat as he let go of her and groped around his neck. Mira realized belatedly he must have a protective charm. She shouted out her last note as the glass smashed around them and the room flooded with water and stingrays and fresh blood.

Once Mira returned her pelt, Iona went straight to the marine courts under protection of some of Mira's contacts. She would be immune from the seawitch's spell until the court had come to a decision and Mira was confident of what side they would fall on.

Steve on the other hand, had gone missing.

Pouring herself a drink, Mira sat on her office armchair and decided not to let it bother her—she deserved one night off before she started worrying about him. She dozed off but woke with a start when the phone rang. It sounded like pounding on her skull at first and took Mira a while to answer it.

"Mira? Mira are you okay?" Kai asked.

"It's going swimmingly, what's up?"

"The lines have gone crazy. I've had half a dozen reports of a man who has approached every seawitch in the city to learn how to kill a siren. If this goes down the balance is screwed!"

"The balance? Always about the balance! It's already screwed. You are about the only one who has stuck to the letter of the amnesty agreement. We were fools to ever agree to curtail our powers when they were the one who polluted our waters!"

"I think you should come here for a few days, until it blows over. I would just feel better if—"

The pounding started again. But it was different this time. Someone was trying to break down her door.

"Eh, I need to go Kai. Someone is knocking."

"Don't open the—"

She hung up the phone and rubbed her temples. She didn't have a head for alcohol anymore and confrontations were a huge annoyance.

Steve smashed in the glass of her window with a huge fish hook. He was carrying a fishing net in his other arm. "So," he said, as he unlocked the door through the broken glass, "this is where the harpy lives?" The stingrays had had some revenge. Barb punctures riddled his arms and face.

"You honestly thought my own animals could kill me? I'm not that stupid. And all for Iona? Really? She has nothing to do with you. She's my wife!"

"It's called domestic abuse. Holding someone against their will. There are laws," Mira said as she slowly stood up.

"Screw the laws, no human jury has ever taken the side of seafolk. You are all asking for it."

"And that's why I still have a job," she said, realising her words rang true.

He threw the net towards chair but she moved easily away. Too easily. A second net wrapped around her head, tightening immediately so that the mesh pressed against her face in stinging lines. He wrapped the fish hook around her neck.

"Try to sing now, you mermaid whore," he said smugly.

Mira's voice would not come. The net had choked her breath, like drowning. But he had forgotten she had tools other than her voice. She grabbed at an ornamental conch and smashed it hard against his leg so that spike dug into his flesh. Steve swore and let go.

"You slag! I'm going to make you pay!" he shouted and flung the conch to one side.

Mira peeled the net off her head and grabbed the hat stand—even Kai would consider this one self-defense, she thought grimly. Her voice was still hoarse and numb and Mira could only hope the enchantment would wear off quickly. As Steve sliced down toward her with his weapon she whipped the hat stand in the way. The hook cut the bathrobes into shreds but became entangled in curved arms of the stand. Steve screamed and pushed with his shoulder, forcing Mira back against the wall, pinning her there.

"Make me want you so badly I drown myself? That's your game, right?"

Nothing would've revolted her more. Mira kicked him as hard as she could but she didn't have the physical strength to do any real damage. Steve laughed cruelly and seemed to be enjoying himself. She saw the violence in his eyes and knew that whatever happened, it was worth it to save Iona from this. Mira let herself go limp so that Steve leaned in closer and then cracked him hard with a headbutt.

Then her voice came back.

She sang a single note, higher and louder than she had done in years. The power pitched through her and slammed Steve to the ground. Right now if she told him to stop breathing, he would.

"You wouldn't dare," he hissed through the enchantment. "The amnesty forbids you from harming me."

Mira sang a simple refrain and watched the blood drain from his face and his conviction falter. Her body ached so much she barely registered the heat from the nape of her neck.

"Oh? Really? But I'm not doing anything, you are," she said. "I want you to relive it. Every hurt you gave your wife: every emotional, physical and sexual piece of shit you subjected her to, you are going to do it to yourself with this lovely fishhook." She picked up the hook from the rug and put it reverently in his hands.

Then she turned her back on him, humming her song under her breath and put the kettle on to drown out the noise. She tidied the charmed net into a drawer, wondering if she could use it against the mercenary seawitch—she would have to deal with that little problem sooner rather than later.

When she checked on Steve he was holding the fish hook in both hands, fighting her song for control. And losing. He looked shocked every time his own hands opened up another cut. Trails ran down his body and pooled in bloody footprints on her rug.

Mira remembered why she had stopped doing these jobs. And how many rugs she had gone through. She remembered how the power made her feel and she wasn't sure if she liked it.

"Go. Go and get cleaned up," she said.

Steve screamed at her but he could not control his body. It pulled him over to the window, yanked it open and he stepped off the edge into the raging sea below. The tide was low and he fell two floors before he hit shallow water. The water blushed with flow of his blood and as he thrashed, Mira could already hear the carnivores of the sea honing in on him. His protection charm wouldn't work this time.

"No direct harm," Mira reassured herself. She looked at her bloodstained rug and the cooling mug of seaweed tea in her hands. She shook her head and headed for the door, reaching it just as it was flung open. It was Kai.

"Are you ok?" he said, breathless and dripping wet.

Mira smiled and pushed them both out of the room, closing the door firmly behind her. She slid the brass door sign to "closed" and put her arm through Kai's.

"No rescuing needed today. But it won't affect the balance if we eat, right?"

"What happened?" Kai said.

Mira pulled out some very damp cash and waved it under his nose. "No questions, I'm paying."

"Mira…"

She smiled back at him once as she walked to the stairs. With a brief pause, Kai followed.

'Til Death is Done

Chadwick Ginther

DYING

The sky became crows. A black rainbow of talons scratching, beaks biting, caws shrieking, and I knew the world was lost. *I* had lost it.

The Crow Queen. I'd called Her and She came. To save me. To save the world.

Crows swarmed the Lonely Tree, flapping wings louder than the distant explosions. Back home, I could've never told the difference between one crow and another. Here, now, was different. One bobbed its head side to side and cawed—gently—against the cacophony of its fellows in the sky, and I knew it. It recognized me too, and it landed. It brushed my face with the broad of its beak as if to comfort me, but staring into its black eyes was no comfort at all.

A peck.

Gentle, inquisitive.

Probing.

Another, firmer. Insistent. It liked my taste. My heart thudded, pushing life from every cut and wound to mingle with the already blood-sodden ground, steaming against the surrounding snow.

With the third jab, it plucked my eye from the socket, gulped it into his beak and flew off. The pain.

The *pain*.

Enough to bury every hurt I had now, or had ever, received. A thousand glass shards scraping over a blackboard. A dam burst inside me and I screamed myself raw in one yell. I kept my good eye crushed shut, as if that could stop the pain. Hoping not to see the state my body had been left in.

But, I *could* still see.

I saw myself, a speck, from above.

A second crow took my last eye, unleashing a new reservoir of screams. Their friends landed in the tree and took the rest of me. I watched from above until I could watch no more. I saw Her then, through the eyes the crows had stolen, a cloud of fluttering darkness. Snatching souls liked I'd sniped food off a friend's plate a world away. Murder spread across the sky and She took me home.

FIRST FIGHT

It was the end of the world. *This* world, at least.

I'd been sent here to save it. To stop it.

To fight.

And fight I had. I'd never learned the world's name. Maybe it no longer had one; its name could've been lost, cut up in the Rising when the dead started to walk, and eat again.

I could save this world—every world—from what waited in the dark. I couldn't fail. I had to show Her my gifts had found the right home. How many good people would have followed Her to Her cave? How many would've accepted Her gifts? How many would've made the Bargain.

I couldn't say. I'd never know.

All I knew was *I* had. And I wouldn't fail.

Who would've thought, as I got lost in the woods, I'd have stumbled into Her. Into this world, staring at the summit of Marrow Hill. There was no avoiding it. It drew the gaze like a black hole eating light. We'd been trying to take it for years.

I'd left my Sally back across an ocean of worlds, so far I couldn't find a memory of home in the night stars. Her locket hung against my skin; a small portrait filled the silver heart. The only silver I hadn't melted to fight the End King's army.

I spat in mud black with blood and offal. Long before this war began, men fought over this hill, for empires long dust. I'd seen what happened to the worlds where champions failed to rise. I wondered how She chose when, where, to send Her champion, when there was so much pain and hurt and conflict in existence. Why had she sent me *here*?

A scream and the stink of burning meat jolted me from reverie. I forced myself to listen. We burn our dead now, the dying too. Fresh wounds, old wounds, infection, trench fever. That used to be that. They were given Gods' Rights, and put in the ground. Then they started coming back. The soldiers had protested the fires, until our dead clawed from the earth to join the enemy. Christ, that'd been a lifetime ago. A world away, I would've protested too. But not here. Not now. Not after what I'd seen. And done.

Our sorcerers, hunted and Turned, became necromancers in the End King's army, accelerating the assault against us. It was hard. Hard for the soldiers. For me. We had to kill friends. Brothers and sisters. Again.

Now you're wounded and the doc don't like it, on the pyre you go.

It's a hell of thing to have to do. To have a dying person's hand clutch your wrists, nails scraping your skin as they go screaming into the fire. Cursing you, your family. Cursing their fate. We used to give them a soporific so they wouldn't go in awake, but we ran out of drugs two years ago. There was no other choice. Kill them before they go in, and they shamble off the stretcher to gut you. Another scream.

You wonder what you're losing trying to stay alive. If the fight is ever worth it, given *how* you must fight.

Once, I would've felt the same. Here it made me believe She was with us. We hadn't died yet. We'd fought hard. If I pleased her, this world might be spared.

We fought in shifts, but we always fought. No one had enough sleep—not even the dead. There was no escaping the sounds of battle as you planned the next attack. Explosions rang out against the din causing earth and detritus to rain down, peppering my neck and sliding under my jacket.

My friends waited.

I saw Eyes first. He guarded the entrance to our planning area. His dark skin blended into the shadows, but the white ink tattoos covering his body, and which gave him his name, shone as they took me in. His crossed arms unfolded, pointing two bone-handled pistols at me.

"C'mon, Eyes. You know it's me."

"Hat off, Morgan. You made the rules, not me."

He had a point.

I tipped back my hat's brim and let Eyes see my face. Assuming he could see any of the man he'd met years ago under the shaggy beard and long hair I'd grown. His tattooed eyes blinked and turned toward me. He could see through any living creature, see what they saw. That he could see through mine, told him I was alive. It didn't tell him I wasn't the enemy. Neither did my face alone. We'd dealt with enough shapeshifters and fetches over the years.

Satisfied, he nodded.

I clasped his hand and glimpsed what he saw: battles, hot with blood, skirmishes still unfolding, and further up the hill, what my crow spies were seeing. No one saw more of Marrow Hill than Eyes, but I doubted he could see a way we could win this.

"A few prisoners are still alive, for either torment, fuel, or food for the Turned, I don't know." Eyes' shoulders slumped. "And the End King."

"We won't get another shot."

Eyes released my hand and turned his back. I followed him into the Specialists' bunker. There used to be a lot more Specialists, those of us with gifts defying natural law. Sorcerers. Paragons. Tallmen. Now our paragons were broken, our tallmen cut down, and our sorcerers dead. Or Turned.

All but one.

Diahann, a muscular woman who preferred the axe to the sword, chewed her lip as she washed the body of her wife, Vonn. The cloth was red as if it had been dyed. Diahann rung out watery blood from the cloth and stared at her hands. She was no stranger to someone's life staining her fingers, but this time bothered her more than any other. While Vonn's wounds didn't look bad in the dim light, I knew they were mortal. Our last sorcerer. She meant something different to us all, and yet, most of all, she was loved. *I'd* been sent to save this world, *she* represented our last hope of victory.

"I can do this," she rasped. Sweat damp hair, once a lustrous yellow clung to her scalp in thin, grey strands. The shadows made her sunken eyes look more hollow,

"Better you stay behind," Diahann said. "Rest. We'll have a drink and a smoke when we've won."

"If we win, I won't live to see it."

Diahann shook her head in protest, but couldn't stop her tears. She clutched Vonn tighter. "Don't say that."

"This way I go out by your side. That's something, at least."

Diahann turned to me. "She can barely speak. No fucking way she's getting up Marrow Hill."

"She's coming all the same."

Diahann scowled. She didn't want to back down. Her misplaced guilt for allowing Vonn to be hurt in the first place could doom us. Doom the world. Not that I blamed her.

"We can win this," I said to Diahann, as much as the other Specialists. As much as to myself. "We *have* won this by fighting. We've bought time for countless families. Every day we've breathed and fought is victory, a middle finger in the face of entropy and the End King."

Diahann asked, "How can we possibly defeat them?"

"The End King is up there," Eyes said.

"Then we're doomed," Diahann said.

I shook my head. "No. We've faced the worst he's had to offer. And we've survived. We take the fight to him. Take him out."

I knelt next to Vonn's bed and held my hand out. Eyes clasped it first. Vonn raised a shaking hand and placed it over ours, then, finally, Diahann topped the clasp.

"Save the world," she said.

Easy, right?

All around Marrow Hill, crows filled the few dead trees still standing until they looked lush with leaves. Legend said the hill was no natural rock and soil, instead built entirely of bones, and it would keep coughing up bodies until the world's end.

The hill shuddered and the crows left their trees, circling overhead. I chose to take the quake as a good omen. My Queen watched. Between my crow spies, and Eyes' gift, we avoided any patrols as we climbed. We took breaks as necessary. Vonn needed them. We all needed them. Specialists or not, we'd all been ground away by the war. In those moments when we could sigh in relief, eat some old cheese or hard tack, wash it down with weak cold tea, or fortified wine, we were ourselves. Who we'd been before the war.

Those moments never lasted.

An explosion on the other side of the hill rained dirt on our heads, and peace evaporated like fog in the sun. Sometimes, the wind whistled around the Hill, dissipating the mist. Sometimes, those high-pitched gusts weren't air at all.

"Gaunts!" Diahann screamed, shielding Vonn with her body.

Black tendrils, only visible where they hid the stars, gaunts found any cut or scrape, and turned your body septic. Made you kill and devour yourself until you became one of them. A soulless shadow. A flying hunger. And they'd found us.

They smelled Vonn's blood. Wanted her. I couldn't let them have her. I ran my sword edge across the back of my forearm, and flicked my blood into the air.

"To me!" I hissed at the gaunts, backing away from Vonn. "Keep going. Eyes, keep them safe."

Eyes blinked, his tattoos scanning the horizon. He grabbed Diahann's shoulder and pointed. "There!"

I led the gaunts away, toward the fighting. My gifts couldn't kill them. They wanted my blood and life, but both were pledged to my Queen. Their corruption would find no root in me.

I hoped.

One of my crows stayed with me, the other with Eyes to lead me back to them. Again, I hoped. I ran pell-mell through the night, zig-zagging on instinct. Marrow Hill was riddled with traps; some planted by our sorcerers, others by the End King's necromancers. The traps could swallow a person whole. Turn them into a vampiric bloody mist. Possess them with a trapped spirit. Buried on Marrow Hill were nightmares worse than its current reality.

I wasn't running *from* the gaunts, or, at least, not *only* running. I wanted to lure them into a trap that would hurt them, not me.

They caught me first. Swarmed me. I bit my lip to muffle my scream as they touched my cut. I tensed, hoping I'd guessed correctly, and released a breath. They recoiled as they tried to Turn me. I *had* guessed right. When they tasted the Crow Queen's power, they tried to take it, to take me, but couldn't.

I was still too close to Vonn. Many gaunts melted into the night, back on the hunt. The rest: they couldn't Turn me, but they *could* kill me.

A mote of light, like a firefly, twinkled as it buzzed past my head, and around the gaunts. I turned away, and closed my eyes. With a muffled, "*whummph*" it exploded. I knew the tactic and both cursed her for expending the effort, and blessed her for coming. Through my clenched eyelids, I saw the daylight glow as a dome of power encased me and the gaunts. They shrieked, and came apart like a sweater with a loose thread pulled.

Vonn stared, leaning on Diahann, breathing raggedly. "We have to go. Now." She looked to the hill's top. "That won't have gone unnoticed."

I agreed. We were better together, which I should've remembered. My fear of Vonn's weakened state could've ruined our plan.

"To the summit," I said. "Let's end this."

We crept past walls formed from bodies too disarticulated to do more than bite or scratch futilely at us. I fought the urge to command Vonn to burn them to ash. We couldn't afford to be seen, and she needed to preserve her strength for the End King.

Beyond the walls, we found time for one more respite, where I caught Diahann alone. "If you suspect she'll Turn, finish it yourself. We can't allow Vonn to fall to them."

I hated myself for saying it, but not as much as Diahann for hearing it. Her face was hard as my Queen's when she turned on me. "If you find it so easy for us to die, do it yourself."

Marrow Hill's peak loomed. Prisoners whimpered in paddocks more suited to pigs. Free them now, and they'd get us killed with them. If we lived, they'd be free, if not... It hurt to creep past soldiers we'd served with, but their eyes barely registered us.

At least, that's what I told myself.

"Waiting," a chorus of voices said from beyond the paddocks.

Former friends, now Turned; unrecognizable walking corpses, faced us with skeletons' eyes, and hands crackling with purple lightning. Plumes of smoke and ash billowed where their flesh had been. Their clothes—gone to rags—gave no indication of which friends they'd been. I could read the future in their dead eyes: my friends would fall until I was alone.

There were too many. A score, at least. More than us. There had always been more than us. Lightning wrapped around Eyes, lifting him into the air and hurling him aside. He rolled into a crumpled heap. His real eyes cooked from his head, and his tattooed ones scorched black, closed forever. He groaned, still alive. For now.

Vonn screamed "No!"

The Turned whipped their dead gaze to her as one as she gathered her power and wailed. It was as if she held the sun in her hands. Eyes raised his bone-handled pistols in shaking hands, firing by instinct in the direction of the cries.

"Go," Vonn said. "Finish him."

"No," Diahann begged. "*No.*"

"You can't keep them from me." Vonn slashed a blade of fire in a wide arc, burning the Turned around her to nothing. There were more. Always more. "We can't win if we all die."

"We're all going to die if we don't fight," I said, interposing myself between the Turned, and Diahann and Vonn. Their lightning danced over my blade and I spun it back toward them. My sword looked as if it were made from metal, but it was forged of magic and blood.

The sword scythed through their magic as easily as it cut through their bodies, and disrupted both. They could hurt me too. My blood froze. My will slipped. I slumped to a knee.

With a snarling yell, Diahann was at my side in an instant, an axe in each hand. She whirled like a tornado, spinning the cold iron blades through our enemies. Gaunts poured from the sky, enveloping Vonn. She jammed her staff into the ground, dragged herself upright, readying her magic.

"No! You won't have me. You won't have us. Never." And she turned her power on herself.

The blast threw me into the air. I couldn't see for the smoke and debris. Couldn't hear for the ringing in my ears. I hit something hard, unyielding. The impact stole my breath and I fell, cracking against other surfaces, until I felt a pressure on my leg. I screamed as my ankle snapped. Blood rushed to my head as I hung, upside down, above the ground.

When the smoke cleared, I was stuck in the Lonely Tree, the last thing standing on Marrow Hill other than necromancer fortifications. My crows would roost there from time to time. I fought back a bitter laugh. Now *I* roosted there. The first time my Queen had sent me out to fight for Her, and I'd failed.

Failed everyone.

My friends were gone. My body broken. Near the summit, but I hadn't made it. Close. Close wouldn't cut it. The Turned—Vonn among them, cracked ribs yawning out of her body—circled the tree, but didn't attack. I didn't know why—until I saw him.

The End King had come. He was a yawning void, not a man. Where the Turned and his gaunts had covered the stars with their darkness, he seemed to pull starlight into himself. His forearms narrowed to a sword's tip, and as he incanted, they stabbed the air leaving arcane gouges in the world's reality. As if, through every symbol more darkness, more hunger seeped into a world already flooded by it.

I couldn't see my sword, but I could sense it. The fight wasn't over yet.

"Night has fallen and the dead are hungry," he whispered as I called the sword to my hand. When my fingers closed on the grip, I cut off my leg below the knee.

I fell in a heap, new pain lancing my entire body. I braced my back against the Lonely Tree and pushed myself upright.

I spat blood from my mouth and levelled my sword at the End King. "Fight me."

He laughed at me. *He laughed.*

If I couldn't kill him, maybe *She* could. Her names tickled my tongue and knew they were three, and She would only answer to them once. I called.

"Great Giver. She Who Decides. Mother of Dead Men."

Once I'd called for Her, Her rules locked into me, like creeping vines burrowing into every crevice in my soul our Bargain had touched. I knew the rules because I couldn't *not*—the platitudes were burned into my soul, when She'd made me Hers.

At the sound of Her names, the symbols the End King had cut into the air whirled tightly around him, orbiting like a protective cloak.

Crow shrieks cut a hole in the sky, and She came. But She didn't come to save the world. Or me. We were all carrion and She came to consume the corpse.

FIRST MEETING

When I was a younger man, still a boy, really, and a foolish one, I went looking for magic. For Sally, so she might live the life she deserved. I found her: the Crow Queen. Beautiful. Dangerous. Magical. She came to me in the night. Dressed in shadows and blood.

She led me through a forest in the centre of my home city. We walked until I didn't recognize the trees, the sky, or stars. I followed because I needed to. Needed to know where She would take me. To understand something greater than myself. I followed Her until I lost my way home.

In a cave with a vaulted ceiling and tree roots breaking through the roof, a skeleton dangled from a noose dancing on a breeze that wasn't there. The remnants of its body held together by a will beyond death.

Her shadows melted away when we entered the cave, and the Crow Queen came to me clad in gown of Her subjects, their feathers so black they seemed iridescent and chattering as if alive. She smiled as she took in their music.

I asked Her, "Are you a god?"

She smiled, as I tried to keep the fear from my face. "A small word to contain me, but it will suffice."

I'd never believed. Not in the God my parents gave me. Not in fate. Or astrology. But I'd always searched. And all the harder after Sally got sick.

"You wanted magic. Yearned for it. How does this feel? You have walked between the worlds. Are you ready to go home, or do you need more?"

I don't remember saying anything. Not yes. Not more. Not no. And yet I must've said something. I must've said yes.

The hanged body crumbled to ash that swirled in a tornado around the Crow Queen's body, until She gathered it all in a bowl. One crow in Her cloak tore the throat from another and its blood spilled into the bowl.

"Sit," She said. Her request had the weight of a command, a one word avalanche.

She set the bowl before me, and two more birds stole away from Her cloak and landed, balanced upon the bowl. The dipped their beaks into the black slurry of ash and blood, and into my chest. Again and again, until they'd outlined a tiny crow. Then another. And another.

"A knight must bear his Queen's device." She ruffled the crows' feathers. "They will always be with you, so I may find you when you have need."

The crows nipped at my cheeks and I winced, thinking they wanted my eyes. Maybe they did, and only Her power stopped them. She stepped toward me and clutched a crow in each hand and spread Her arms wide. A sword formed between the crows as the birds turned to mist.

The blade was single-edged, with a gentle curve, alike a cavalry sabre, but not so slender; its metal black as a crow's eye. She set it atop a black suit; a jacket and trousers, no shirt. A wide brimmed hat and a thick leather belt with a scabbard buckled to it. She gestured for me to take the blade, I did. All the weight of a mountain and yet lighter than a dream.

"What do I do with this?"

"Will you fight for me?"

"Fight?"

I wasn't a fighter.

"Your Sally will live. 'Til death is done with you."

She touched my forehead and I saw what She needed of me. She showed me worlds ending in fire and blood. Worlds where the dead walked. I heard civilizations scream themselves into oblivion. Heard them beg for an end that took longer than I could bear to arrive. I heard a voice from my home calling my name as if I were lost.

I'd come for this. Wanted to make a difference. Wanted to help, and here were people without number, crying out. I wasn't sure I could trust the Crow Queen, but I'd never trusted old employers, those meant to protect me, cops or government. I trusted myself. I trusted no matter who *She* was, I knew who *I* was.

"These worlds will be reduced to ash in an instant without my intervention."

I had to try. I couldn't go home knowing I could do something. It was too late. Her mark was on me. I'd said yes even if I hadn't said the word.

"I'll fight for you."

"When you have done all you can, call my name three times."

"What is your name?"

"I have three names. Always three." She smiled. "You will know them."

AGAIN

My body whole again, the Crow Queen sent me to a second world. It fell faster than the first. I died again, never facing its nemesis. The third, a world buried in an endless winter, face more than the killing cold. A walking bestial frostbitten corpse, half-man, half-wolf, controlled the winds and the snow. He had brought the winter. His end would bring back the sun, and the spring.

Crows were a bad omen here. They followed his servants, wolfmen, like himself, ate their dead, and their kills. I built no army. Joined no battles. The locals too few to take to the field, were too concerned with staying alive for the day, than to dare dream for tomorrow. I helped them where I could—until I found the enemy. I had a new way to win: creep into his mountain palace, past his cannibalistic worshippers and his snow maidens, to kill him. Alone.

But that wasn't why I was made to live and die again and again. I wasn't a hero. Or a savior. Not even an assassin.

I was a sacrifice.

The snow maidens caught me before I reached their master. I called.

"Thorn of Sleep. Discord's Daughter. Queen of Damnation and Dread."

The sky opened, the veil lifted. My crows turned on me. I fell. Only me. The crows came only for me. The world fell without me, to ice, to fang. To despair.

AND AGAIN

My eyes blinked open. I hung from the tree in the Crow Queen's cave by one foot. Long hair and a beard tickled my face. Always the same. I felt dizzy and sick, but better than how I'd last remembered feeling. Outside Her cave, outside time and space, the happy hunting ground—heaven, paradise—teased, but my steps never take me there.

Never.

Maybe one day if I do enough. Pray enough. Kill enough in her name, She'll let me rest.

If I was awake, another world would die. I'd given up on going home, but Sally would live so long as I fought. I pulled myself up and untangled my foot from a forked branch. I dropped to the cold floor.

The Crow Queen wasn't here to greet me this time. She wanted the struggle, not just the end. Her cave reeked of Her displeasure, but one crow greeted me. It held a ring in its beak, a ring that'd belonged to one of my dead companions a world away. I put the ring on the silver chain with Sally's locket.

Finally, my Queen arrived. She wore a sundress, cowboy boots, and had a light, long-sleeved button up sweater covering her shoulders. A pleasant image, but one that couldn't obscure an oily slick of death clinging to Her pale skin.

She'd made me a revolver to pair with the sword. I spun the cylinder and it seemed to roll endlessly. I saw no bullets in its chambers, and yet, I knew it was loaded. In my hand, it would *always* be loaded.

"Will you fight for me?"

"Yes."

I took my mantle and I walked to another dying world.

AND AGAIN

"Your last efforts have not impressed me."

I hung my head. She was right. I'd been an abject failure. All my sacrifices. All the death, the loss, for nothing.

"What will you respond to better? The carrot? Or the stick?" She ran her fingers through my hair, grabbing my beard to pull me closer. "Let's try the carrot, shall we? The stick might break you."

She snapped her fingers and two spirits appeared. I recognized their shapes. Friends from other worlds. Friends who'd lived until the end. Until I'd failed them.

"Where you fight on my behalf, I will spare *one* soul. Which will be yours, rather than mine."

The first spirit, Diahann's, touched my chest where the bare tattooed crow outlines were and disappeared from view. The tattoos, once merely outlines were filled in black. The crows' eyes blinked back at me from under my skin.

If I couldn't save a world from the Crow Queen, I could at least save one person. Even if it was never myself.

"You may call them from your body to serve you."

I put my hand over my chest, feeling my heart, and theirs. Two tiny hearts beating like jackhammers. I had no idea what to say to the Crow Queen besides, "Thank you."

It was the tiniest bit of hope for me; a glass of ice water in hell, having my companions back. A short-lived feeling. My friends were trapped in their own hell. They'd be watching me die, feeding on my corpse until the end of all days, the end of the Crow Queen, or until She grew tired of me.

The third option felt most likely.

"They will need blood to be called." Her eyes narrowed. "Now go. Find some."

Part of me feared what would come when She was done with me, as much as, in my pain, I welcomed the idea. I knew if I woke again, I'd try again. I'd fight.

We hadn't said the words yet. She hadn't asked. Maybe She wouldn't.

She did. "Will you fight again?"

I barely heard Her as I stared into the face of a crow that'd once been called Diahann. While the Crow Queen hadn't explicitly asked me if I would fight again, I knew Her request was implied.

Save one life or none.

No choice at all.

"I will fight for you."

AGAIN AND AGAIN

It was easy to build an army, and I found it easier every time the Crow Queen sent me to do it. When the End Times come, people always look for someone to say, "Let me shoulder your burden." An easy thing to do, to *build* an army, every time, while it grew harder every time to *lead* it, knowing I commanded them toward death. To *pointless* death, with no hope for victory. Feeding them to a monster as bad as the one I promised to fight.

When the end came, we held each other knowing we'd die, and the world with us. I carried the extra weight of knowing when we did, my fight wasn't over. It would merely be moved to the next world waiting to die.

Lifting me in Her arms, the Crow Queen took me home—Her home, not mine, though I could no longer tell the difference.

My weapons waited.

Every time, the same.

I lay bleeding, last living witness to a dead world. It wouldn't last.
The peace of the grave coming, but it wouldn't last. It never did.
There'd be another world. Another fight.

I remember flying and being cast down.
I remember crawling chaos and the sounds of teeth on plaster.
I remember the pounding of shells, so intense, the din would drive
you mad.

"Will you fight again?"
"Yes."

Whenever the Queen dropped me on a new world, I instinctively knew
what I needed to survive. Not everything. History, language, enough
for me to do my work, were provided. I'd learned something else in
my time: her enemies were like her. Those Who Dwelled Beyond,
some worlds called them. Gods, demons. Angels, devils. Old ones. No
one knew for sure. But I knew we couldn't beat them. Couldn't beat
Her.

The Thunder killed the Serpent. Wolves ate Fathers. Dead and dreaming gods woke and joined the conflict. Titans cowered as their creators fought Deaths. Baleful Eye met Silver Hand and all the while the Underfolk and Overfolk fled and fought and perished.

Dead gods rose to die again. Second comings did not lead to thirds.

Oceans of blood. Stars burned out. Another fight, another world lost.

"Veiled One, Horned One, Winged one."

There were always more gifts. More *carrots*. I get close to victory, and never taste it. In the end, it will be me. Alone. Against the horde of The End. And they will die and die and die. Until they kill me. And maybe, if I kill enough worlds for Her, She won't bring me back. Maybe if I please her, I'll never see the stick.

"Will you fight again?"

"No." I was done. It was too much death. Defeat.

"No?"

"This wasn't the deal."

"You owe us."

"I served until death, as my oath commanded," I said. "I didn't ask to be brought back."

"But you were. And death was *not* the deal. The deal was ''til death is *done.*' And the fight goes on." She held up my weapons. "There's no end to your oath. Not in this life, or any after. Not in this world, or any other. Until I allow it."

She jangled the chain of rings and tokens saved from all my lives and deaths. I thought of Eyes, Vonn, and Diahann. My mom, my dad.

Sally. I thought of trees. Of blues skies. Of birds that sang instead of squabbled over the dead. I couldn't go back there for Her. Not there.

Never there.

"Will you fight?"

My head dropped. "Yes."

NOT AGAIN

Another world.

I stepped out onto a barren plain. Blue mountains disappeared into the clouds in the distance. I could sense the battle She wanted me to fight was beyond those mountains, but in those mountains—or under them—there would also be many ways to reach the Crow Roads that led me to other worlds. Worlds that might be, should be, or should *not* be.

Worlds free from Her interest. Free from *Her*. I'd told the Crow Queen I would fight, but I never said I'd fight *here*.

I wondered sometimes what was better. To have your sun ignited and spend the terrified minutes watching the glow burn brighter before turning to ash. Or, fighting a losing battle for days, months, years, decades, only to succumb, as all worlds do. Either way, they were food for Those Who Dwell Beyond. For those like the End King, or, I supposed, my Crow Queen.

My crows stared as if reading my thoughts, and cawed shrilly, demanding I follow them deeper. There was no life for them on this world, and in case I failed, I didn't want to damn my friends' souls too. I nicked my thumb on my sword and traced the outline of my crow tattoos. They burst from my body, fluttering through the sky, revelling in their freedom—their life. I hoped they kept both.

"Go," I said. "Live."

They didn't go. They circled overhead, they rode my shoulders as I walked. They took their human forms and watched me as I slept. But they never left me.

Every world has its own seers. Fates. Norns. Augurs. What they were called didn't matter, I found them in a simple mud hut where three rivers forked. Inside the hut, woven in gold and iron and wool, the entire history of their world. But no future. These three had been spinning out heroes to combat their world's end.

That's why I came to them, in another world nearing its end. It was foolish thinking; save *one* world, I could save them all. Change luck, fate. Change everything. They were…less than thrilled. They looked at me with one face, separated by tides of years, raven hair going to grey and white.

"Another dead," Mother said, looking into the pool in the hut's centre.

"This is beyond our sight, beyond our knowing," Grandmother said, turning away from the pool and returning to her bed. "Fate's weave comes undone. Our work unraveled, twisted. Every hero we spin out to face our foes, goes mad and joins them, giving strength to the End."

"We are done then," Mother said.

"I will not quit," Daughter said. "We *cannot*."

"What do you suggest, child?" Grandmother asked, placing a wet cloth over her head.

"We use the enemy's tactics against it."

"Side with the chaos?" Mother slammed her drink on the table, and the strong brew slopped over the edges of her stein and onto her hand. She frowned as it stained her dress. "Side with him? He's marked by *them.* We bring order. If we change that, we've already lost. What are we fighting for? What are we doing?"

I saw my chance to sway them.

"You're fighting for another moment of life," I said. "To live. For everyone to live."

Mother watched me over her cup. "You look too young to be seasoned by such loss."

"I have fought on more worlds than I care to count."

She looked at me over her stein. "And all have fallen."

"I wasn't sent to this one. It isn't my fate to fail here."

She sniffed. "You bring only death, not salvation."

"Death can be salvation." I hadn't meant to speak the words. I pulled my locket chain from under my shirt, displaying Sally's locket and the many rings from dead lovers and friends the crows had brought back for me. "I want it to end. For once I want to win, and I don't care if it kills me."

"Your death will not save us."

"Nothing your enemy does to me will sway me. Not with what I know awaits me for failure."

Daughter shot a defiant glance at Mother. "What we set *is* set. What the enemy makes, is fluid, changeable. What if we unravel *their* champion, and set his fate against our enemies?"

"I like it," Grandmother said.

Mother asked, "And if it doesn't work?"

Daughter shrugged. "What have we lost? At the least we've spared one mortal from becoming its puppet."

"Aye. Spared," Mother said. "For how long?"

If I failed, I wondered which of their souls the Crow Queen would gift me, or would the time for gifts be over? Would I be done?

Daughter smiled, and drew down a golden thread and held her scissors over it. "Won't it be interesting, not knowing how it ends?"

She cut the thread, and all three Norns watched me walk out to die.

On the Norns' side of the rivers, the forest was lush, full. Alive. On the other, the trees were bare, dead, their tops wrapped in silken webs. The Norns wove fate, and their enemies were weavers too. Deeper in, their dead heroes were strung up, lifeless husks missing their arms and faces, warning future fools what fate waited.

I cut and shot my way through abominations without number. Until I came to their queen. A massive bloated thing, combining the worst features of human and worm. The heroes' missing arms lined its sides, skittering it around, slashing with swords or axes, while their faces, covering the worm's belly, gibbered and wailed in a thousand voices, snapping and snarling.

I broke its swords. I filled its mouths with lead. I stabbed its belly as it slashed me, tearing it open. Gore and ichor poured over me. As did its young. My crows snatched them up, halving them, and leaving their bodies to fall. I'd never get them all. I thought I'd saved this world. Killed its monster.

It stung me as it toppled. I dropped my sword and gun as my body convulsed. A kind of peace came over me.

At last, it might be done. No more being wrenched from the grave. No more outliving all I loved. No more watching the world die. At least, this time, my end could be *the* end. The pain was as excruciating as ever, but my only consolation, that I would die before my world, that I would not live to see this last good place twisted into foulness was enough.

Not the end I'd wanted, but it was *an* end. The spawn my crows hadn't killed feasted. Eyes gone. Light gone. Breath gone. Life gone…

My crows cried out in alarm as a thousand thousand worms stirred in my chest, I gurgled a cry from deep within. No. *No.* The crows flew into my mouth, the inky slurry that'd formed their tattoos forced its way into my lungs. Forced me to form the words. Her names.

"Wish Giver, Wound Giver. Life-Taker."

The Crow Queen came.

And I would pay for my trick. Assuming I woke, my world would pay, regardless. Soon enough, all the world—all the worlds—would be food for her. It was only a matter of time.

'TIL DEATH IS DONE

I saw through the lie I might ever win. She didn't want me to fight for victory. She needed me to prolong the worlds' suffering. Force them to fight, not die in an eye blink. She wanted hardened souls to throw at her enemies. And when I show up, the Crow Queen's herald, it's already too late. The world will die.

She came to me in a cobweb dress and a plague doctor's mask. When the mask came off, she seemed haggard, as if coming to that world had weakened her.

"I see it is time for the stick." Her words cut like a snapping beak.

She tore me from the tree. No new crow waited for me. The only soul she'd brought home was mine.

"Will you fight again?"

How could I say no? Live, and walk away, knowing—having seen—what ends would come, how could I say no? How could I stop?

Home. Paved streets. Speeding cars. Golden arches. The world of my birth.

And I would fight.

Vestige

Annie Neugebauer

Sam tipped her head back, simultaneously polishing off the tiny bottle of okolehao and watching the last of the Petrels on the beach— multitasking at its finest. The bird banked in front of the sliver of moon before swooping low over the water. The sweet liquor burned Sam's throat, and the bird caught its prey. The fish did not flap and struggle. The "survival instinct" was a true concept that had become little more than an over-applied catch phrase. Most prey in the animal kingdom knew when they were beaten and gave up life gracefully.

She pulled out her last mini-bottle, stumbling closer to the water. Always closer to the water. The smell of salt was pure and sharp, the waves crashing violently. Near midnight, the hike-access-only beach was deserted. A few yards ahead she saw a pile of debris, maybe the melted remains of a sand castle, but shiny. As she stared, it moved.

Sam's pulse ratcheted. She stopped, swaying against the wind, fighting for balance.

Something lay on the sand. Small, maybe a foot and a half long. Slick and wet, although it was several feet from the incoming waves. Something alive.

Her eyes watered. She blinked rapidly, trying to clear the alcohol haze. She tucked the bottle back into her jacket pocket unopened. Morbid curiosity took her a few steps closer.

It squirmed. Definitely an animal.

Two more steps. She gasped. A face. The thing had a face. A little round face. A baby?

"Oh fuck, oh fuck, oh fuck *me!*" she muttered to herself, dropping to her knees beside it. Why had she waited so long to check? Was it dying? Who leaves a baby abandoned on the beach?

"You poor thing," she cried, reaching to pick it up. At the last moment, she snatched back her hands. She leaned forward to get a closer look. "What the…"

She scrambled back before her brain could fully process what she'd seen. A pale face the color of the sand, but too flat. The nose didn't protrude so much as the whole face swelled forward at the mouth. The eyes were closed.

This wasn't a normal baby. Maybe a fetus? An infant with a birth defect?

Sam looked around, fighting back a wave of nausea.

Did some woman give birth to this child, see its underdeveloped condition, and leave it on the beach to die?

"Oh God damn it," Sam sputtered. She didn't have time to be repulsed. She had to get over this horrifying feeling; this baby's life was at stake, if it wasn't too late already.

She crawled back over, the knees of her jeans soaking through, and looked down again.

It drew another gasp. It wasn't just the face. The whole child was deformed. Its arms were too long somehow, or bent wrong—she wasn't sure. Its back legs were stubs, barely the length of thighs. And, oh mother of fuck, it had a tail. A small, useless tail. A vestigial extension of the tailbone.

Its arms twitched, and Sam jumped.

She dragged a hand through her hair. "Stop shitting around, Sam. Help it. Do something." She pulled her phone from her purse, but there was no reception out here. She turned on the flashlight feature so she could see it better, check if it was still breathing. She told herself this was necessary, but she knew the truth was she couldn't bring herself to touch it.

The bright white light clicked on and the infant was illuminated. Thick blue veins ran through its sallow skin at the surface of its oddly smooth stomach. She did her best to hold still, but the light trembled so much she couldn't tell for sure if its chest was moving.

Her hand moved forward as if it were someone else's, and her fingers felt a cold slime as she pressed against its long, thick neck for a pulse.

Faint, steady, there. It was alive.

The knowledge didn't bring the relief she'd hoped for.

Its chest wasn't rising, so it wasn't breathing. It wouldn't be alive for long. "Mouth to mouth," she heard herself say aloud. "Mouth to mouth, then get it to a hospital."

Her brain told her no. No way. But she ignored it. If she let this child die because she was drunk and thought the poor thing was creepy, the guilt would haunt her for the rest of her life.

But its mouth was so oddly shaped…

She leaned over, put her mouth over its nostrils, and breathed into them. The taste was sharp and bitter, the texture putrid, but she concentrated her attention on getting it to breathe.

Two puffs, inhale, two more.

Nothing. She sat up for a moment to wipe off her lips. Sam looked down in time to see it gasp.

It's whole face parted at the mouth, a black gaping hole sucking air in a heaving, tiny wheeze. Its eyes flashed open: round, large, the pupils odd and impossibly dilated. On its neck, the skin parted with the breath, slashes of bright red blood on both sides, but neither spilled.

It was an instant. One breath. Its little body expanding with the new air.

Something moved in her periphery.

As Sam turned, the infant wriggled, waving its arms, squirming, gasping, but it was background information. Something large was coming at her from further inland.

Something human-sized, long and unnaturally low to the ground. Front arms moving fast and sure, sand flying up on each side as it propelled toward her. Bald, no hair, the face colorless and wet. Two bulging eyes glistening in the night. Its mouth, at the front of its face, opened wide to show two rows of tiny, sharp teeth circling back to the side of its head. It snapped its jaw shut and opened it again, a warning as it rushed her.

Sam screamed. She bolted up and over the flailing infant, surging, falling, getting tangled in her purse. Up, finally, sand shooting out behind her as she raced for home.

As she ran, Sam looked over her shoulder.

She saw one heavy groove in the sand and then a tail—long and thick like an alligator's but smooth and slimy like a newt's—slide into the sea.

The infant was gone.

She ran inland until she hit the trail, not even caring that she'd left her shoes and lost her phone. She charged the two miles home, not stopping until she'd climbed the stairs to her garage apartment, slammed the door behind her, and bolted both of the locks.

She panted, heaving, feeling the urge to vomit, a strange tingling spreading around her mouth. She brushed her lips with her fingertips, but they were numb.

Sam went into the bathroom and splashed water on her face, staring in the mirror, but all she could see were the flashes of that thing—those things—especially the infant and its pale belly with the veins running through it, smooth, so unnaturally smooth, and she suddenly knew why.

It didn't have a belly button.

It was too much. With one blissful heave that promised some relief, Sam threw up.

In the morning, Sam lay in bed staring at the water stains on the flat ceiling. The breeze from the open window pushed around the room's smell of stale mold. She felt weak and vaguely nauseated, unsure if she should call in sick, but her mind was alight.

The animals. What were they?

The slits in the side of the infant's throat had been gills. She knew that now, after sleep and sobriety. Gills.

All fetuses have pouches in the womb that later develop into tonsils. Some babies are born with these slits still visible, but they're not really gills. It was simply an anomaly. As a girl, seeing a picture of these slits in a library book, Sam had inexplicably longed for them. As she grew older, it led her to the concept of human vestigiality, and eventually steered her into the field of biology.

One theory of the hiccup proposes that it's actually a remnant of amphibian respiration. Some amphibians use a motor reflex similar to hiccuping to gulp water, and thus air, across their gills. Perhaps this evolutionary trait is still stuck in human DNA, seen only as the now-useless hiccup. The tail, too, could be explained away as vestigial.

So the infant on the beach could have been an underdeveloped baby who hadn't lost its tonsil sacs or tail yet. But no belly button meant it wasn't a placental mammal. It is possible for humans to be born without a naval due to intestinal defects, but that requires surgery, and the infant's stomach had been perfectly smooth.

Whatever those things were, they weren't human.

Sam scrolled through the last page of the essay and closed it, frowning. She was grading the undergrad reports on extinct species for her Ecology and Conservation 101 class online, connected to CU back home. This one was about the Thylacine, or "Tasmanian Tiger," and it broke her heart. The Thylacine was a unique marsupial apex predator that humans decided was a threat. Fear, ignorance, and over-hunting drove it to endangerment, until the only remaining Thylacines survived miserable existences in zoos. Then, in 1938, the last one died in captivity.

The student's facts were well-researched, but he hadn't taken it the last step toward critical thinking. How could the history of the Thylacine serve as a lesson for better treatment of other species, for example? Instead of proposing a thesis, he'd simply regurgitated.

She typed "B-" into the grade slot and closed the screen, rubbing her temples.

"Rough night?"

She jumped, glancing over her shoulder to see Dr. Cindy Endicott standing behind her, grinning, her short gray-blond hair spiked from running her hand through it. Cindy was the reason Sam was here in Kauai doing a one-year field study on The Hawaiian Petrel. It would complete her Ph.D. in endangered species.

Sam sighed, pushing out the chair across from her with her foot. Cindy sat, thumping a stack of books and papers on the tabletop.

The sound made several of the students in their tiny shared office glance their way. The only redeeming quality of their building was the abundance of windows that showed off the spectacular view. Outside the air was fragrant with rain-soaked blossoms.

"Yeah, I let some of the new volunteers talk me into going barhopping."

"You? Barhopping? No wonder you look so queasy. How many bars did you guys hit?"

"Just one." No matter how she tried, Sam never felt a part of any social circle. She'd left early to be by herself as the others went on.

Cindy laughed. She was technically Sam's mentor and boss, but they'd gotten pretty friendly over the last seven years. Cindy was head of the Biological Sciences/Applied & Health Sciences department at Clayworth University, and would ultimately be on Sam's review board. "That's not hopping," she said. "That's bar-squatting."

Sam put her head down in her arms. "I actually feel pretty bad."

"Hey, you okay?" Sam felt the weight of Cindy's hand settle over her own, but the skin felt tingly and distant, as if she had on latex gloves.

She heaved a sigh and raised her head. "Yeah, just a little light-headed."

"Whoa. What happened to your mouth?"

Sam lifted her fingertips to her lips, recalling last night. "What? Nothing. Why?"

Cindy gave her a strange look and pulled a compact out of her bag, handing it to her. Sam opened it and peered at her face.

Her lips looked so bloodless they were almost white, with an aura of paleness around them that flushed into large pink blotches that spread across the lower half of her face.

She gasped. It hadn't looked that way when she left the apartment this morning.

Cindy's voice dropped lower and took on the authoritative tone that always made Sam want to call her Dr. Endicott. "Sam, are you sick? What's going on?"

"You'll think I'm crazy. *I* think I might be crazy. But the rash proves it..."

"Proves what?"

"Proves that it really happened." She looked around, making sure no one was watching their conversation. Something strange and tight and unknown began unraveling deep inside her. "Cindy, I think I might have discovered a new species."

Sam told her almost everything: the infant, the mouth-to-nose, the large, low thing that carried it off into the water. The lack of a belly button, the tail, the gills. The words came plunking out of her like a series of skipping stones, and she felt lighter when they were gone.

The only thing Sam held back was her odd suspicion that whatever these animals were, they were humanoid if not mammalian. Maybe even a *Homo sapiens* predecessor—a missing evolutionary link. She wasn't sure why she held that part back.

Cindy gave her the narrow-eyed glare of doubt. "How drunk were you?"

"Drunk enough to handle it less than well. Not drunk enough to have hallucinated it all."

She could sense Cindy's belief. Why would Sam lie? She expected Cindy's next words to be along the lines of, *You could be seriously ill. We need to get you to a hospital.*

Instead, they were, "Where was this, exactly? Somewhere on the north shore?"

Cindy's eyes were bright and alert, eager to pick up any detail Sam would throw at her. It made Sam think of a few years ago when her stern but usually mild-mannered mentor had snapped during a classroom debate. Sam had seen this same strange gleam in Cindy's eyes as she'd attacked a student's position to the point that he'd had tears in his eyes. Finally, to drive home a point, she'd slapped her metal pointer across the student's desk—and his hand. He'd left to seek medical attention. Cindy apologized, but Sam had always secretly wondered if it was really an accident.

"At the far east end, close to Kīlauea." The national wildlife refuge was over fifteen miles from where Sam had been.

"Really? I can't believe no one else has seen them before! Do you think they're fully aquatic? Or maybe ectothermic? Some sort of amphibian?"

"I don't know," Sam said, running her fingers around and around her lips. "But hey, why don't we keep this to ourselves for a while? I'm afraid that if the news gets wind of it before the right researchers, this could go badly for the animals."

"Sure," Cindy said. "Sure." But she was already looking into the future, her gaze unfocused over Sam's shoulder.

Muscles contracted and shuddered around Sam's spine.

At three in the morning, Sam stood on the west end where she'd seen the animals. She was wrapped in two sweaters and a windbreaker and still she shivered. Her heart beat erratically and she rubbed her palm over the skin, trying to soothe it. By the time she got off work it'd been too late to go to a doctor, and she didn't feel ill enough for the hospital. She'd make an appointment tomorrow.

She thought of all the times she'd stood on this beach since moving here. She'd been so lonely, yet she'd sought the most isolated beach she could find. Even though her studies here on the coast made her feel the most immersed and at home she ever had, she still didn't fully belong.

The perfectly blue water looked black in the cloudy night. The waves glinted like moving obsidian as they rolled and broke. She had always been drawn to the ocean. She'd often wondered if some hidden part of her DNA remembered evolving from the water—if she was drawn to the coast because her biology remembered once crawling from the waves. It felt like they were calling her.

It was only at the ocean that she felt nearly whole. It was only by the sea that she felt a desire so strong it left her content and aching in the same moment. It was only here that she felt she almost belonged. And in spite of this new fear that fluttered inside her at the unknown species, the closer she got to the water, the stronger her feeling of belonging grew.

Jerky movement to her right, low to the ground.

Sam turned her head slowly, not wanting to draw attention to herself. It was heading away, at an angle toward the water. It had something bright white and feathery between its jaws. A Petrel?

Its long, thick tail made no sound as it dragged through the plane of sand.

Hands buried deeply in her pockets, Sam followed.

She tracked it down the shore until the large rocky bluffs at the end of this stretch of beach came closer, closer, and finally Sam decided that it must be where the things lived. Her skin felt suddenly warm and flush. But as it reached the lowest outcropping, it veered left and slunk smoothly and soundlessly into the sea.

Her building fear and anticipation sunk, leaving her colder. "Damn," she whispered.

If she had on a scuba suit, and didn't feel so weak, Sam probably would have gone in after it. Instead, she wiped saliva from the corners of her numb mouth and hiked up over the rocks in the dark. The undeniable pull of discovery dragged her along.

By five in the morning, Sam was too winded to keep climbing around the bluffs. Her heart was knocking like a fist pounding on a door. She walked to a protrusion in the rocks and lowered herself against it. She leaned her head back, closed her eyes, and sighed. The waves washed calmly below her, their sigh echoing up over the bluffs.

Something splashed. Sam jumped. It somehow sounded both distant and right next to her. She opened her eyes, confused, but there wasn't water directly around her.

The sound came again, echoey but vibrant. It was distinctly living, different than the rhythmical crash of the waves. Sam cocked her head to the side. There was a slick pop and the tinkling sound of water dripping into more water.

Sam pulled her flashlight out of her pocket and got to her knees, shining it behind her. She scooted around, peering into the rock formations until she saw a small opening, about the size of a thick tree trunk.

"I'm insane," she told the air, but she was already shimmying inside.

Sam crawled down the tunnel, and her heartbeat echoed around her, like the tick of a clock that no longer kept even time. Future bruises settled into her elbows and knees as she scooted along while holding the flashlight in one hand. The dark rock grew from volcanic rough to wishing-stone smooth, and the sound of lapping water echoed louder, louder, until she could no longer hear her own pulse.

Then the tunnel opened into a cavern filled with a soft, diffuse light. In spite of the adrenaline making her tremble, Sam turned off her flashlight. She didn't want to alert the animals to her presence, and there was enough light once her eyes adjusted. The room smelled strongly of salt mixed with something rank.

She scooted forward, out of the tunnel mouth, and sat up, moving toward the edge of a natural shelf about twenty feet above a vast, bowl-shaped underground room. She tucked her flashlight back into her pack and pulled out a can of pepper spray, just in case. Her vantage point was above the water, which lapped occasionally at rocks that flattened away from it like a stone beach.

The shelf was maybe four feet deep, though it curved in a semicircle partway around the room. There was enough headroom to stand, and the ceiling was made of a smooth, melted version of the same rough rock outside.

It was a sea cave of sorts, but the opening was below the waterline. As the sun rose, the light filtered through the water and turned it a semi-translucent green, making the inside of the cavern glow in a study of light and shadow.

At first she saw nine of the animals. But as her eyes continued to adjust and she looked further back into the darkest recesses, she couldn't be sure. A dozen, maybe more. Her hand tightened on the pepper spray, but there was no way they could get to her up here. Most of them were large, probably fully grown, although they were of roughly two different sizes that suggested sexual dimorphism.

There was one that was half as long as the others. It dove noisily into the water, swam down deep enough to become a vague, dark shape, and then circled around. It resurfaced with a violent splash, loping toward where two of the larger ones lay tangled together. It clambered right up over them, eliciting two loud puffs of air. Then it ran back to the edge and propelled itself into the water again.

It was a juvenile, playing with its family, almost like otters. They were social.

A smile crept across Sam's face, and she silently took off her backpack, retrieving a pen and notepad, and settled in to take notes.

A loud smacking sound woke her. Sam startled, sitting up, and bumped the back of her head against a jut in the rock. She shook herself and looked over the ledge to witness some aggressive posturing by one of the smaller adult animals, which she took to be the females.

This one was backed into an extrusion in the cave, her mouth open, rows of tiny teeth bared, and her large, powerful tail slapped loudly against the wall, making the smacking sound. A larger male skirted her, snapping, and then Sam saw the infant behind the female. Small, pale, squirmy—the one Sam had seen on the beach. This was its mother, protecting the baby.

Sam stayed long enough to watch the confrontation die down. She dutifully took her notes, keeping track of what was fact and what was conjecture, although it was mostly conjecture at this point. She believed they were ectothermic and semi-aquatic, going underground to cool. It was likely they were slimy looking because they had to stay moist to breathe through their skin. The adults didn't appear to have gills, which made her think that they probably also breathed underwater in this way.

Regardless, they were a fascinating species and a once in a century find, which was exactly what worried Sam. She thought maybe if she could document them well before anyone else found out, she *might* have a shot at getting them protected species status before the general public learned of them. They were obviously rare, if not the last of their kind, or someone else would have discovered them by now. Which meant that there was no room for error. These were not Great Whites, with a large enough population to recover after human over-hunting. These were even less populous than Tasmanian Tigers had once been. A few zealous hunters could destroy them.

Sam packed her backpack and left through the tunnel. When she stood, dusk was settling. She'd been in the cave all day. No wonder she fell asleep. Her limbs felt weak and heavy, and she knew she needed medical care, but she felt an indefinable pressure tailing her.

Time, her instinct told her, was ticking down. Faster, faster, as irregular as her heart. A shudder wracked her.

One good night's sleep, and she'd be okay. She'd call in sick and come back in the morning.

Sam stood, panting, near the aboveground entrance to the cavern. It could only be seen from the perfect angle, which had made it difficult to find again. And rather than waking refreshed, she was even sicker this morning. She felt as if someone had replaced her blood with liquid lead and covered her skin with saran wrap. Her head pulsed and her heart pounded, so she waited a moment to catch her breath.

"East end, huh?"

Sam whirled with a little yelp. "Cindy! What are you doing here?"

"I knew you weren't sick."

Sam crossed her arms over her chest, wondering if Cindy had already seen the opening. She tried not to look at it. "I am sick."

Cindy narrowed her eyes, scanning her, but then her scowl softened and real concern flittered across her features. "Okay, you are sick. Damn, Sam, why aren't you at a doctor's?"

Sam's eyes flicked down to the opening, and Cindy's followed.

That glint lit her from within. "They're in there, aren't they? You found them!"

Regret roiled through her. There was no point in denying it now. "Yes."

"Can we get in? Is it dangerous? Will you show me?"

She hesitated, her heart tattooing out doubts and defenses. But there was no way around it. If she left, Cindy would go in without her. That would only be worse.

Sam sighed. "Yes."

The animals had found some prey. Sam and Cindy watched as a medium-sized brown dog—already dead, thankfully—was squabbled over and consumed. Wet ripping sounds echoed through the cave, followed by the scent of copper. Sam had a moment to wonder if the pet disappearance rate was higher than usual in this area, and then Cindy said, "My God, they look almost… hominid."

A few of the animals looked up at the sound, but when they saw nothing around them they returned to their meal.

Cindy shuddered and said, "We have to tell someone."

Sam felt a responding shudder through her spine, but fought it. "No."

Cindy turned to her, eyes wide. "These things are dangerous! The people around here have a right to know."

"The population here is very small. Otherwise there would have been sightings reported sooner."

"But look at you! You're obviously ill. Do you want this to happen to someone else?"

"I'm only sick because I touched them with my mouth. They probably have some sort of toxin on their skin. The chances of this happening again are slim to none."

"People have a right to know," Cindy repeated. She ran a hand through her short, spiky hair, rearranging the bangs, and Sam thought she could discern the pattern of her thoughts.

"Who would you tell?"

Cindy shrugged. "Kauai news, to start. To get the word out."

"You want to be on the news."

Cindy's eyes flashed as the green light of the cave bounced off her pupils. "I want to keep people safe from dangers they don't even know are lurking around these shores."

"If that were true, you could tell the mayor and let him decide. Or the CDC."

"That would be too slow. The world needs to know about this now. Just think of how this will change our field! We'll be famous!" As she spoke, Cindy pulled her phone from her pocket, pressed a button, and lifted it up.

Sam's heart paused, wilting, then surged to action, leaving her feeling dizzy and flushed. "What are you doing?"

"Taking video. This needs to be documented."

"I've already been documenting."

Cindy stepped closer to the shelf's ledge to get a better view of the den below.

"Cindy, stop."

Cindy glared at her. "Don't be selfish, Sam. Knowledge is meant to be shared."

Sam stepped forward. "No, if we don't handle this right you're going to cause a panic. If you go on the news with footage of these things eating Fido and say they're dangerous before we can put out any education about them, you'll scare everyone. They'll hunt them down, kill them, capture them, study them in zoos and labs." Her chest actually hurt from the pounding of her heart. She rubbed it.

"They should be studied. Who knows what miracle cures their genetics might unlock? What evolutionary history?"

Sam could think of nothing but the Tasmanian Tigers—the last one dying uselessly in a zoo. She spotted the infant, small and fragile, wiggling in the corner. A wave of protectiveness crashed over her, and her tone grew stern. "I said stop."

Cindy ignored her.

Sam knocked the phone from her hand. Cindy gasped as it went spiraling end over end, then plopped into the water.

Five of the animals looked up from their meal, staring at the water where it had landed. Seconds passed where all Sam could hear was blood rushing behind her ears. Then one of them broke away and dove noiselessly in, and the other four turned back to their food.

Cindy whirled. "You bitch."

Sam tried to look defiant instead of scared. "I told you to stop. These animals are probably already endangered, Cindy. We can't be casual with their existence."

"I don't need you to remind me what they are. I would remind you that *I* am the one with a doctorate in endangered species genetics, not you." She stalked one step forward. "And you're going to pay for that fucking phone." Cindy grabbed her by the arm.

"Don't touch me!" Her voice came out high and shrill, echoing through the cavern. There were more water sounds below.

Cindy's hand tightened painfully, and she reached with the other for Sam's backpack. "Are your notes in here?"

Sam twisted back and forth, trying to dislodge Cindy's grip and keep her from grabbing for her pack. Why did she want her notes? What was she going to do with them? Destroy them to get even, or steal them and run to the news?

Cindy let go of her arm, shoving her shoulder to get at the pack. Sam's heart was screaming within her chest. She felt she would collapse at any moment.

"I said get *off* me!"

Cindy grunted and lunged.

Sam's thoughts moved like a misfiring circuit within a slow jelly-roll of time, faulty and electric and impossibly fast. She had a clear vision of what her options were: duck, or push.

Sam pushed.

Cindy screamed. She windmilled wildly, her mouth forming an oval of darkness, and then she fell.

Her scream pierced the cave, then was cut abruptly by a splash and a gurgle. Sam held her breath as the echoes of the cry died, and then she heard water moving. She stepped to the edge of the shelf and looked down.

The last of the adults slipped into the water. Their silhouettes moved deep in the green like limbed eels, eerily silent once underwater.

The dark shapes moved inward, knotting into an indecipherable cluster of parts, a perfectly synchronized underwater dance. There were sharp motions, the cluster tightened, and blood slowly spread through the water.

Sam wept.

She needed to lie down, but she knew deep in her gut that once she did she wouldn't get back up. Her back spasmed violently, spreading to her limbs, which flopped with the convulsion. Fatigue seeped through her like anesthesia. This was a systemic reaction to whatever neurotoxins were on their skin. It was probably too late for a doctor even if she'd wanted one. Yet there wasn't time to question why she wanted what she wanted—only time to do it.

She added some final thoughts to her notes and left them out, open, where anyone who might ever come through the upper entrance to the cave would be sure to see them. Would her thoughts about preservation and caution do any good? She had no way of knowing, but it was all she could do.

She left her backpack behind as well, tucked unobtrusively against the wall. Then she slowly made her way outside and picked down to the beach beneath the bluffs.

It was near dusk by the time she sucked in the deepest breath she could, fought off another convulsion, and dove into the sea.

Sam's lungs felt like two giant, weeping bruises when she surfaced inside the cave. If they couldn't breathe underwater, they sure as hell could hold their breath a lot longer than she could. Still, as she met air, she fought not to gasp but to inhale quietly. If she could avoid startling them overmuch, she would.

As the oxygen hit her lungs, her whole body convulsed and she swallowed water, coughing and hiccuping. Several of the animals looked at her from the flat rocks that served as their home. They appeared calm, many sleeping, probably full from their meal. Sam tried not to think about that as she paddled slowly closer.

They might attack her. Probably, even. Her hope was crazy. But even so, it would be worth it. She was dying anyway. If she could spend the last moments of her life witnessing these magnificent creatures up close, she would die content. It was the epitome of what she'd dedicated her life to.

Her legs had lost sensation, so she had to drag herself ashore with arms no longer evolved to work as forefeet. More of the animals looked her way, and the juvenile turned to face her, but none of them came forward.

A few yards from the water, Sam collapsed. A violent convulsion wracked her entire body, and she struggled not to cry out. When it passed, she opened her eyes.

The juvenile had come a few feet closer, but was still yards away. It smelled of algae and blood. Several of the adults had turned toward her as well, but they sat peacefully, watching.

A strange, fierce joy seared through the pain, and her wild hope was affirmed. These animals, they were her predecessors from millennia ago. She knew that she had come from the sea. Hadn't she always felt its vestiges somewhere deep in her marrow? Hadn't she always felt it calling her home? She didn't belong anywhere else, and this was why. Some of them had never left.

The juvenile inched closer, and a few more of the adults roused.

Maybe these animals sensed that. The scientist in Sam argued that they were probably full. Or maybe they could see that she was already dying; perhaps they were waiting for their poison to make her an easier meal. But she allowed herself to believe that they somehow sensed her affinity for them. Maybe they could tell that for the first time in her life, Sam didn't feel out of place. She felt that for once she was in the *right* place.

A series of convulsions took her, so strong that her head bounced and cracked on the stone floor. Then she curled onto her side facing the animals, sobbing, hiccuping, smiling.

The juvenile darted closer, and Sam stared into his alien, animal eyes, and she thought she discerned a glint of intelligence there. Almost familiar. A source of humanity, perhaps. It snapped its jaws.

Her heart stopped. She felt it still, and she gasped in a breath before it started again. Pain laced her torso, but her arms, too, had gone numb.

All of the adults were up now, walking toward her with their strange, horizontal limbs. A few of them yawned, bearing small sharp teeth.

Sam flopped onto her back, heaving a last sigh. Her heart stopped again, and dark shapes moved in from three sides.

It felt like she had finally come home.

Gift of the Kites

Jim C. Hines

The first time Jesse saw the black Buka was in the park. He was flying a plastic Superman kite, dueling against his step-father's rainbow box kite.

Jesse yanked the blue nylon string, swooping his kite toward his step-father's.

Kentaro dodged easily. "Too broad a strike," he called, laughing. "A true fighter kite would loop around and cut your line."

"Get him, Jesse," cheered Jesse's mother, sitting in the shade on one of the picnic benches.

At twelve years old, Jesse felt a mix of pride and embarrassment at her enthusiasm. Flushing, he unwrapped a bit more line, sending his kite higher. He dove again, missed, then tugged the kite in a tight turn that nearly clipped Kentaro's kite. His mother whistled.

"Much better," Kentaro said, grinning. He pulled his kite through a long 'J' in salute. "Amazing control from a plastic store-bought kite. You're sure you have no Japanese blood?"

A shadow caught Jesse's attention. A black rectangular kite leapt from the horizon, corkscrewing through the sky. Jesse ran toward the fence, hoping to glimpse the kite's owner. His Superman kite followed like an obedient blue and red puppy.

"What is it?" his mother called.

Higher and higher the black kite flew. The string was invisible to Jesse's eyes, but given the angle, the owner had to be by the highway. The wind carried exhaust fumes to Jesse's nose.

"It's a Buka kite," Jesse yelled. The black fighting kite moved like no kite he had ever seen. It flew and bucked like a thing alive.

Kentaro shielded his eyes. "I see nothing."

Jesse's bowels grew cold, and sweat beaded his forehead. He felt exposed, a rabbit trapped in the open as a hawk swooped down. He wanted to run away, but his legs trembled, and he could barely stand.

The Buka turned slightly. Jesse's breath caught. Something within him knew he wasn't the kite's target. "Mom, look out!"

Kentaro was still searching for the kite, but the terror in Jesse's voice brought him sprinting. His box kite crashed, forgotten. "What is it?"

Jesse shook his head. There was no time. The Buka was moving faster. It was so big, a window of darkness the size of a bus. How could anyone control a kite that huge?

"Jesse, I'm here." Kentaro squeezed his shoulders.

The wind blew harder. Jesse's kite tugged its line, like an animal struggling to escape its leash. Jesse twisted away from his step-father, circling his kite around to intercept the Buka. He couldn't see the other kite's line, but he knew where it had to be. Closer and closer it flew. It began to block the wind, forcing Jesse to shorten his line to keep his own kite aloft.

Jesse backed away from the fence, trying to stay between the black kite and his mother. The Buka paused in its flight, then dove. Jesse yanked his own line, hoping to tangle his kite with the Buka and bring them both down.

The blue line quivered. Ice shot through Jesse's fingers. He cried out, and then his line was falling, cut cleanly a short length from the kite.

"Mom!" Jesse screamed.

The Buka touched the earth, an enormous sheet of blackness that blotted half the park from view. When it rose, Jesse's mother was on the ground, shaking uncontrollably.

"Susan!" Kentaro shouted. He reached her side before Jesse, catching her shoulders and moving her away from the steel legs of the picnic table. "Jesse, get her medicine from the car. Quickly!"

Jesse cried as he ran, knowing it was too late. Whatever the black kite had done, no pill would fix it.

Beside the parking lot, his Superman kite sat torn and broken in the branches of a spruce tree.

One year later, Jesse sat in his bedroom, painting broad, garish stripes over the paper of his newest kite. He longed to add tassels to the corners, but such decoration would be too obviously Asian.

After his mother's death, the courts had given full custody to his biological father Sam, a man Jesse hadn't seen in years. But Sam had kept current with his child support, and Michigan law said that was enough to tear Jesse away from Kentaro.

Jesse jabbed his brush into the paint, remembering how Sam had thrown out Jesse's ebony chopsticks, his anime collection, anything with any trace of Kentaro's Japanese heritage. He hoped this kite would slip past Sam's radar. Jesse needed a kite, and what better design than the Hata, a diamond-shaped fighter traditionally painted red, white, and blue?

Jesse pushed away from the desk and stretched. The small bedroom still didn't feel like *his* room. Faded patches marked the wood-paneled walls of the former den. Several cigarette burns marked the carpet.

He glanced at the picture taped to the window, the one of his mother after one of her bike races. The hospital said her death last year was a reaction to her epilepsy medicine. Jesse knew better.

He returned to the desk and examined the bamboo splints. The wood flexed into a perfect arc. He tested the curve and the balance, then used string to bind the splints together.

By the time Sam's car door slammed in the driveway, the paint had dried enough for Jesse to begin gluing the paper to the frame. The paper rustled, tasting an unfelt wind.

The bedroom door opened. "You got a card or something," Sam said. Jesse wondered if anyone else would have heard the slur in his voice.

"Thanks." Had Sam been drinking to mark the anniversary of Susan's death? Why such grief for a woman he hadn't seen in nine years? Jesse shoved the bitterness aside and grabbed the envelope. There was no return address. His pulse quickened, and he casually tossed it onto his desk.

"Aren't you going to open it?" Sam asked.

"I'm busy."

Sam grabbed the envelope. "Open it."

Forcing a smile, Jesse used one of his Exacto knives to slit the envelope. Inside the card, Kentaro's precise handwriting read:

Jesse,
It's been a year since Susan left us. I want you to know you are still in my thoughts, and in my heart.

That was as far as Jesse got before Sam snatched it away. "I knew it. Why can't he leave us alone? You're *my* son!"

Jesse grabbed for the card and missed.

"Bad enough he took Susan. You're my son." He glanced past Jesse, studying the half-assembled kite. "What've you been working on?"

"Nothing much." Jesse held his breath.

He scowled. "Where'd you learn how to build these?"

"The library," Jesse said.

Sam's forehead wrinkled as he stared at the kite, like he was trying to dig up a long-buried memory. "Weren't you out flying kites the day Susan died?" His face tightened. "You and that Jap were both flying the things."

"You don't understand. I *have* to build this."

"Why?" Sam snapped.

Jesse bit his lip. He had never told anyone about the black Buka and his own failure. Sometimes he spotted the Buka in the distance as he mowed the lawn or walked back from the bus stop. It was waiting for something. Waiting for him. Jesse didn't know why. All he knew was that he had to find a way to beat it. "Sam, please."

"I'm your father. When are you going to start calling me Dad?" He grabbed the kite, breaking the spars and using the jagged ends to tear the paper. He crumpled it into a ball, then forced the whole thing into the garbage. "The sooner you stop living in the past, the better off we'll be."

The door slammed. Jesse counted to twenty, first in English, then Japanese. When Sam didn't return, he went to the trash and pulled out the remains of his kite. One look told him it was unsalvageable.

"*Kentaro* was my father," he muttered as he retrieved his Exacto knife and tried to cut the few bits of undamaged paper from the frame. It had been four months since his last letter to Kentaro. Sam had almost caught him sneaking back from the public mailbox down the street. Jesse didn't dare use their own mailbox. He even had to buy his own stamps from the machine at the grocery store. Sam noticed missing stamps as quickly as he spotted long-distance calls on the phone bill.

Jesse glanced down and found he had cut the paper into a rough hexagon, like a Rokkaku kite. He trimmed tiny sticks of bamboo, fitting them to the lines of the Rokkaku. A strange warmth flowed through his fingers. The glue dried impossibly fast. He grabbed a spool of black thread and tied a small four-point bridle.

As he finished the last knot, the kite leapt from the desk. The spool of thread bounced to the carpet.

Jesse held out his hand in amazement, and the tiny kite returned. The thread tickled his fingers. Abstract shapes of red and blue covered the back, like an exotic butterfly.

"Hold still," Jesse said. The kite obeyed, hovering on an unfelt wind. Smiling, Jesse cut the thread, leaving a yard or so dangling from the bridle. "Fly around—"

Before he could finish the thought, the kite flew a fast circle around the room.

Fingers shaking, Jesse scrawled a quick note on another scrap of paper. He tied it to the thread.

"Can you find him?"

The kite flew to the window and spun like a top. Jesse slid the pane to one side, then pushed out the bottom corner of the screen. Distance soon swallowed the little Rokkaku, leaving Jesse to wonder how long it would take to traverse the forty miles to Kentaro's home.

Later that night, Jesse heard a tapping at the window. He climbed out of bed and flipped on his desk lamp. Pushing the window open, he helped the kite inside. A tight tube of paper was knotted to the thread.

Jesse,

I won't pretend to understand the miracle you've created, but I thank God you did. Tonight it was like having you here with me.

You have a gift. I've known it ever since you flew your first kite. I'm more proud of you than you can know.

I trust this little Rokkaku will find you again. I wish I could do the same.

I love you.

Kentaro

Grinning like it was Christmas morning, Jesse grabbed pen and paper and began to write.

It took two months to build another Hata fighting kite. He worked on it in the attic and hid it behind the artificial Christmas tree. Whatever power had guided him with the Rokkaku remained, and he could feel the Hata yearning to soar through the clouds. Finding time to fly it was difficult, though.

Jesse grabbed his lunch and his backpack as he headed for the door. "See you tonight, Dad." The word burnt his mouth, but it kept Sam happy.

Outside, Jesse crouched behind the bushes and waited. He froze as the front door swung open, and barely breathed until Sam's car disappeared down the street. Only then did he sneak back inside to fetch his kite.

More than an hour later, he was exiting the bus near the park where his mother had died.

Jesse searched the park as he walked. He knew Kentaro wouldn't be there, but he looked anyway. Jesse had said when and where to meet, but Kentaro refused. He wouldn't violate Sam's rules.

"Why do you care what Sam thinks?" Jesse muttered, more hurt than angry. "He's *not* my father."

He was worried about Kentaro. The last few letters had been different, somehow. Longer, almost rambling. And Kentaro's handwriting had decayed ever so slightly. It still looked like he drew each letter with a ruler, but the spacing was more ragged.

He spotted a black shadow among the clouds. He felt no surprise. He had seen the Buka more and more often lately. It always stayed in the distance, watching.

Jesse tugged on the leather work gloves he had swiped from the garage, then hoisted his diamond Hata kite. Red and blue Kanji characters marked the kite's center: tanchi, the symbols for heaven and earth.

There was little wind, but it didn't matter. Jesse could feel the Hata pulling skyward. He held the stiff thirty-pound line. The first hundred feet were the cutting line, coated in glue and ground glass. Holding the line carefully, Jesse allowed the kite to rise, and soon it was flying above the trees.

He ignored the Buka as he practiced. A sharp dive here, followed by a wide loop, then another dive to slash an opponent's line. He visualized the cutting line as a blade slicing through the air. He couldn't tell how much of his control was physical and how much was like the little Rokkaku, an extension of himself that obeyed thought alone.

Jesse had spent hours staring out the window at school, watching the birds and memorizing their movements. The small sparrows banding together to drive away the crows...the jostling of pigeons as they fought for scraps by the cafeteria...the hummingbirds hovering and darting at the feeders by the fence.

Time slowed as he imitated those movements. He stilled the Hata in the midst of a breeze, then darted a short distance. He circled, taunting an imaginary crow. Faster and faster the kite danced through each attack.

The wind changed, bringing the smell of cigarette smoke. Before Jesse could move, a strong hand clamped his shoulder. "I've spent two hours trying to find your worthless hide," Sam thundered.

Jesse kept his grip on the kite string, trying to reel it in without being too obvious. "I'm sorry. I—"

"Kites again." Sam shook his head in disgust. He flicked the cigarette to the ground and stomped it out. "He told me this was where you'd be."

"Who?"

"What is it about him?" Sam rubbed his scalp, making his hair stand up in spikes. "How did that little Jap turn you against me?"

"He didn't." Jesse caught himself before he could add, *You did.*

"I figured I'd be nice. Give you a chance to say good-bye. You know what it's like to walk into that school and have your secretary tell me you were out? To look at me like I'm an incompetent father because I don't know where my own kid is?"

"What do you mean, say good-bye?" Jesse asked. He could feel the cold in his gut, and his hands began to shake.

Sam sighed, and a bit of his anger seemed to dissipate. "Sam, Kentaro's got himself a nasty case of cancer. He's been in and out of the hospital for months. They didn't catch it in time, and—"

"You're lying!"

Sam's expression hardened. "I wouldn't lie about this."

Jesse looked up. The Buka had moved closer, silently confirming Sam's words. The black kite was like a window into darkness, swallowing the sky itself.

"He can't be sick," Jesse said. "He would have told me."

"So you *have* been talking to him." Sam reached into his pocket and pulled out a Swiss Army knife. The blade clicked open, and for a second Jesse thought Sam was going to stab him. Instead, he grabbed the kite line.

"This is the only fighter I have!" Jesse stared at the Buka. "You have to take me to the hospital. You have to let me save him!"

"*I'm* your father. It's time to let him go, son."

Jesse yanked the line hard. This part lacked the cutting glass, but the waxed line still cut deep into Sam's palm. Sam swore, but didn't release his grip.

"Dad, please," Jesse said.

Sam pressed the knife blade against the line. Taut with tension, the line snapped instantly.

"You're grounded until I say otherwise. And if you take one step out of my house, except for school, I'll put you in the hospital myself."

Tears stung Jesse's eyes as he watched the Hata spin downward. "No," he whispered. Thinking about his little Rokkaku, he reached toward the Hata, trying to control it. "Don't fall."

"Come on," Sam said, tugging him toward the parking lot. "Behave yourself, and maybe I'll take you to visit Kentaro next week."

"Next week will be too late." Jesse concentrated, imagining he still held the Hata's line. He could feel the wind beneath the kite. Ever so gently, he shaped the air itself, creating updrafts to lift the kite higher. Slowly, the kite responded, floating on nonexistent winds. "Wait for me."

"What's that?"

"Nothing." To his left, the black Buka dipped in salute and disappeared.

Sneaking out of school that afternoon was absurdly easy. The principal would call Sam, of course, and Jesse would be in even more trouble, but that didn't matter. All that mattered was getting to the hospital.

As the bus pulled to a halt, Jesse spotted the black kite hovering over the parking garage, drifting slowly closer. He grabbed his backpack and ran to the back of the hospital. At the fire escape, he climbed the dumpsters to reach the bottom rung. Minutes later, he was on the roof, unzipping his backpack to free his little Rokkaku. He doubted it would do much against the Buka, but he planned to fight with any tool he could get.

The Rokkaku began to orbit Jesse's head, spinning like a top to shed the drizzle that had begun to fall. Jesse clenched his fists, praying the Hata still flew and calling it with all his heart. "Please..."

The Buka drew closer. It was smaller than Jesse remembered. Maybe four feet high and twice as wide. Jesse's little Rokkaku leapt in response, like an angry kitten.

Where was the Hata? Had it fallen? It had taken Jesse several hours to get out of school and make his way here. Whatever strange magic connected him to the kites, maybe it hadn't been strong enough to keep the Hata aloft.

And then something tickled his hand. Jesse clamped down, feeling the familiar line tug his fingers. The end was frayed from Sam's knife, leaving only a few hundred feet. It would have to be enough.

The Rokkaku darted out of the way as Jesse flew the Hata into position, sweeping the red and blue diamond in a wide figure eight.

The Buka streaked toward the hospital, as if it had been waiting for this moment. Jesse ran along the roof, pulling his kite down to intercept. His shorter line was an advantage here, giving him speed. The Hata ducked beneath the bigger kite, then flew upward. The Buka pulled back, barely escaping Jesse's cutting line.

How long would the line last in the rain? he wondered. At least he hadn't used the traditional mix of rice paste and broken glass. Wood glue might be too modern for Kentaro, but it should endure the water better.

Jesse moved to intercept another attack, sweeping his kite like an enormous saber. Each time the Buka approached, Jesse was there, using every trick he could think of to drive it back.

His arms began to ache. He pulled in a bit of slack, hoping to lure the black kite closer. If he could just get his cutting line within range, he could try to cut the other kite down. Even though he couldn't see the Buka's line, he knew in his blood where it had to be. But the Buka moved impossibly fast, and every one of Jesse's attacks came up short.

"Jesse! How the hell did you get up here?"

The line dug into his fingers as he turned to see Sam and a security guard stepping on to the roof. Someone must have seen Jesse on the roof.

The Buka took advantage of Jesse's distraction, swooping down at a sharp angle. Jesse ran to block, but the Buka veered, dragging its invisible line toward Jesse's own kite. The Buka's line brushed the edge of Jesse's Hata. Terrible cold burned Jesse's hands, and then it was all he could do to keep the Hata aloft.

"Kid, watch out for the edge," the guard yelled.

It gave Jesse an idea. He hurried toward the corner of the roof and hopped onto the ledge, a low, foot-wide wall of concrete. The cars in the street looked like plastic models. Jesse wavered slightly, yanking his kite to correct his balance.

"Jesse, no! Get down *now!*"

There was real fear in Sam's voice. "Stay back," Jesse yelled. His little Rokkaku buzzed anxiously around his head. He could hear Sam and the guard talking, but at least they weren't coming any closer. They wouldn't risk him falling. The next time he spared a glance, the roof was empty.

Jesse pulled the Hata in, trying to assess the damage. The bamboo spar had cracked near the left corner, causing it to flap back and forth.

The Buka attacked again, moving to block Jesse's wind, then streaking down as the Hata fell. Jesse dragged his kite closer, until he was pulling the cutting line itself. The glass scraped skin from his palms, but he kept pulling, avoiding the Buka's attack.

He loosed his hands suddenly, allowing the Hata to leap higher. It swung in a broad, flat arc, seeking to decapitate the other kite. The Buka circled away.

Attack and parry, feint and counter. The sparrow and the starling. Every move put more strain on Jesse's damaged kite. He had water-proofed and layered the kite, but there was only so much it could take.

"Jesse, come down this instant, dammit!"

Sam had returned. Jesse ignored him, but he couldn't ignore the second voice. Weak and hoarse, Kentaro yelled, "Listen to your father, Jesse."

Jesse glanced back. Kentaro stood supported by Sam on one side and the guard on the other. A trailing tube connected him to an I.V. stand. The rain-damp hospital gown emphasized the boniness of his shoulders. His bare arms were little more than sticks. Panic clenched Jesse's chest. The Buka was so close, and now Kentaro stood exposed.

"Get out of here," Jesse yelled. "Kentaro, please!"

Kentaro reached out. "If you won't obey your father, obey me. Come down."

"I'm trying to save you!"

"I know." Kentaro smiled. "But not like this."

Sudden fear made Jesse turn. The Buka had already begun its attack. Jesse jerked the line with all his strength, but it was too late. The Buka's invisible line cut the Hata a second time. Jesse had kept the Buka from cutting his line, but it made little difference.

"No..." The Hata began to fall, little more than a crumple of silk and sticks. He heard footsteps behind him.

"No," he said again, more firmly this time. His little Rokkaku shot backward, and he heard Sam cry out in surprise.

Jesse tightened his grip, forcing his broken kite higher while the Rokkaku kept Sam back. Jesse battled the wind and the kite's own weight with for every inch.

"What's he *doing*?" Sam demanded.

"Trying to save my life," Kentaro said.

"I don't understand."

"I don't either," Kentaro said. "But that is what he's doing."

Jesse relaxed his fingers, feeling blood pound through the cramped muscles. His kite bucked harder as the wind tossed it about.

"We are family, Jesse," Kentaro said. "Nothing can change that. Not the court, not even death. Your little Rokkaku showed me the strength of that bond. You don't have to do this."

"He's not your son," Sam snapped. "I swear, if you weren't dying—"

"He's not going to die," Jesse said, newfound determination in his voice. The Rokkaku shot past his ear and disappeared into the rain. Jesse didn't need to see it. He could sense it spinning through the air.

The Rokkaku collided with the black Buka, punching a hole in the blackness.

The black kite bucked, but Jesse had already brought the Rokkaku around, tearing a second hole, then a third. The slender spars of his Rokkaku splintered with each blow, but Jesse forced it to attack again and again until it disintegrated.

Only then did he allow his Hata to fall. His line intersected the Buka's, and he pulled so hard he fell onto his back, knocking the breath from his lungs. The last thing he saw was the black kite dropping out of sight, followed by his own ruined Hata.

Sam's fingers dug into Jesse's arm, hauling him upright. Fear, confusion, and fury all battled across Sam's features. Jesse wondered which would win.

The guard yelled, forestalling the argument. "Hey, you can't come up here."

A young girl stood in the doorway leading down into the hospital. The guard shook his head. "When did we get a revolving door on the rooftop?"

The girl wore a black leather jacket and torn jeans. Her black shoes gleamed wetly, even though the rain seemed not to touch her. In her hands, she held a small black Buka kite. She touched the guard with the corner of the kite. "Leave."

Blank-faced, the guard retreated back into the hospital. Jesse started to shiver, sensing the power in that kite.

"You know the traditions?" she asked, her eyes never leaving Jesse's.

Slowly, Jesse nodded. He clasped his bleeding hands together to stop them from trembling.

"What traditions?" Sam snapped.

"When fliers battle," Kentaro said, "one who cuts down another's kite often claims and flies that kite as his own."

"No more kites," Sam said. "If I catch you with another one of those damn—"

"You won't catch him," the girl said, grinning.

Jesse pulled free of Sam's grasp and walked toward her. "You killed my mother." He couldn't feel anything at all. Kentaro's hand came to rest on Jesse's shoulder.

"A chemical reaction killed your mother," she said. "I helped her spirit on the next stage of her journey. It's what I do." She frowned. "What you do, now." She held out the Buka.

Jesse put his hand on Kentaro's. "What about my father?"

"His body is failing. If it's any comfort, you'll be with him at the end. You'll be the one to ease him on his way."

"No," Jesse said. "You can't make me—"

"I don't understand," Sam said, coming around to Jesse's other side. "It's just a kite." He reached toward the girl.

From the center of the kite, a black line snapped out to hit Sam in the chest. He fell back, gasping.

"Stop," Jesse said. At once the kite obeyed, and the line vanished. "Sam, are you okay?"

Sam nodded, though his face was pale.

"You will have power and responsibility both," the girl said. "Most importantly, you will have freedom."

Kentaro started to speak, but a coughing fit took him.

"Leave them alone!" Jesse took a step toward the girl, but she shook her head. This wasn't her doing. Jesse caught Kentaro and held him until the fit passed.

Jesse's eyes watered. "I won't kill Kentaro."

"I'll return for him if you don't," she said. "Which would bring him greater peace?"

Slowly, Jesse reached for the kite. It was surprisingly light. The black paper was dark as night, with no sign of damage, but he recognized the Buka he had fought. The bamboo spars were yellow with age, and the bridle was simple hemp. A sparkling of light trailed from the bridle to his hands, hands which no longer bled or hurt.

"Jesse, what are you doing?" Sam asked.

Before anyone could react, Jesse pressed the kite into Kentaro's hands. The girl started to protest, but Jesse cut her off. "It's *my* kite now. I choose to give it to him." Already he saw new strength in Kentaro's fragile frame. "Give it to me when I'm older, if you want. But at least this way...this way you could still visit sometimes? We could fly kites again." He glanced at Sam, daring him to argue.

But Sam said nothing. More than anything, he looked lost.

Kentaro gave Jesse a quick hug, and Jesse marveled at the strength in those arms, even as the contact sent frigid chills through his body.

"Are you sure, Jesse?"

He nodded.

"I almost forgot." The girl reached into her jacket and pulled out a small scrap of blue and red. "You'll want this, I think." She took Kentaro's hand, leading him away.

Seconds later, Sam and Jesse stood alone in the rain.

Jesse cleared his throat. "Thank you. For telling me about Kentaro."

Sam stared for a long time, until Jesse began to fidget. "That was...that was pretty impressive," he said finally. "The way you handled that kite."

"Thanks."

"Kentaro—" Sam hesitated. "He did a good job with you, didn't he?"

Jesse flexed his hands, studying the newly healed pink skin. "He's family. I had to save him."

"Yeah." Sam squeezed Jesse's shoulder. "You did a good job, son."

As he followed Sam inside, Jesse stopped to look into the sky, where the black Buka saluted with a broad 'J' before disappearing into the clouds.

Surveying the Land

BD Wilson

"Fifty-five meters by forty of high-grade cropland," the surveyor said, and Robanni recorded the measurement on the partially covered sheet of parchment. He had six almost identical but completed sheets back at the village office. The Plains of Aslinea hadn't changed in the six years of his apprenticeship, and he didn't expect them to change in the last two remaining on his service debt.

Not that it mattered to Jekaar. The surveyor would have him record the same information this year and the next. And then he would buy some other poor nomad child to keep track of the eight years following that.

"High-grade cropland," Robanni repeated as he finished writing the words.

"Such waste," Jekaar said as he stood, brushing wet soil off his hands. "Crown land, of great value, just sitting here, rotting."

Robanni looked at the low grass of the plains around them. The ground could be seen through the scattered patches of earth-saving growth. It was dark and healthy, and the grass was the light green of spring leaves. The area was level enough that he could see across the wide fields to the fences of the surrounding farms and holdings. He

searched for signs of rot—it would be something different after all—
but there were none.

"It seems just as healthy as last year," he said, "and the year before."

"Large packets, undistributed, undeveloped," his master continued
without acknowledging the words. "It's an affront to business, to progress."

"And yet, it's respectful to nature." To nature, and the secrets the
world still held. There were reasons the crown would do nothing with
these lands. There were stories and warnings that kept even the no-
mads from resting here when they passed between the farms.

Robanni raised the hand with the quill and caught one of his two
braids. His fingernail stroked over the black bound hair, running between the beaded charms and feathers worked into the strands. The
movements made a whisper of sound that stood in for words he was
no longer allowed to speak, and only half remembered.

Ashaantali d'annan, spirits of life, otalidiel savon. Bless those who
bless you. Istel.

"Look around you!" Jekaar stood in the middle of the cropland sec-
tor and spread his arms wide. "Just look around you."

Instead, Robanni read back over the notes he'd already made so
far, and compared them to the mental copy he had of the previous
year. His handwriting had improved.

Jekaar's words picked up speed as he pointed far to the south.
"Farmland, profitable and useful, feeding the people of the kingdom,
bringing in revenue." He spun to face the west, the light of the sun
hitting his bronze skin, emphasizing the age lines on his face. "Pastureland, filling the stomachs of the finest wool-producing flock in the
kingdom."

Robanni's own stomach growled. They'd been out here all day,
and Jekaar's obsession prevented them from stopping for lunch.
They'd be out all night without dinner, too, if they didn't start moving
again.

"Sire, we'll lose the light," Robanni interrupted as Jekaar spun to the north. This, at least, was heard.

"Quite right. Onward." He marched in the direction he'd been pointing, his gaze focused on the ground before him.

Robanni rolled his eyes, adjusted his satchel of supplies, and then followed the measured steps. From the previous year's records, they should hit the change right about —

"Ah ha! From cropland to pastureland again, just like the surrounding areas. Mark these co-ordinates." Jekaar scowled at the almost imperceptible line between the grades of quality. "She'll listen this year. She has to listen. No more of this superstitious nonsense getting in the way of development."

Robanni tuned out the willfully ignorant rant, shaking his head over the familiar obsession. The king wouldn't listen this year any more than she had the year before. There were laws even she had to uphold, after all. With good reason.

Jekaar started moving again, still muttering to himself. "Protected territory. Nonsense. Such a waste. Eh? What's this?"

Looking up from the parchment, Robanni frowned. They should have been able to walk to the edge of the Plains uninterrupted now. They should have been able to finish this ridiculous waste of time, abandon their trespass of the land, and return to the office. He should not be staring at his master's bald head as Jekaar crawled around, face lowered like a bloodhound.

For the first time in almost six years of employment, Robanni had no idea what the normally predictable man was doing. His hand twitched, causing an errant mark on the clean onion-colored surface of the parchment. He stopped writing, taking his braid in hand again. The quiet rasping noise helped stop his rising nerves, calming him.

Keethanval who guards the mind, otalidiel risan. Let mind find an answer. Natef istel.

"Sire?" he said, watching the man on the ground. "Is something wrong?"

"Look at this," Jekaar answered. "Come here and look at this. Tell me what I'm seeing."

Robanni rubbed the braid one more time before letting it go and then tucked the sheet of parchment and the quill safely into his satchel. He knelt on the ground next to his master. For a few moments he saw nothing, and then he blinked.

"Is that—?"

"Yes, yes?" Jekaar prompted.

He took a breath. "Is the ground glowing, Sire?"

"Yes!" Jekaar sat up. "Hand me my kit," he ordered, holding one hand out.

Robanni looked up from the glowing ground, glanced at the outstretched palm, and then at his mater's satchel. "It's in your pack, Sire."

"What? Oh, right." He shuffled back and opened the satchel, pulling out balls of twine, stakes of various lengths, strips of colored cloth, and finally, a small leather box. Jekaar left the other items scattered across the ground, and opened the box to reveal securely packaged vials of potions.

Robanni looked down and sighed at the scattered mess. He was going to have to clean those up.

He frowned. The light glow on the ground had increased to a sparkle, like the sun on frost in winter. The sight was at once familiar, and completely alien to the warm weather.

"Now then," Jekaar said, "let's see what this is." He knelt on the ground, opened one of the vials, and dipped an eyedropper into the liquid it contained.

"Sire, are you certain this is wise?" Robanni asked, aware of his master's movements, but still focused on the playful light of the soil.

"Of course it is." The answer was snapped, terse, but sounded so very far away. "Something has happened to the land. It is our duty to determine what it is."

"Our duty," Robanni repeated. The sparkles seemed to be spinning. His hand caught his braid again, as his mind pulled back the stories he'd heard as a child, sitting around the cooking fires with his mother as her mother spoke to them in a voice withered by age, warning them of the dangers in the wild. He tried to focus on the quiet sound his scratching made, but the lights called to him, tricked his voice into joining the whisper.

"Lotali en'iva," *entrancing sprites*, "otalidiel vitomali. Free me from your spell." *Kisamidi istel.*

Over the sound of his prayer he could hear a hiss and sizzle as Jekaar let a drop of the liquid fall to the ground, but he still couldn't tear his eyes away.

"I should be taking notes."

"Of course you should."

Had Jekaar moved? Walked away, farther into the field? Robanni couldn't tell. The pinprick lights were brighter. They were sharp little stars, playing on fallen sky before him, dancing in the darkness.

"What are you—Who are you?" Jekaar's tone was outrage tinged with fear.

Robanni frowned, trying to make sense of the words. The darkness behind the lights grew deeper, started to move forward, creeping around and over the lights toward him.

"This is crown land. You can't be here! Do you hear me? You can't—"

Jekaar's scream seemed even farther away than his words. Robanni felt his eyes roll, his hand releasing his hair as his legs gave way. The darkness swallowed the last of the lights, and him along with them.

A sound woke him. By the time his mind registered consciousness, it had stopped, but it left behind a shiver-touch of panic that raced through his heavy limbs. He fought the need to move, to open his eyes. Instead, he strained his ears, trying to find the sound again. All he could hear was the pleasant crackle-snap of a nearby fire. Once his attention was drawn to it, he could feel the brush of heat on his cheeks, and around his body.

It was thick and heavy as a blanket, like standing beside the blacksmith's forge. He drew in a breath, but he didn't smell smoke. Instead, the air brought with it the scents of dust, hay, and horse dung. Over all of that was a tangy, metallic smell he almost recognized, but it was buried underneath the overwhelming stench of bitter sweat that surrounded his head, forced its way into his nostrils with every breath. He gasped, trying to draw air while escaping the smell, and heard a rustle of movement.

The sound came again. This time he was awake enough to recognize the blubbering whimper for the plea it was. His body reacted, goose bumps breaking out over his skin despite the heat of the fire. Jekaar's scream came back to him, loud enough in his memory that it might have come from the same room. Though he tried again to fight them, his eyes won this time and snapped open.

Orange and yellow. The entire area seemed to shine with the colors of the fire in its centre. Through the dancing flames he could see light reflecting off bronze skin and a slumped bald head. Jekaar was hanging down from the ceiling, wrists pulled above his head. Thin, dark, dribbles curved down from the too-tight bindings to the awkward twists of his shoulders. His bared skin was streaked with dirt and rust-tinged blood. There were small scratches, long gashes, pokes, punctures, all of them fresh and still bleeding out. He was sweating in the heat of the fire, rivulets running down his body into the many injuries, forcing them ever open and oozing. His eyes were wide, color pushed away by black irises, and when his gaze meant Robanni's, he moaned. Before Robanni could move, a shadow figure approached the bound man.

"Shh, now," a voice beyond the fire whisper-hissed, and Robanni felt a chill shiver down his back. A bright dagger shone yellow in the firelight as the figure tilted it one way and then another. Its back was to Robanni, but he could still see the thoughtful angle of its head.

He tore his eyes away from Jekaar's and looked around himself, eyes darting from point to point. There were wooden beams, and piles of hay at not-entirely safe distances from the roaring fire. A bridle hung down from a hook on the ceiling to his left, and to his right he thought he could see sky through the open door of the barn. It seemed very far away, out of reach through the fire.

"No, no, no," Jekaar whined, "no more." Despite himself, Robanni felt his gaze pulled back to his master, just in time to see the dark form beside him shift.

"There's always more," the strange voice said again. After a few moments of consideration, it brought the dagger to the skin just under Jekaar's right armpit and pressed it in. "Even when you think you can't take anymore, you can. It's quite remarkable, really."

Jekaar shrieked as a new torrent of viscous liquid poured from the incision, splattering the closest walls. "Spirits, stop." The wailed words were ignored, and the figure drew the dagger down. It reached forward with its other hand to catch the top of the thin strip of skin it peeled off the man. The metal scent grew stronger as the strip grew longer and Jekaar's cries louder. The slice continued until the dagger reached his hip, and then with a quick flick, separated the skin from the body. Holding the strip up to eye level, the figure nodded, and then turned to lay the flesh out on a sawhorse as though it were laundry left to dry.

When the strip was positioned, the figure turned and reached toward the fire. Robanni froze, eyes wide open. Though the thing now faced the flames, none of the warm light penetrated the hood of the cloak it wore, giving the impression there was no face within its shadows. Drawing its arm back, the figure pulled a poker from the embers. The tip of the metal glowed orange, almost pulsing now that it had been removed from its heat source. The figure turned back to Jekaar, its head once more at that considering angle.

"No, please. Let me go," Jekaar's words were slurred. When he managed to raise his head, Robanni could see his split and swollen lips. "Please."

The figure moved the poker, placing the top lengthwise across the gaping, bleeding patch of raw flesh. Jekaar's mouth opened, his lips torn anew, but only thin blood poured forth, no sound. The figure pulled the poker away, leaving behind a rough black line between the mushy fields of red. Taking the poker, it adjusted the position, and pressed the hot metal against Jekaar's side again, one end touching the tip of the first line, the other just slightly off.

Line after line, until it had forced the silent scream into shrieking sound, the figure continued to press the metal against Jekaar's flayed skin. When it finally stepped back to consider the results, Robanni could see in the injury a fan of oozing meat spread out over charred spokes. He felt bile rising acidic in the back of his throat, but couldn't bring himself to move. As he waited, frozen in place, the scent of the Jekaar's burnt flesh reached him. Though he knew the source to be his master, it was still the smell of well-cooked meat, and his treacherous empty stomach growled.

The figure spun. With the masking shadows, Robanni couldn't see eyes, but he could feel its gaze land on him. For a moment he froze, pinned by that oppressive force, and then the figure moved. Robanni cried out and scrambled backwards, clawing his way to the end of the stall. It was only when his back slammed against dusty wood that he realized the poker was in the fire again and the figure still stood beside it.

"You are excitable, aren't you?" Its voice carried a note of amusement, and he felt his cheeks flush with shame. Then it did come closer, stepping around the fire and walking with deliberate steps to the mouth of the stall, and Robanni's fear returned.

The light still could not penetrate the cloak, which now fluttered around the figure like burning parchment, blocking his view of Jekaar, and the fire cast a bright halo around its dark shape. Robanni pressed himself against the wall, feeling splinters digging into his skin. He whimpered.

"Shh," the figure said, drifting closer, "it's far too soon for that."

Robanni wanted to move, to keep away from the shifting fabric, but his body would not listen to his commands. The figure raised its hand, and the strength went out of his arms. He felt himself flop against the wall. The muscles under his skin shivered and twitched.

The figure's hands drew back in a gesture that would have been a clap had it made any sound. "Oh, wonderful. You will be fun."

Robanni stared, feeling his jaw drop. He moved it a few times, unable to make a sound. He didn't know what sound would have come out, anyway.

"You're all so different, you see." It tilted its head in a contemplative manner, and then let its arms fall limply to its sides. "I'm trying to learn."

Still nothing came from his mouth. He tried, and a thin reedy whimper crossed the space between them. The figure sighed.

"Stop being so impatient." It looked back over its shoulder at Jekaar. "I don't expect him to last very long, after all. Some of you expire sooner than others."

Jekaar began to blubber, a snotty, dripping sound thicker than the smoke in the air around them. Robanni shuddered, feeling the cry drip down his skin with the sweat. It froze on his skin when the shadow turned back.

"We'll play when he's done, all right?"

Robanni's head tossed back and forth.

"No? Well, we can play now if you like."

Robanni's hand grasped his braid as the figure stepped closer. He heard the familiar scratching rasp as he traced from beads to feathers, the sound low and rough as a cat's tongue.

"Oh," the figure breathed, as even the cloak ceased its dancing movements, settling into perfect stillness. "Do that again."

Robanni's mind blanked, body refused. Then his finger spasmed, twitching as nervous tension sent it scratching across the surface of his hair. The nail dug down into the centre of the bound strands before pulling back out and starting over. He felt the tight braid begin to loosen, but continued.

The figure leaned forward, raised a hand and brushed it over Robanni's head before taking his other braid and rubbing the surface. It was so close now, close enough to see the shadows were no illusion. There was no face within the hood, and the stories loomed within his mind again, chastising him for walking on the lands of the Plains for so long. As a prayer formed in Robanni's mind, the figure pulled the braid, just hard enough to hurt, and startled the words out of him.

"Tishaani annaval—"

"What is that?" the figure asked, with the curious head tilt, and Robanni's frozen mind spoke the next line as his answer.

"Night's mischief maker." He caught his words, and then stammered, "You."

Otalidiel vitomali. Please don't hurt me. Kisamidi istel. Istel.

For a moment there was no answer, and then the figure sat back and laughed. The sound was sparkling cool water in the heat of the barn. It floated around Robanni, light and bright as the sparkles on the earth of the Plains.

His hand dropped, shocked, into his lap. The figure leaned forward, stroking his braid one more time. "So I am. Wonderful."

Robanni stared as it looked between him and Jekaar. When it stopped on him again, the contemplative tilt was back.

"For naming me, I think you deserve a reward, don't you?" It stood, stepping back far enough for him to see poor Jekaar. "I have two to offer, but you may only have one. You must choose."

Blinking, Robanni looked up, mouth gaping once again. "W— What?"

"Reward the first: I let him go now, and you stay. Your night will be long, and so very painful." Its tone was light as sun-sparkles on snow. "You'll never be the same, but you'll be alive, and so will he."

Jekaar struggled against the ropes, thick blood clawing out fresh from his wrists. His eyes met Robanni's, pupils still wide enough to swallow the color.

"Reward the second: I let you go now, and he stays. You'll be free and clear and whole. But he'll play, and then he'll die."

Bubbles of spittle burbled over Jekaar's lips. Sounds flew out with the spit, but they didn't form any words Robanni could understand. He pulled his eyes away from the other man, only to have them land on the figure instead.

"Choose." Its hands were raised to its hood, almost in prayer position. It waited.

Robanni turned back to Jekaar. His master's eyes were wild, tinged with madness, pleading. He was trying to speak again, the bubbles on his lips popping. Spittle flew in tiny globs, vanishing in the light of the fire. Whatever words were to have accompanied them disappeared into squeaked gibberish. Robanni's gaze skimmed the bruises, cuts, and seeping gashes which now marked Jekaar's skin. The fan seeped blood out over the constraints of the cut, dribbling down the surveyor's leg. The acid taste returned, and Robanni choked. He bucked forward, gagging as his empty stomach tried to force its natural juices out in lieu of food. His throat burned. His vision began to shimmer and fade as air refused to enter his lungs. His eyes stung, water taking what remained of his sight.

The figure giggled. The sound skipped around the room, from Jekaar around the fire to Robanni, and back again. When it stopped, even the gibbering noises from the other man were silenced. Robanni forced one breath in, and then another. When he could see again, he looked up, avoiding Jekaar this time, looking instead at the cold shadow of the mischief maker.

"Well," it prompted, "have you made your choice?"

"The second," Robanni coughed the words. "I choose the second."

A low moan began in the Jekaar's throat, rising in pitch and tone until it stabbed Robanni's ears. The figure made the clap motion with its hands again, and the cloak rippled. It skipped forward, moving in a blink. It knelt on the ground beside him, and leaned forward to whisper in his ear.

"Run. Now."

Robanni jerked back. His eyes shifted from the floor to the figure to his master. Jekaar's head was slumped again, and he hung limp from the bindings. Robanni stood, felt his legs tremble. He forced them to take one step, and then another, and another. His steps rang on the floorboards before he hit the muffling dirt outside. Cool fresh air soothed his cheeks, filled his aching lungs with the scent of farmland and night dew. Each step away from the barn came faster than the last until he found himself running across the edge of the cursed land.

The screaming began behind him as he turned his feet away from the Plains of Aslinea and toward the village. His hands trembled too much to grasp his hair, denying him the comfort of the sound. His breath whistled in his ears, and he focused on it instead, concentrating until he managed to block out the suffering of the man he'd left behind.

Zhandaan loval, who measures the scales, otalidiel savon. Forgive me. Forgive me. Istel.

Rooks

Dan Koboldt

For three weeks, Lord Matellan and I had watched the dark columns of smoke march steadily toward his estates. Two armies, one broken and fleeing before the other, left only devastation in their wake. It didn't matter which army was ours. They were both headed right for us.

For three weeks, I'd cajoled and chided and cursed him to retreat to safety, with no result. He wanted to see the apple harvest through. Now the first harbinger of death and destruction had come, and faced me through the wrought-iron gate of Matellan orchards.

He wore a soldier's uniform, but the sun had bleached it of any color. The shirt was untucked, the sleeves threadbare. I couldn't help but notice his boots. Standard issue was a plain black boot, good leather but nothing fancy. This man wore fur-lined boots of expensive suede. Custom made, but poorly fitted -- and clearly not his.

"Lookin' for the lord 'o the orchards," he said. His voice grated against the placid morning air, like an avalanche down the side of a mountain.

"Lord Matellan will want to know who's calling," I said.

"Name's Rouch," he said.

It fit him, somehow, a thick name for this burly ox of a man. Fever-bright eyes glinted at me above a greasy unkempt beard.

I gave his uniform a pointed glance. "Would that be Captain Rouch?" I asked him. "Lieutenant Rouch? I don't see a badge of rank."

He smiled, showing teeth that had yellowed like old parchment through his beard. His eyes never changed, though. "Just Rouch'll do."

Something about his manner really put me off. "My master is a busy man. Perhaps you should be on your way."

The burly man ignored my dismissal and sauntered forward, until he was just on the other side of the gate. He stared at me, unblinking. His breath stank of sour wine and something worse. It was all I could do not to cover my nose with a handkerchief.

"You think this here rattletrap's gonna keep us out?" he asked. He grabbed the gate's cast iron bars with and shook it. The gate clanged loudly against its hinges. I fought the urge to step back. Now was not a time to show weakness.

"That's not the only thing keeping you out," I said.

"I ain't alone," Rouch said. "And I ain't leavin'. So go along now, and fetch me this Matellan."

I wanted to turn him away, or at least to wipe the sneer from his face. But the man had sixty pounds on me, and he'd invoked my master's name. I had no choice.

"Wait here," I said.

The Matellan family home nestled atop the highest point in the landscape, surrounded by the rolling tree-topped hills of the apple orchards. Our grandfathers had built the place, and they weren't going for elegance. Every wall doubled as a rampart; every window could house a bowman. It was a building of apparent style but hidden readiness, much like the Matellans themselves.

I knew better than to look for Matellan in the house. Not with the harvest so close. He'd sent the orchard crew out again this morning to trim deadwood from the trees where they could. Fire was a constant threat. High summer in the western provinces brought dry, windy days with little rain. Matellan worried about it, and about the drought, and about a thousand other things that promised a bad year for apples. But never about his own safety.

I found the crew in the old orchard, which wasn't surprising. It grew along a cliff at the southeastern edge of Matellan estates, near the ruins of an ancient keep. The trees near those moss-covered stones were unlike any others. They were tall, rounded, and majestic; their apples were the pale gold of winter's rising sun. Golden apples commanded three times the price of red ones. They were the prize of Matellan orchards. And their seeds were poison.

It was midmorning by then, and intolerably hot. I'd sweated through my light linen shirt, but I refused to take off my dark tailored jacket. It was better to be uncomfortable than improperly attired, in my line of work.

The men of the orchard crew were a hard lot. Years of labor outdoors gave them thick shoulders and leathered faces. Theirs was a tough occupation, but a simple one, and I envied them that. I think Matellan did too, for he joined them whenever he could. He stood atop a ladder balanced by two men, trimming the tops of trees with a pair of long-handled shears. Even in the rough-spun work shirt, there was something noble about him. The sharp nose and high cheekbones, perhaps. Or the pale, silvery-blond hair that often marked men of the Matellan family line.

"Have a care not to break your neck, my lord," I said by way of greeting. He was always taking unnecessary risks, despite my express requests to the contrary.

"Ah, Jarrett," Matellan said. He paused long enough to give my sweat-soaked attire a brief inspection. "I believe you've ruined your finest jacket."

"There's a man at the gate," I said. "A soldier, by the look at him."

He got back to work as I neared the base of the ladder. "Just one?" he asked.

"As far as I could tell. But he says he's not alone."

The shears never stopped. Twigs and dried leaves rained down on me and the two crewmen holding the ladder. I stumbled back to brush myself off, cursing. It seemed to amuse the crewmen. No doubt they thought me softer than ever.

"He's asking for the 'lord of the orchards,'" I said. "I assume that means you."

Matellan sighed. He made a final snip, gave the tree a nod of approval, and climbed down. "I'll have a chat with him, I suppose."

I found his jacket folded over a branch, and tossed it to him. We started back on the hard-packed dirt trail on which I'd come, as the snip-snip of the shears took up again behind us.

"What's wrong?" he asked, as soon as we were alone.

"I don't like the look of this fellow," I said quietly. "Something's off about him."

"Tell me what you saw."

"He looks like a bruiser. Wearing a soldier's uniform, but no badge of rank. Unshaven."

"Is that all?"

I hesitated. "There was another thing. His boots. Fine leather, professionally cut. Expensive."

"Sounds a lot like my boots," Matellan said.

"Not everyone can afford to dress as you do."

"Are you saying you'd like a raise?"

I shook my head in exasperation. But Matellan gave me a sidelong glance, his face unreadable, and I realized that he was probably just having fun with me. He'd been doing this little naive-noble game since we were boys. Well, two could play at that.

"Thank you," I said. I gave a small bow. "My lord is most generous."

He blinked in surprise. Then he chuckled, and clapped me on the shoulder. "And well earned, old friend."

I grinned despite myself. Then I caught a glimpse of the columns of smoke in the western sky and my humor faded. He saw me looking, and changed the subject.

"Jarrett," he said. "What happened to the rooks?"

"What rooks?" I asked.

"The ones in the attic."

"Oh, those," I said. Somehow the dark birds had gotten the idea to turn Matellan's attic into a rookery, and defied every effort to keep them out. They'd lifted shingles, bent wire mesh aside, even pecked through a few boards with those clever beaks.

"I noticed that they're gone," he said.

"Yes."

"You could have let them be, you know."

"It wouldn't do for someone of your station to have a rookery in the attic," I said. "They're carrion eaters."

"Ah, well, I knew you'd outsmart them eventually."

"Your unflappable confidence is appreciated, m'lord."

We reached the gate an hour after I'd left it. Rouch had taken to lounging in the shade. Droplets of water glistened in his beard. I cast a suspicious glance at the old well just inside the wall. I couldn't prove the trespass, but the grin on his face said it all.

Three more ragtag men had joined him - wide-eyed fellows in faded uniforms. No badges of rank on them either. I couldn't help but notice how thin they were; even Rouch's skin hung loosely about his frame. He spat over his shoulder and stood, then swaggered forward to meet us at the gate. The three other men stood back, watching us like buzzards near a dying animal.

I coughed into my hand and offered a brief introduction. "My lord, may I present... Rouch." I gestured vaguely at the hungry-looking men behind him. "And company."

Matellan's smile and easy manner were gone. He was Lord Matellan, now, and he surveyed them all with a faint air of distaste. "You look like soldiers," he said.

"We was," said Rouch.

"And your commanding officer?"

"Don't have one."

"You reported to someone, if you were a soldier. Where is he now?"

"Dead," Rouch said. A haunted look flashed across his eyes. "All dead," he repeated, almost to himself.

"I'm sorry to hear that," Matellan said. There was real sympathy in his tone. "But I don't know how I can help you."

"You can feed us, first," a man blurted out. The face under his battered steel helm was youthful, but haggard.

Rouch shot him a dangerous look. The man fell silent.

"Food, aye," Rouch said. "And shelter. And maybe a few other provisions."

Matellan nodded, as if he understood. "These are hard times. What makes you think we have anything to spare?"

Rouch barked a laugh. "We see what we see. Big manor house. Orchards with plenty of apples."

"We have those things. But we don't feed deserters."

The grin slid from Rouch's face. "Is that a fact?"

"That's a fact."

"It's a mistake to turn us away." Rouch glanced back at his men, his lip curled in a half-snarl. "Might get rough for your lordship."

Matellan shrugged. "Things are rough all over."

He and Rouch stared at each other for a long moment while the rest of us shifted around uncomfortably. The other men eyed the apple trees and licked their lips.

"We'll give you a day, to think it over," Rouch said at last. "To-morrow, same time. The gate opens one way or another." He turned his back abruptly and walked away.

I bristled at his impudence, but I didn't want to make things worse than they were. It seemed we'd have a respite, if a brief one. Maybe long enough for me to get Matellan away to safety. If I could only convince him to leave.

Matellan turned swiftly on his heel, and strode off in the direction of the manor house. "They're not getting my orchards."

I tried to slip out of the manor house at dusk. I'd prevailed on Matellan to send the crewmen and the household servants east to safe-ty. They'd taken a couple of horse-drawn wagons, and most of my master's worldly possessions. My bootsteps echoed in halls made empty without them.

"Jarrett?" Matellan called. He stood at the railing above, with a quizzical look on his face.

Damn. He'd caught me right on the threshold. Five more seconds and I'd have been gone. There was no hiding the longbow and quiver I held in one hand, or the sword I had in the other.

"Thought I'd go keep an eye on the gate," I said.

"The man said he'd return tomorrow."

"Even so," I said.

He mulled this for a moment. "I'll join you," he said.

Before I could protest, he was down the stairs and beside me, with a longbow of his own. It was nearly as tall as he was, and the quiver at his shoulder bristled with white-fletched arrows. My eyes fell to his waist, and the sweeping, silver hilt of a rapier.

"Just happened to have that around, did you, m'lord?" I asked.

He gave me that little smile of his. "As luck would have it."

The rapier belonged to his father, once upon a time. Until the man died, clutching his chest, when Matellan and I were little more than children. It was a fine weapon but I hoped he wouldn't have to use it.

I let him pass through the door ahead of me, and followed him out into the orchards. We walked in silence for a while. Only a sliver of sun remained above the horizon, like the last ember of a dying fire. Matellan ran his hand along the trees as we went, whispering something. Maybe it was a trick of the light, but I could have sworn the leaves trembled at his touch.

"You never told me what happened to the rooks," he said.

"They went away," I said.

"After so much effort to get in?"

"Perhaps they found a better place to roost."

"Perhaps," he said.

When we reached the western edge of the estates, twilight had deepened. The moon was rising, and painted the trees around us in a pewter glow.

Matellan unshouldered his bow. "Quietly now," he said.

We crept forward to the edge of the open ground and crouched in the shadows of the apple trees to wait. The minutes stretched and the darkness grew. The gate was a silent patch of darkness in the white stone wall.

Then came a soft sound from the far side. A rustle of leather, perhaps. I held my breath and strained my ears. Another rustle. Then the hushed baritone of men whispering. A shadow appeared on the other side of the gate. Metal clinked as he fastened a chain.

"Just thought you'd keep an eye on the gate, eh?" Matellan whispered.

"Something was off about him."

From the darkness beyond the wall, I heard the slap of a hand on horseflesh, then galloping hooves. A heartbeat later, the cast-iron gate wrenched free from its hinges with a screech of twisting metal.

Matellan stood and nocked an arrow. I did the same. Everything hung in silence and slow motion. He drew the white fletchings to his cheek just as the first deserter came through. I heard the bow's thrum, saw the feathered shaft slam home. The man grunted and tumbled backwards into the darkness.

"That should get their attention," Matellan said.

Two more shadows rushed through the gap. They bent low to the ground, to offer smaller profiles. But in the moonlight at forty paces, they were like lambs in the slaughter pen. I drew, squinted, loosed. One man clutched his throat and stumbled, gurgling blood. His comrade ducked behind him, letting the dying man take the next arrow. A veteran's trick.

We both cursed and fumbled for more arrows, but the man closed too quickly.

"Devan!" I shouted. I dropped the bow and threw my dagger instead. It flailed right past Matellan's ear and caught the charging man just beneath his breastbone. He went down in a heap at our feet.

Matellan nodded his thanks. "You're just full of surprises."

"I spend a lot of time in the kitchen, m'lord."

Then more men came through. Five or six of them, and the bows were useless against so many. I put my hand on Matellan's shoulder, meaning to pull him away into the shadows. But he shrugged me off, drew his rapier, and charged right at them. I cursed. I drew my own sword. And I waited.

A squad of trained soldiers might have taken him. But it was nearly dark, and these men had long been out from under discipline's yoke. Too busy looting and burning things, I suppose. Matellan swept into them like a whirlwind, his rapier a blur. Two men were down before they even knew what was happening. His was the swift, deadly grace of master swordsman. He made it look elegant, too, as only a nobleman could.

The others moved to surround him. Putting their backs to me, just as I knew they would. I threw my second dagger as I came up behind them. A man screamed and fell, clawing at his back. I parried another man's cut and threw a shoulder into him, shoving him over the dying one. He stumbled, cursing, and I ran him through. No mercy. The last deserter circled my master, still unaware. I didn't hesitate, or try to keep it fair. I snuck up and cut him down from behind.

"Jarrett!" Matellan chided.

"Looked like you needed help," I panted.

"I could have handled him."

"No need to take chances, m'lord."

We could still hear Rouch shouting at his men on the other side of the gate. Cursing them in some of the foulest language I'd ever heard. But no more ventured through.

"Seems like we've won for the night," Matellan said.

I was too busy vomiting in the weeds to answer. The blood, the killing, it wasn't normally part of my job description.

Matellan had hardly broken a sweat. He bent to clean the blade of his rapier on one of the fallen men's tunics. I shuddered, and looked away. As much as I wanted my daggers back, I left them.

"Perhaps they'll go away, before the morrow," he said. "Just like the rooks did."

"Perhaps," I said. But in my heart, I doubted it.

Back at the manor house, I let my master inside, and barred the door behind him. He stationed himself at the table in the kitchen to draw up his plans. "Tomorrow we'll set up on top of this hill, just in case," he said.

"Just in case?" I asked.

"In case they try again."

"Wouldn't it be safer to ride east? We surprised them once. We won't again."

He ignored me. "Plenty of arrows, and the road running right between us."

I listened with half an ear while I fixed him a cup of our best applewine. He'd earned it, tonight.

"Makes sense," I said. I gave him his cup; he drank deeply of it. I didn't make a drink for myself.

"We can fall back to the manor... house," he said.

The last word had a delay to it. His brow furrowed. He looked at his cup, and then to me. "What- what's in this?"

"A sleeping draught. Did I forget to mention that?"

"What... why?" he managed.

"You have your priorities, m'lord. And I have mine."

"Jarrett, don't-" he began, and then he slumped forward.

I admit, I'd made it a touch stronger than necessary. I eased him out of the chair so he wouldn't fall.

"I never could get the rooks to stay out of the attic, my lord," I said. "So I let them in, scattered grain on the floor. With golden apple seeds among them."

The rooks were hungry. They were careless. And they'd underestimated how far I was willing to go. A single seed from a golden apple was enough to kill a horse.

After that, no bird ventured near the attic. The sense of death had lingered.

I brought the wagon around and got it ready. This was it, the last of Matellan's things and mine. We'd lock up the manor house, of course, but there was nothing that would keep any determined looters out. For that I had another idea entirely. I just hoped I had the stomach for it.

My master finally roused at midmorning, by which time we'd covered some ground. The sun beat down on us without relenting, but I was grateful for the doom the heat ensured. Matellan groaned and sat up, surprised, no doubt, to find himself beside me on the wagon bench.

"Where are we?"

"Morning, m'lord," I said. "We've come about ten leagues or so, by my guess." Every one of them east and closer to safety.

"We've got to go back," Matellan said. "Protect the orchards, and the manor house."

"They can't steal those things."

"But they could burn them!" he said.

"I don't think they will," I said.

In this heat they'd need to drink, first. And Rouch had already helped himself to the well. Ground appleseeds made for a fine pow-der, one that dissolved in water. And they'd need water first, in this heat. I doubted any would live out the morning. And the bodies would serve as a warning, to any who might trespass while we were away.

Matellan must have seen something on my face. "What did you do?"

"I took care of it," I said.

"How?"

"I'd just as soon not talk about it, m'lord," I said. I wouldn't let it haunt him, the way it would haunt me. He got to live the clean life of a noble. Someone had to handle the dirty work. I clung to that until the nausea passed.

At midday we crested a rise, and I chanced a look back. The rolling hills of Matellan orchards were distant, but still in view. No smoke marred the landscape, so I guessed the house and the orchards were unspoiled.

High above them, the rooks had already begun to gather.

Cold Spells

Diana Hurlburt

It is with some reluctance that I set down the events of that winter—of the Liberator's devotees, and how snow first came to Lykosoura. Not being a wordsmith by trade, there was little thought in my mind that I might do the whole strange business justice, but Markos laughed and said at least I would not lie, in that case. At any rate, the principal player no longer among us and Demetrios determined not to speak of it, they deserve to have the story told.

We are generally agreed that it began when Demetrios returned.

"See," Agdo said with a sweep of the hand, "the garden knows who is about and who forsakes us."

Agdo had long been perishing for love of Demetrios, this all the countryside knew, and the gardens of the Liberator's temple throve or wilted according to his will. Agdo's will was strong, such that six new anemones had appeared as droplets of blood on the black earth, one for each day of Demetrios' absence. Agdo's will was not so strong as to compel love, for not even gods may seed passion where the ground is barren.

Demetrios admired the poppy blooms and went into the temple to deliver what news from the city.

Now, a person of that countryside in a position such as Agdo's might weep, or complain to a friend, might plot, might adorn themselves in borrowed linen, might walk into the Well of Forgetting and forsake the earth entirely. They might come groveling to the Liberator's temple for a sweet-scented posy to freshen their cheeks or a philter to drown their desire, for the Liberator's devotees command all manner of herbs and craft to deliver a baby into the world or a heart from beating too powerfully.

(Markos laughs at this point and says, grandly, *physician, heal thyself.*)

Agdo was one such, and so how to proceed? That which could be cured or banished in others was out of reach, the clean waters of Lethe sinking away as Agdo reached for them. Had Demetrios been cruel with it, perhaps Agdo's heart might have turned; if Demetrios had mocked, or ignored, or whispered, the rose within Agdo's breast would have grown thorns. But Demetrios is a kind man, friendly and hard-working, gentle with children and devoted to his gods, and his patience for Agdo was noted. It is a simple matter to water such qualities with the sweat of passion—though, myself, what Agdo saw in Demetrios escapes me.

The news Demetrios brought from the city began to trickle out. Some of it was temple business and sacred, but there were bits of politicking, of the harvests and a new plough, of a war far to the south and of a traveler who had entered the gates and flung herself at the feet of the Huntress in the city's greatest temple and not moved. Indeed she could not move, so the priestesses found; she was shrunken and shriveled, her extremities an odd and mottled purple, and she fell into a deep slumber before remarking to anyone where she had come from. When she woke after three days, Demetrios said, it was hailed a miracle of the gods' mercy, for the Huntress smiles upon itinerants, adventurers, and wanderers of all variety.

"May she smile upon me in two nights' time," said old Kharis, and the assembly laughed, but kindly, to imagine Kharis among the processional throng of the annual wolf-hunt.

The traveler claimed to have mounted the City of the Gods itself, the tallest peak for leagues, to satisfy her curiosity. Curiosity has never seemed to me an adequate defense of anything, and the gods rarely reward anyone for being curious near them. In this case, the reward had been reddish streaks growing up the traveler's ankles, dark and bloated feet, and fingers stultified and useless.

"From cold!" Demetrios said.

The assembled people were quiet. He is not much of a storyteller, as I am not much of a scribe, but his face was aglow. He described how the surgeon of the temple had amputated several of the woman's toes and two of her fingers, and that this had been enough to stem the rot growing from exposure to such cold temperatures as no one in the city or here among the assembly had experienced. The traveler had not seemed to mind it, somehow. Her eyes, so Demetrios said, were those of people who have seen gods. She had returned from the City's slopes only to deliver the tale, for was it not right that people should know of the blanketing cold of the mountaintop? She'd pointed to the peaks, distant and pale gold beyond the city's walls, and asked in the voice of prayer whether no one knew why they seemed so strange, compared to our own dark and pine-swept crags.

Now the Huntress is the mother of mountains; all rocky places and secret caves belong to her, and she is best found striding from peak to peak with her bow, surefooted as a goat. So the traveler dedicated her quest to the goddess and implored the temple's keepers for funds to return to the City of the Gods, to measure the strange cold substance found only on the bare rock of the highest peak.

"Perhaps she'll get it," Demetrios said, and the story was ended. People talked among themselves for a moment, conferring over the traveler's evidence—her hands! Her poor feet! But who had ever heard of a white matter both hot and cold in the moment, soft on the wind and hard enough to break bones when fallen upon?—and then the evening turned toward wine and song, as evenings do.

But Agdo leaned against the temple wall, threading black strands of hair with linden blossoms, and a spell was cast.

There is an argument between Markos and I whether Agdo meant to cast the spell. Sometimes we do not know the deepest intents of our own hearts, and whether Agdo meant it comes to naught: the doom was laid. I have some pity, being one of the Liberator's people in spirit if not in practice, and Markos might do well to ponder his own humanity now and again.

That night the cold came.

It was the proper time of year for a chill, for shimmering halos around the moon between midnight and dawn, but this was a blistering wind no one had felt in living memory. Furs piled high on pallets and people clutched one another, drank heated wine and bundled their children's feet in rags as needed. There was something of a festival air through the countryside already, as the Liberator's hunt drew near, and the strangeness of the weather only added to it. Bonfires roared high; children blew out their breaths and traced shapes through the cloud before it dissipated into the air; if people took to their beds, it was not to sleep. The temple gardens seemed impervious to the cold, though outside the walls trees were looking rather sorry for themselves, and a song wafted through the night air, just loud enough to draw one into a corridor, believing the singer was around the next corner.

Agdo's voice was counted among the finest of the Liberator's devotees.

People saw cheeks bloom scarlet where before they had been wan with longing, though the bones of the body grew sharper seemingly overnight. It was as though whatever Agdo's soul subsisted on had ceased providing physical nourishment as well. When the heart eats itself, the belly forgets to hunger. The Liberator is a god of the body, and those rituals that are carried out in his temple embrace richness, fat feasts and liquors, fine draperies, pleasure. Some thought Agdo had grown only more beautiful, that perhaps the love for Demetrios had finally run its course. Others listened closely to detect pain in the voice lifted high, and tutted about the tunic grown baggy around hips and shoulders.

"Are you not cold?" I asked on the eve of the hunt, surveying that tunic and a pair of new sandals, not even a cloak to fight the chill. But then, a shimmer hung in the air around Agdo, as of a great heat.

The processional, as you know, begins in the temple's sanctuary and exits the outer gate in a great flood, the stream of the Liberator's people bursting forth and gathering bodies as it goes, swelling to a river undammed. On that night everyone is a devotee, and people all over the countryside come bearing flower-twined staves and arrows dipped in aconite to lend their strength as an offering. The chants and rattle of the tympanon blended with laughter, wild ululations, and the rhythmic thud of feet on earth, knees and foreheads pressed to earth, bodies tussling on earth. Breath steamed in the air before every member of the troop, and above it all, throughout, Agdo's voice rang in unending song.

The forest ate us up. It is not a very good way of hunting wolves, truth be told, but the meaning is in the making, and the Liberator has his reasons. If one of those poison arrows finds its home in a furry ruff, so much the better, and then the victor may proceed into the sanctuary on their fellow's shoulders, draped in a wolfskin as the god occasionally wears when he is feeling modest—but it is as well for the people to commune with him, and with one another, for he is a god who accepts all manner of sacrifice.

(Markos is a former soldier, a lover of austere deities. We understand one another well enough.)

"In echoing hills and wooded combs," sang Agdo, with an answering clatter of drums. "The ethereal gales, the deeply spreading glades, the rock which is stricken and gives birth."

Ah, but there is little lovelier than the processional of the wolf-hunt, its sweat-glazed bodies and eyes fervent, its hands and knives and garlands. I remember stumbling, my knees and fingers stiff with cold. I thought then of Demetrios' story, the traveler in the temple and the surgeons with their blades. My bow would be useless, thought I, gripped in clumsy hands not expecting the possibility of wolves.

"Look!" someone cried, and then the forest path was canopied in upturned palms, faces raised and shining, as the firmament dipped close. This was how it seemed, for who among us had seen snow, and we had no other recognition for the sparkling mites sintering down through the pines.

"Sing hail to the lord of tragedy," Agdo's voice continued, "who is called Chthonius and Psilax. Liberator of the slave, eater of men, who gives birth to himself and his people."

My tongue burned, as it is said the tongues of people do when divinity is near and wishes to speak. The processional slowed, all thought of wolves forgotten, and people milled in the woods. Hands cupped the cold white sky and red mouths licked at the substance, and wild laughter thrilled through the trees. The music did not halt. Shouts rose—prayers, perhaps prophecies—and the snow fell. We had found ourselves in a glade open to the sky, a natural round of clearing where youths came with their sweethearts and hasty rituals were held, and the stars did not cease plummeting. We had all heard the story of the traveler and her exposure, but that seemed unimportant in the face of such strange glory. If you are witnessing a miracle, matters of climate fade a bit.

Agdo was dressed perhaps poorest of all for inclement weather, and it seemed to me that the tunic was not there at all, that the Liberator had stripped his devotee of all but the most basic necessities of dignity and love. The snow fell, in piles that seemed outrageous, frosting the tips of people's noses and gilding eyelashes, and it was agreed later that Agdo was the most beautiful among us. This had always been true, but especially now, clothed in deep winter and keening the praise-song and stepping, sandals discarded, up the sudden slope of white.

"To be trodden underfoot," Agdo sang, "of the first vintage and the last, to be supped and dined upon," and the prayer was so piercing, the tenor so lovely, that we noticed only late that voice was all that remained of Agdo.

When the song had at last fallen away too, we stood there in the glade, in that muffled embrace of stars, and knew not to continue our hunt.

There were some in the Liberator's temple skilled in the craft of reading the movements of birds, and some who knew what weather to expect from the sky at dusk and then dawn, and some who collected stories of people like the traveler, to compare our countryside with lands north and west. Much squabbling took up after the ascension of Agdo, for that is the way of the religiously inclined, not to mention how most things get done in the realms of politics and natural arts. But it was one of the sky-readers' apprentices who said, cautiously, that the heavens had settled themselves once more, after the weather returned to something like normal. It was a clear cold night—a *normal* sort of cold, Markos emphasizes—and the apprentice pointed to the thick swath black as old wine that cradled the highest of our modest mountains. She traced the star-map of the Goatherd, as she had been taught, and the arcing cluster of the Horses of the Sun. And then she pointed south of them, to a milky patch where rested stars which, though gem-bright and numerous, she had no name for.

It was simple enough to find them a name, as easy as recognizing a childhood friend whose eyes remain open windows, though their face has changed with the years.

So it was that snow first fell in our woods, and again every year after in the weeks between the wolf-hunt and the curing, and so it was that the star-map called Agdistis came to hang in the winter sky over Lykosoura.

The Moon

C.S. MacCath

Three dreams of sorrow were given to Serkleit, Goddess of Art and Fermentation, Keeper of Caves at the Heart of the World, before her deification.

On the night of the first, she was a small boy running barefoot over grey dust. A veil of ice clung to the fine hair on his arms and legs. Chest muscles heaved a prayer for atmosphere that went unanswered. Above him a dog crouched, inverted, to the left of a winding road, yellow teeth bared in a downward snarl. A wolf stood to the right, suspended, howling from a place of air and sound. Serkleit reached up as he passed, hands thick with baby fat, to grasp the merlons of the towers hanging out of the meadow above. But they were far, far away, their topsy-turvyness a mockery of the safety they might have offered.

Boy. The word was a slickness under the heel. Boy, boy, boy, an edge on the blades of grass above. Boy, the wrong body in the mirror. Boy, the hated clothes in the press. It tolled like a bell in his mind, lived under his skin, in his bones, a corruption from the time he had emerged out of the Cosmic Mother's womb into the stars. He stopped, blood on his hands and feet, flesh under his little nails. *Don't call me that!* he wanted to scream but could not and wept instead. The tears turned to diamonds on his cheeks and fell away.

On the night of the second, Serkleit learned there were thirty-two paths to the towers; sixteen greater and sixteen lesser, each one blocked by a beast. The Goddess Nephropidae descended from the surface of the sea, at the edge of the winding road, and beckoned upward with a clack of mighty claws. "You must travel them all," she signalled in a wash of pheromones, "or they will say you have not passed."

A willowy youth in a kirtle of petals from every blossom in creation, Serkleit traced the scars on xyr palms and tried not to despair. Instead, xe sang to the Beast of Mouths a dulcet lullaby. But the melody was silenced by the airless expanse of space while the beast declaimed in a gabble of tongues, "You will never be her. You will never be free."

For the Beast of Faces xe painted xyr own in the kohl of the void and the crimson light of a dying star. A terrible thing of square-jawed hate, the beast leered back at xem in a caricature of the man xe might become, trapped and defeated. The Beast of Limbs pulled xem into a dance. Naked and hairy, a thick cock bouncing between his legs, he made a puppet of xyr body. We do not speak further of this.

But these lesser beasts were shades of their greater kin, whose paths to the towers were narrow tracks between the moon and the meadow above. The Beast of Curses, lacking a body, slipped around Serkleit's neck like a noose and whispered execrations into xyr ear. His brother, the Beast of Blows, beat xem with fists heavy as mountains until he grew weary of xyr immortality and lumbered away from his post. Xe crawled from there to the Beast of Knives and begged for his touch, fearsome but welcome. He cut into xyr flesh while xe remembered the Cosmic Mother's loveliness and the Goddess Nephropidae proclaimed that all the paths had been traveled at last.

On the night of the third, Serkleit lay in a cloth-of-silver gown, listening to the call of a nightingale. The meadow was blessedly beneath her, soft and green, the moon blessedly above, low and full. Curled into the curves of her out-flung arms, the dog and wolf guarded the

mistress they had menaced in her boyhood. She drew breath and exhaled a sigh, long and low, grieving for what she beheld above.

A set of footprints marking the dust where a child had taken flight,
trailing the blood and diamonds of his sorrow. A brave youth's kirtle
of petals trampled beneath the feet of a beast. Serkleit lifted a graceful
hand as if to gather those younger selves close to her breast. But they
were already within her, solemn and joyful by turns, and they were
safe.

So when the Goddess Nephropidae, pereiopods resting in the glory
of her hair, gestured left and right at the looming towers, Serkleit drew
herself up and away from them. There was no airless cold she could
not endure, no beast whose name she did not know. Behind, a bright
star shone beyond the moon. Ahead, a rosy sunrise chased the darkness from the sky. Serkleit bade the lobster goddess a grateful adieu,
whistled for the dog and wolf to follow, and continued down the road
toward apotheosis.

The Words of the Sun

Sarena Ulibarri

The sun spoke to me today, and I can tell no one. I am telling you, dear Zinnia, my beloved sister, because you know me well enough to know I am not prone to flights of fancy, that I am not the type to speak with birds or see portends in the clouds or prophecies in my dreams. And yet, the sun spoke to me. As our army marched toward Ryland this morning, dawn broke over the mountain peak and I lifted my face to its warmth, reveling in the chance to burn away the chill of the night. One sunbeam seemed to shine directly on me like a tunnel of light. I looked into it and saw the face of an old man, frowning sternly back at me. He spoke, but it was not in any language I have heard before. When I turned to see if anyone else had heard, the vision and voice disappeared, and everyone strode steadily as though nothing had happened.

Now I know what questions you will want to ask me: Have I been sleeping enough? Am I well-nourished? Have I been checking my drinks for contaminates? And the answer to all of those, of course, is no. I am a soldier, marching toward the destruction of the enemy who seeks to destroy all worship of the sun god. I sleep fitfully on the cold, hard ground, surrounded by the snoring, farting bodies of the rest of my platoon. I eat and drink whatever is given to me with little regard for taste or substance, choking it down as fast as I can. So perhaps that's all this vision was: a tendril of dream sneaking into my waking hours, a bit of delusion brought on by moldy bread or sour juice. I would be grateful to realize that's all it was, for I was not meant to be prophet or priest.

We draw closer to our enemy's borders. I hear whispers among the ranks that the Rylanders hold dark, violent rituals meant to defile the sun god, that they commit terrible crimes against their own children and animals. I wonder how much of it has been exaggerated in the retelling, but I bite my tongue. To speak any doubt would be treason and blasphemy. It may still be treason to write the words here. But by the time you receive these letters, Zinnia, the war will be over. I hope. I have to believe.

Today was the Festival of the Sun God. It was a cloudy and miserable day for us, and we did not see the sun once. Though we sang the festival songs while we marched, they took on a somber tone, unaccompanied by instruments or the voices of children and the roar of bonfires. Though we march in the sun god's service, we feel disconnected from him, so far from our sun-blessed homes.

I hope the sun god was with you today, and that the whole town was wild with celebration. I found comfort in recollections of climbing on the statue together when we were children, and sharing the fiery spice-bread until we had to run for the water tank, and dancing around the bonfires at sunset, our arms flailing in ecstasy, hair slapping across our sweaty faces.

I almost wish no one had reminded us that the festival was today. These memories of marching under a cold sunless sky and reciting songs like rote lessons do not belong in the same category as those memories of festivals spent dancing with the people I love. Though every step takes me farther away from you, I try to tell myself that each step actually brings us closer to our goal, and therefore closer to our trip back home.

The sun spoke to me again today. This time, I am sure. It was no dream or hallucination: the clouds parted and the face looked down on me as real and solid as any of my fellow soldiers, the voice steady and clear. Except I still could not understand the words. When the sun disappeared behind the clouds again, I repeated the sounds under my breath, trying to memorize the shape of them, match them to any kind of meaning. I could fathom none. Until...

Oh, Zinnia, this must truly be blasphemy for me to relate what I am about to, but it is true, as true as anything I have ever known. We reached the borders of our enemy's lands today, and set up camp to prepare for tomorrow's siege. I imagine it must look quite threatening from down in the village of Ryland, all of our orange and red banners lined up on the hill that overlooks their valley.

Near dusk, a small band of emissaries climbed the hill, riding on gray horses. I thought at first that they carried torches, but they were small glass orbs that shined with light. Part of their heresy, some of the soldiers whispered, bits of the sun captured for their personal use. A few of our officers went out to meet with them and the rest of us crowded as close as we were allowed, straining to hear what was said. And, Zinnia, I swear, when the enemy spoke, it was in the very same language that the sun had spoken to me. The words were not all the same, but I recognized a few, and the *sounds* of the words...I'm certain they were the same tongue. One of the officers spoke back to them, haltingly, with all the sharp edges shaved off, and then the emissaries rode their gray horses back down into the valley.

We march in service of the sun god, to preserve his traditions, to destroy those who would seek to destroy his worshipers. But what does it mean that the language of the sun god is the same as the language of our enemies?

The siege was delayed. We awoke in the night to a perimeter of fire that pushed us farther back up the hill. Zinnia, you might be ashamed of me for saying this, but I was glad. Or maybe, you more than anyone would understand, since you were always the one pulling me away from fights, since you begged me not to join this foolish crusade in the first place.

I couldn't sleep, and my stomach was sick every time I recalled the sharp consonants and swallowed vowels of the Rylanders who had come to speak with us. I kept hoping that morning would bring some kind of sign, another vision from the sun god that would assure me we were on the right and righteous path as we had been told we were. But then the fire came, and I was already awake when the guards sounded the alarm, tossing fitfully in my camp, and Zinnia, I'm sorry, but I did something I never thought I was capable of: I deserted. In the chaos of the retreat, I grabbed my pack and slipped off between the trees, following a rocky goat trail down into the valley.

Perhaps this choice means these letters will never reach you, and if so, I regret that almost as much as I regret breaking my promise that I would return home unharmed. Yet I must continue to write, as I have found myself in a place where my spoken words have no meaning to those around me. Well, the words of our language, anyway.

At the edge of Ryland, I was accosted by an enemy platoon, and I fell to my knees and repeated the words the sun had spoken to me. The soldiers lowered their weapons instantly, and looked uncertainly toward their sergeant, who was a hard-faced woman perhaps ten years older than you. She stepped toward me, and asked me something in their language. I shook my head to indicate I didn't understand, and repeated the words of the sun again, straining to be precise with the syllables, clear as I could be, though my voice shook with stress and I did not know if I pronounced them all correctly. The sergeant frowned, but no one raised weapons against me. Two of the soldiers grabbed my arms, pulling me to my feet, and marched me into the village.

I realized as I followed them that Ryland was not a village at all, but a city, dense and complex, with ancient stone buildings and modern marketplaces, and those glowing orbs I had seen the emissaries carrying were everywhere, lighting the streets like it was daytime, though it was still before dawn. And yet the symbol of the sun god was stamped everywhere. It looked a little different than ours, but it was indisputably the same deity.

They led me through an orb-lit plaza, and into a building larger than anything I'd ever seen back home, with great marble columns and statues flanking the entrance. Inside, I was tossed into a small cell with steel doors and windows. And here I wait to see whether I will be killed by those who have captured me, or by those I betrayed.

Everything is different now, Zinnia. These letters will reach you after all, I have been guaranteed. And perhaps I will return to you as well, though there are still many risks between now and then. But if all goes according to plan, then I will return home, not as a deserter or a prisoner, but as a hero. As the one who stopped an unnecessary war. I will ride into town on a white horse with a crown of sunflowers, ready to lead everyone into a time of peace and prosperity, an era free of the petty prejudices that have driven us apart and obscured the truth.

As I languished in the cell, sure of my own imminent destruction, a woman came to visit me. She was a priestess, with gold robes that were embroidered with the sun god's face—that very face I had seen twice, which had spoken to me and only me. She knelt before me, and asked me to repeat the words I had spoken to the soldiers. She spoke our language, but not well, her accent thick, vocabulary limited, and grammar confused. But still, we struggled through a conversation, and I told her of our army's goal to protect the worship of the sun god. She explained that the claims of blasphemy and oppression were a pretense, that the army really intended to gain access to a mine rich in a mineral that could store the sun's power—the source of the orbs I saw all over Ryland, which could do much more than simply light a nighttime city. I believed her. We were the ones marching into their territory, after all, and nothing I had heard about Ryland matched what I had seen of it. The reports that they wanted to destroy us for worshiping the sun god seemed much more distant and far-fetched than a simple conflict over scarce resources.

We are the enemy, Zinnia, you must understand. We were led astray by lies, and we have deviated so far from the sun god's path that he cannot even speak to us. But there is time to change. To negotiate for this mineral without bloodshed. To communicate although we cannot understand everything the others say. To make right all that has gone so very wrong. The siege has not yet begun, and with my help, it never will.

I will see you soon. Meet me in the village square with a crown of sunflowers to celebrate our victory, and I will bring you the sun god's light.

My Brother's Keeper

Beth Cato

Half the county figured my big brother Samuel had bricks for brains. There was mighty good evidence in favor of that, like the time he decided to walk through downtown naked simply cause it was a hot day and clothes just plain didn't feel good. But I knew Samuel wasn't a dummy, just quiet, with his mind in a different place than the rest of us.

So when I heard him with two speakers of dark words, I knew to hunker down and listen. Here by the barn was the most private spot on our property--or would be, if I wasn't up in the rafters.

I smelled the bad guys before I heard them. Mama didn't get to teach me much, but she did teach me to heed my nose when it came to good and evil and all the grey in between, and those men stank like the septic tank being sucked out on an August afternoon. I gagged against my wrist to keep quiet, Mama's old chain bracelet warm at my lips.

"I want to kill Macaulay," said Samuel.

That name made me inhale with a hiss. Kill Macaulay?

"It's easy to kill someone you hate that much," said one of the men. "But if you want to join our circle, you can't simply kill for vengeance. It's too easy."

There was a long pause. "He's got a wife and kid," said Samuel. I recognized the scuff of his bell bottom jeans dragging against the dirt.

"Three," said a deeper voice, "There's power in that."

"Yes," agreed the other man. "You must kill the entire family, on the equinox, with this knife. Then you can join our circle."

"I want them books of yours." Samuel's drawl was slow, every word dragged out like his puffs from a cigarette.

"You'll have access to our knowledge in stages. It takes time."

"I can do it," Samuel said.

When Samuel took that knife blade in his hand, I felt the wrongness of it rattle down my spine. That knife was an ugly, cursed thing. The other men left, heading back down the trail towards the base of the hill. Samuel stood there, holding that thing, assessing it in his quiet way. I barely breathed. I kept a pencil frozen in my hand, same as it was when I first smelled them come my way.

After a while, Samuel thudded back down the hill. The stink of evil faded. Why was Samuel doing such a stupid thing? If Mama knew, she'd whip his hide. She'd been the only one to ever keep him in line, the only one who understood he was so smart underneath all that stupid. But Mama was dead and gone and beneath feet of red iron dirt, and now Samuel was set out to kill the whole Macaulay family tomorrow night, and for magic, too.

Anger got all tight in my chest. At least Samuel had some magic, had some words to go by.

I stared down at my half-done math homework. I hated math something awful. All those numbers danced around in my mind and the answers never came out right, but I'd rather do a full fifty pages of algebra than save those Macaulays.

Old man Macaulay was the one who killed Mama, blowing past the stop sign at Templeton Hill and crunching our car flat as a griddle. They said in town that Macaulay had enough whiskey in him to pickle him like a frog for science class, but he hadn't been the one who died.

I scampered up and left my math for the mice to nibble on.

Given my druthers, I'd rather help Samuel out than save those Macaulays, but Mama loved everyone. She used to be close to Grandma Macaulay, too.

Mama wouldn't want Samuel to meddle with darkness, wouldn't want that blood on his hands. I just had to ignore whose blood it was.

Most all the other men around came back from Vietnam and fell into the bottle, but not my Papa. Nope, he fell straight into Jesus's arms.

Papa had the table covered with books for his seminary course and was all hunched over, muttering to himself. He didn't notice me going by, or flinch when I opened up a can of RC. But the second I headed towards my room, his pencil stopped scratching.

"Deborah?"

"Yes, Papa?" I turned around, the cola fizzling on my tongue.

"We're out of bread."

"I can go by the Pig later."

His head bowed over his work, and I moved on. I didn't have any kid brothers or sisters underfoot. Didn't need them. I had Papa and Samuel, and the fact that I was twelve didn't matter a doodle. I cleaned, I cooked. If it wasn't for the fact that I made Sunday dinner just like Mama, Samuel might have never visited the house at all.

I can't even say I held any fondness for Papa, not anymore. He was more like an extra piece of furniture around the house, something to take care of because it'd always been there. Just looking at him made that anger rise up again, all because of what he did the day after Mama's funeral.

He burned her books. The family books.

Mama never said that what she did was magic. It was as natural as breathing. The words were all for focus, she said. So she wrote down what she learned, just as her mama had, and her grandfather, and her great-grandmother. From the way Mama told the tale, her great-grandma was all sneaky about learning to read and write as a slave, and did it all so she could preserve the words and pass them along.

Papa burned every last shred of those books, a full century of songs about growing okra in a day, warding away mosquitoes, making babies form all perfect, and calling on rain. Papa sobbed as he did it, said that it was an awful thing that Mama was burning in hell right now, but he'd save us kids. I woke up because I felt the flames inching along Mama's old ink; it woke up Samuel, too. Mama had already started teaching Samuel. Me--she said I was too young.

Now I'd never know how to focus or sing the words, not unless Samuel taught me, and he didn't know much.

But I had been learning from Papa. Not that he knew those kinds of words, of course, but he had been writing down his experiences from Vietnam. Called it his "spiritual cleansing." Course, those weren't the kinds of things a girl my age should be reading, but it was an education in the ways a man could die and the way eating half-cooked chicken could make him pray for death as he spewed out his guts for days and days. I had the latest book tucked under my mattress, and just the other day I read something that would come in mighty useful.

Samuel was a big fellow at seventeen. I couldn't overpower him. I didn't even know where to find him now, though I guessed he was sleeping somewhere in the woods, somewhere within easy walk of our place.

Keeping Samuel away from the Macaulay's house would require some military strategy.

It would have been a brilliant plan if it hadn't involved math.

I spent the rest of that Saturday gathering supplies, so I headed out after dark to set everything up. I figured I had to establish a perimeter around the backside of the Macaulay shack, which would be the most direct way for Samuel to sneak up on them. Any car on the drive would be too loud. So, I snuck a full reel of fishing wire from Darrel Craigshead's garage, and a pop cap gun from Lewis David's back shed, and I dragged myself through the woods to make a tripwire.

See, Samuel had this thing about particular loud noises--the pops of guns or firecrackers or car backfires. He'd cover his ears and hunker down and freeze. I figured that I could rig this tripwire and scare him away, and I could do it far enough from the Macaulay house that they might not notice. Turns out that farther away means a bigger perimeter, and big reels of fishing wire aren't so big as they look.

Also, it's cussed hard work in the dark, in September. My skin was sticky as a swamp.

I was so busy muttering that I didn't hear Ralph Macaulay till he was five feet away. He had a shotgun in his hands aimed straight at my head.

"Deborah Kinsey." His mouth gaped. The porch light from his house gleamed off his glasses. "What are you doing out here?"

Now I'd known Ralph my whole life but barely said more than a grunt. That's because from the very start of kindergarten, when I could barely count to ten, Ralph Macaulay knew his multiplication tables. Since 3rd grade, each afternoon he'd gone to the high school across the way to sit in on the advanced coursework. I hated him long before I hated the rest of his family.

"Ralph."

"You didn't answer my question."

I looked around. The pop cap gun was leaning against a tree way far away. I had no desire to confess to him that I was trying to save his no-good family from some sort of dark sacrifice.

His eyes narrowed behind that thick glass. "Is that an empty wire reel in your hand?" He stepped closer, his gaze on the ground. "You... what is this, some kind of trap?" The barrel raised towards me again.

"Oh, what, you gonna shoot me?" I was hot and sweaty and bone-tired. "I'm not setting a trap for you, stupid."

"Then who? Looks like you ran out of wire, anyway."

If I had possessed any understanding of how magic works, I just might have blown him up. "Yes, thank you so much, Mr. Einstein." How could he even tell that in the dark?

"If the wire's not for us... is it for Samuel?"

My jaw almost hit the dirt. "What? How?"

"Maybe you should come to the porch where there's light. We can talk there."

The thought of going near that house made my stomach clench like a fist. "Nuh-uh, I don't think so."

Ralph sighed, all deep and heavy. "Look. We know Samuel's up to something. I thought you were him, that's why I came out." He motioned with the gun barrel. "We know about the magic. Your mom used to come over and chat with Grandma about it all the time, about how it affected my dad, and me."

"...You?"

"It takes different forms for different folks. For me, it's numbers."

"Oh." I couldn't help but ask. "Then what about your pa? He doesn't have any knack for math."

"No. No, he doesn't. He sees shades, and since he killed your mom, she's been clinging to him. She's the one who warned us about Samuel."

"Are you trying to tell me my mama's a ghost?" The thought didn't disturb me as much as it could have. I mean, better for her to be a ghost than to burn in hell like Papa said. I felt a bit of relief, really.

Ralph led the way through the brambles towards his house. "No. A shade is... a shade." Upon glancing back and seeing the dumb look on my face, he continued, "Ghosts haunt out of vengeance. Shades are like a shadow of a person, after the soul's gone on. If someone like my dad is responsible, the shade joins with theirs, like a reminder."

"So, Mama is clinging to your dad, and she can talk to him?" I could talk to her? My heartbeat roared in my ears like a revved lawnmower.

"It's not that easy." Ralph stopped on the porch. "Dad dropped bombs when he was over there. That's why he drinks, to blur the shades all together. There are... a lot of them."

"I want to talk to him," I said, and went right up to the door.

"Deborah...!"

I didn't have Mama's insight, but soon as I stepped in that house, I felt that clog of spirits. Even with box fans bellowing at full blast, there was an extra stickiness to the air, something beyond humidity. Like cobwebs tearing against my face, prying at my hands. Raw frustration scratched at my throat. I wanted to see more. I wanted to see Mama. Hear her. Not just feel these... vapors.

Maybe if I had our family books, I'd know what to say so I could see, so I could understand, but I didn't have squat. I hated feeling so stupid and helpless.

But there was something familiar about the cobweb feeling. The air felt that way around Papa, too--not nearly this thick, but that weirdness was there.

"Deborah, listen. Dad says it's really noisy in his head. It took him weeks to figure out what your mama was saying. All he got out was that Samuel was going to come after us, and that you both needed to forgive and let go."

"Forgive?" I recoiled from Ralph. "Forgive your papa?" Mama *would* expect that of me. Mama always had high ideals like that.

"That's what he said, that's all I know."

"Is there a way to get the other voices quiet, so he can just hear Mama?"

"If he forgives himself and lets them slide away," he said, his voice low. "This point, they cling to him as much as he clings to them."

Ralph's papa lay stretched out on a couch. The blanket ended short, covering the nubs of his legs. At least he lost something when he killed Mama. His head didn't move but his eyes did, widening with something I could only call fear.

"No. Ralph, she can't be here." He pushed himself up on a flabby arm.

Good, he hated seeing me much as I hated seeing him. "My brother aims to kill you and Ralph and your wife tomorrow night. I'm aiming to stop him."

"Go away! You look just like her. God, you look just like her."

"What else has my mama told you? What can I do to stop Samuel?" What words should I speak? That's what I wanted to ask, what I wanted to hear. That maybe she had some legacy to pass along, just for me.

"God, get out of my sight! The shade is bad enough, I don't need you in color, standing there! Oh Jesus." He moaned and blubbered and he hid his face beneath a pillow.

I would have spit on the man but I saw the misery on Ralph's face, and for some reason I didn't hate him near so much now. Instead, I stalked outside and let that the old screen door shriek shut behind me.

Ralph and I stood there, staring at the dark outline of the pines for a time. "So," he said, a quiver in his voice, "How's he plan on doing it? Samuel, I mean."

"Some bad fellows gave him a knife. The thing is stinky evil. He's supposed to kill all you with it, then he's in their club."

"Oh." He took in a long shaky breath. "I can understand revenge against Dad, but... me and Mom, we liked your mom just fine." He hugged his arms close, like he was cold.

"Even I know there's power in threes. You're the math wizard and all."

Ralph shrugged. "I'll shoot Samuel if I have to, but I don't want to. How are you thinking to stop him? What magic can you do?"

I blinked back the tears and frustration, the musk of those burning books flaring in my nose like the fire was fresh-lit.

"You think I'd be laying tripwire at midnight if I could do something special?" My shoulders hunched up like they could hide my face.

"What? But..."

"I can't do a thing, you hear me? I can sense power, smell it, but I can't do anything. And Papa, he burned all Mama's books. I don't even... I don't even know how to learn. When you said her shade was in there, I thought..."

To his credit, Ralph didn't look at me, but at the woods instead. "I'm awful sorry, Deborah."

"Yeah." I didn't say anything for a minute, and just listened as the crickets hollered back and forth. "Why don't you all just pack up and leave the state for the day? Get away? He can't kill you if he can't find you."

"Dad's stuck on that couch, and Mom's working double shifts at the diner. She doesn't believe in this... stuff. She won't leave, and I won't leave either of them behind." His voice shook again, but he stood straight and tall.

I sighed all heavy. "I can't talk Samuel out of anything, either. Mama's the only one who kept him grounded. He only really comes home now to eat my cooking, cause I cook just like Mama. He probably hasn't said a word to Papa since..." I blinked. The cooking. I looked at Ralph. "Whenever I cook, Samuel always manages to show up, even though he's not staying at the house anymore."

"There could be something to that."

"Maybe." Mama always had said that recipes were a way of putting words together in that special way. But once I had Samuel there, I had to stop him somehow. Keep him from his awful ritual. Cooking wasn't the kind of power I wanted, but it was something carried down from Mama.

I thought back on Papa's diaries again, about his awful experiences with food poisoning, and I grinned.

At one o'clock prompt that Sunday afternoon, I set the last dish on the table. It was all Mama's best fixings, done in my hand: country-fried steak strips, fried okra, mustard greens, and cornbread. A lemon pie sat chilling in the fridge. Samuel slammed through the door at 1:05 with all the focus of a cat headed to a can of tuna. He grabbed a plate and started shoveling it in.

As for Papa, he was at the church, and would be all day. His books marked his place at the end of the table. Not for the first time, I wondered what he'd think if he came home to find them all burnt, but I knew it wouldn't mean a thing. He could just buy more.

I worked on dishes and eyed Samuel. He always ate his foods one by one and saved his meats for last. That steak strip coating's where I whipped in a hefty dose of ipecac. I threw together some barbeque sauce for dipping, with the hopes that'd cover up the super-sweetness of the syrup. I wasn't big on steak, so I could skip eating it and he wouldn't think a thing of it. I figured ipecac was made to make people throw up, so it'd do the job better than serving up half-raw meat. Samuel wasn't that stupid.

"Haven't seen you for a few days," I said.

Samuel grunted as he speared okra on his fork. The thick aroma of frying oil lacquered the air, but even so I could smell the stink of that knife. He had it clipped to his waist.

I wanted to watch him without looking like I was watching, so I sat down in an old recliner. Next thing I knew the light in the room looked something funny and Ralph was standing there, kicking at my foot.

"You were sleeping?!" His scowl turned his face red.

"I was up half the night! And what are you doing here, stupid? Do you want to get killed? Where's Samuel?"

"Out in the woods, sick as my old man after a night of drinking. Come on!"

I knew Samuel was up ahead on the trail, and not just because he was a veritable volcano of sickness. That knife stank like a manure truck.

"Ralph, you gotta stay back," I said, shoving him behind me. He had his shotgun, but by the quiver in his hands, he wasn't too steady about using it. Which was good. Samuel was already messing with his soul. If he died now... no, I couldn't let that happen. Not when Mama's soul was already in doubt.

Samuel was all hunched over and on his knees, his head in the bushes. The knife was on the ground right by him. I rushed forward, all sneaky-like, but not enough so. Samuel managed to sit up and clutch that evil thing close. He didn't say a thing, just looked at me, his face a funny shade of pale.

"Samuel, that thing is awful evil. You don't need that," I said.

"I do," he rasped. "If I want to get books that tell us how to bring back Mama."

Despite the sweet heat of the evening, all my blood went cold. "You... what?"

"I see the Macaulay boy." Samuel's thick fingers twitched on the knife's handle. "Got to do this."

"Mama... Mama wouldn't want to come back like that, Samuel, it's wrong."

"She's not going to burn!" Samuel's shout sent birds flapping from the trees.

Oh, no. That's what this was about, what Papa said. My own anger stirred up in my chest, fists balling. "Mama's a sweet and good person. She can't... she wouldn't go there." Would she? I didn't rightly know.

Samuel didn't need to say a thing. He worked to stand up, all slow. His pant hems dragged on the gravel of the trail. This was all about Mama, and not even revenge. He didn't care about his soul, what those dark words would do. He'd do it all to save her.

"Mama'd hate you for doing that," I said.

"Mama never hated a thing," said Samuel. He was right.

The first rock plunked Samuel straight on the forehead. He blinked, furrowing his brows. The second one whapped him straight between the eyes. He kinda tipped backwards and splatted on the trail. I stared a moment before looking at Ralph about fifteen feet back.

He held a palm-full of gravel, the gun at his feet. "Didn't want to kill him," he said. "It's all geometry and physics."

"Dang. If you could go all David and Goliath, why'd I bother poisoning him?" I started forward.

Ralph snorted. "You think he'd have stayed still like that if he felt well?"

The sheathed knife slid right out of Samuel's slack grip. He was breathing, his body still and limp as a sardine. The smell of that knife made me heave.

"What are you going to do with it?" asked Ralph.

I stared at that knife, focusing, trying to find words just like Mama. This was the important moment and all. This is when I needed that insight. Instead, the bugs just buzzed in the trees and my nose got used to the stink of the knife and I was left no wiser than before.

"Guess we'll throw it in the river," I finally said, hating how stupid and uninspired it was.

Ralph didn't say one thing or another. We headed through the trees and to the big river. This was the area where Mama said I could never ever swim because the current was so fast. I handed the knife off to Ralph, as he had math in his favor, and he prettily threw it some twenty feet till it splashed deep. Then he turned around and squeaked like a kitten.

Samuel stood at the edge of the woods. Well, hunkered there, leaning on a tree. His skin had an awful sheen, and a big old bump grew on his forehead.

"I don't get a second chance with them," he said, his words slurred.

It took me a moment to realize what he was talking about. "You shouldn't have even had a first chance with those speakers of dark words." I marched up to him. "Your soul's still clean. That's what Mama would want."

At least he wasn't doomed like her. I hated that thought, but it was still there, sticky to my brain like sweat on my skin.

"Will they come after you?" I asked.

Samuel jerked his head in a no, then leaned into the bushes. I waited till his guts emptied some more, then I grabbed him by the arm. Even with me half his size, I managed to prop him up and we staggered back towards the house. Ralph hung far behind, and I can't say I blamed him. The smell of my brother alone was enough to make a person gag, but at least it was the scent of sickness, not evil.

"How long will I be sick?" Samuel whispered.

That was pure Samuel. Didn't ask or care how I'd done it. "Till tomorrow, most likely."

We were halfway across the yard when I saw Papa's car parked there and heard the clink of silverware carry through the screen door.

I hadn't cleaned up the poisoned dinner. Papa was sitting down to leftovers.

Good, I thought. He deserved to get sick, sicker even than Samuel. This was all his fault, anyway.

Anger festered in my chest, all raw and awful, and that's when it hit me. Mama's shade hadn't been talking about forgiving old man Macaulay, though she'd want that of me, too. No, she was talking about Papa. Letting go of the anger about what he said. Letting go of the books and everything they meant. I blinked back hot tears.

"Ralph, can you wait in the barn?"

"Yeah. Sure," he said.

I wanted to speak the old words, not because I wanted power like Samuel, but because I wanted something of Mama. Cooking wasn't enough. I didn't know what would be enough, but I knew Mama wouldn't want me poisoning Papa. Even if he did deserve it.

Mama didn't deserve to burn in hell, either, but God and Jesus would know her best. Better than Papa, that's for sure.

I let Samuel lean on the railing and I bounded on up the steps. Papa's shades whispered against me, that guilt and grief he tried to push away with Jesus. It was working, in a way. The shades didn't dwell on him like they did Macaulay. I was surprised at how that relieved me. I didn't want Papa to suffer, not really.

I just wanted Mama back, and that could never happen. Not even Samuel's dark words could make everything like it'd been.

Papa was still standing there in the kitchen, dishing up food on his plate.

"Papa, you can't eat that," I said, yanking him back. "The steak, I think it's gone bad. Samuel ate some and is sick as a dog." On cue, Samuel staggered in and past Papa.

"What?" Papa said, blinking at me. Unpleasant sounds shuddered from the bathroom.

I plucked the plate from his hands and in two steps dumped the whole thing in the trash. I didn't trust the whole surface, not after that meat had touched it. I threw away the few remaining pieces of steak, too, not that there was much after a hungry seventeen-year-old boy had had his way.

"Here. Have this instead." I pulled out the icebox pie.

"Is that lemon?" Papa asked. I swear I heard drool in his voice.

"Yeah. Yeah, it is. You listen in case Samuel needs help, okay?"

I walked out of the house. The rage wasn't in my chest now, just emptiness. I hadn't forgiven him, not yet. But without that heavy feeling on my lungs, it was easier to breathe, even in that sticky evening air.

The lights were on in the barn, but I didn't see Ralph. "Hey," I called.

"Up here!"

I climbed up the ladder and found him in my spot, those math sheets spread out. Figured he'd be drawn to the numbers.

"You got a few wrong," he said, voice mild as could be.

I snorted. "A few?"

"I could help you, if you wanted. Not going to cheat on tests for you or anything, but I could give you pointers, maybe."

I plopped down on some old straw, staring at this boy I hated for so long. "Maybe," I said. I stared out the slats at the fading light. "There's something your papa said. Do I... do I really look like her? My mama?"

"Sure, you do," Ralph said. "Probably look more like her as you grow up, too."

I nodded to myself. Maybe the words would come in time. Maybe I'd learn the hard way, like my great-great-grandma did. But for now, I had some things from Mama, and that'd do.

"Come on," I said. "Let's have some pie."

Age of Aquarius

Cat McDonald

Ganymede looked at himself in the mirror behind the bottles, then at his boss, who sat over her glass of wine at the bar. She had been a young lady when she'd found him, and it took a little math for him to realize that had been forty years ago. Her blonde hair had gone white and lines spread out across her face, which had come loose at the edges. He'd barely noticed it.

He, on the other hand, hadn't aged. He woke up from dreams of Olympus some time before getting this job, and he'd stopped thinking about what he was, or how old. Hazy memories gave way to a long void, and then the modern world, and the highway, and the woman who almost ran him over. Carolyn gave him a job at the bar and a room in the hotel, and forty years to try and figure the rest out. He hadn't made much headway.

"Staying late today?"

She sighed and held her glass out to him. "Just needed a drink, sweetheart. Do you remember when we met?"

"I mostly just remember headlights!" He started to laugh, but stopped when she didn't join him. She'd been able to tell he had nowhere to go and nothing to do, and told him she'd just taken over her father's bar if he wanted a job. He remembered the way she'd towered over him, her huge voice and broad smile and straight, golden hair, her stories about college. She reminded him, in her bullish strength and power, of the Queen.

"No, not that. Remember the times?" She gestured with her wine at the TV screen and the end of the news broadcast. "Look at this. When I was a girl...we really thought it would be different. That we could put an end to war. The Age of Aquarius was coming, and war and greed would be things of the past. We'd refuse to be part of it all and choose a new world."

"Like the song," he said, laughing through the stabbing regret he felt every time he heard about it. According to the books, it was him. He was Aquarius, which meant all that boundless hope of Carolyn's student protest days had rested on him. For a time, when he'd discovered how he could affect humans, he'd shared her optimism, but that had been a long time ago.

"Exactly like the song! Now look at us. We all got old, and we went into business, and nothing changed."

"...I don't think you're any different, Carolyn. You're still the best boss I've ever had. And maybe the world's just working on changing."

He could recognize the scent of her sadness, something invisible on the air that dimmed her and everything around her. It was an unpleasant noise, Despair.

Because Ganymede knew Despair well, could name it and recognize its shape, he could nullify it. While he poured her second drink, he listened closely to the ascending chime of wine against the inside of the glass, felt the sound mingle with the Despair on the air, dissolve it, sweep it away. By the time the glass was full, he couldn't sense it anymore.

If he explained his memories to her, and she found out who he was, then he'd have to explain why he'd never been able to do more than cheer people up, and even then only after fumbling with shapes and scents and sounds. Before the void, he'd known them as words and concepts and changes in his breathing, but now he had new senses to learn.

She'd been expecting a revolution. The truth would be unfair to her.

She shook her head with a quiet little smile. "Oh, before I forget, weather channel says there's storms tonight."

Ganymede looked up out the bar's front window at the purple undersides of the thunderheads, and memories swelled in his throat. Memories of the King, and his grip, and the scent of wine on his breath, and the breathless height of Olympus.

"I'll be fine."

"You're too old to be scared of lightning." Carolyn took another drink, then pulled her purse up onto the bar and started wrestling her way into a slick black raincoat. "However old you are."

"It's not that. I'll be fine. Good night, boss."

"Don't burn the place down," she said on her way out the door, just like she always did.

Carolyn disappeared through the door leading into the hotel lobby, letting the door shut behind her and triggering the little digital bell attached to it. When that sound died out it was just Ganymede, a lone drinker at the far end of the bar, a collection of out-of-town visitors seated just under the television, and the beginnings of a hockey game. He'd spent years listening to regulars talking about the game in general and Oilers in particular, and now he could identify the names and numbers taking their positions for the face-off. They'd helped him learn about Disappointment. He liked the Oilers.

Ganymede noticed the empty bottles collecting on the table, and made his way over to start taking new orders. Before he even reached the table, a familiar sound hit him. Those cheerful young men sitting under the television, despite being bronze-skinned like the men of Turkey or Cyprus, were speaking his old language. At least, the new version of it. One of them waved him over to ask for more drinks, in English. Ganymede wanted to answer in the old language, to prove he was still Greek himself, but the old language stuck in his throat, he stumbled, and he answered in English without making a real attempt.

When he'd brought a new round of beers, he stood near the table a while, pretending to watch the hockey game, so he could listen. Even while he poured the young man at the bar another beer, his ears stayed focused on the sound of his faraway past, on laughter that somehow sounded unmistakably Greek to him, like the too-loud laughter of the King's favourite son. His memories from his youth, from when he could live without needing a purpose, blurred together in voices and sensations like a dream that left him anxious all day without a reason.

The feeling on the air started to change shape. He didn't notice until the beginning of the second period, but when he returned to take the empty glass from the bar and replace it, it had become something completely different. Frustration, which he knew and could often dissolve just by getting back to work, had given way to something else, something he couldn't quite name anymore.

The patron at the bar was young, Ganymede assumed. Carolyn had asked him for identification when he'd walked in hours ago. He wore, like most people did recently, a baggy hooded sweatshirt in a greenish beige sort of color, and it completely hid his posture and his figure, which was probably as lean and bony as his pale face. No matter what happened in the hockey game, or how quickly Ganymede brought his drink, his face was distant, tied up in a frown Ganymede couldn't decode.

He couldn't do anything about an emotion he didn't know, so he watched. It wasn't quite Hatred, which he had a limited experience with. It was close, somehow, to Despair, but the more he watched the young man's face, the less he understood the connection. It didn't look like Despair.

"Can I get you another drink?" Ganymede asked, and watched carefully as the customer lifted his eyes, grumbled his assent, then looked back down.

While he poured another beer, a shout burst from the TV's speaker and the distant audience started to cheer. One of the Greek-speakers called his friends' attention to the screen and they reacted as a group, joking, as far as Ganymede could tell, about money wagered and lost on the game. They smiled and clapped one of their number on the back and laughed, and Ganymede came over to clear the bottles, listen to their voices, and take more drink orders. Behind him, he could feel that unknown feeling simmering and taking on its own unidentifiable shape.

Ganymede could feel the exact second that he'd let it go too far.

When he turned around, the man at the bar was standing. He held a gun, like the kind people used on TV, pointed just past Ganymede at the other patrons. The feeling on the air was completely new, however hard Ganymede fought to focus, to tear his vision from that little black muzzle, to look the man in the eyes, to remember a feeling that somehow, somewhere, he must have been introduced to.

"Hey, hey, wait, my friend," said one of the men behind, a well-dressed young man with glasses, in flawless English. A little jerk of the gun silenced him.

Ganymede had no idea what this was. He couldn't speak; the words struggling to take form in his mouth were Greek, ancient Greek, and English faded from his mind even though he'd been speaking it for forty years. That gun! It pointed between Ganymede and the customers now, and he couldn't keep himself from jumping when it veered his way. The man shouted something at them, but Ganymede could only translate a few words; "you", "people", "our", "country".

It could kill him. It would kill him. That journey through clouds on the King's talons hadn't killed him, but this would. In a time before guns, he'd been promised immortality. Olympus, and then the stars, and he would die here to a feeling he couldn't name.

His chest started to hurt, to anticipate the bullet. Everything in his vision drained into that little black hole.

Ganymede took a breath and tried to feel warm again, tried to bring himself back to the bar. He'd broken up fights before. He'd dissolved Anger from the air and swept it away. Despair, too, and Regret, and Sadness and Fear.

With another deep breath, Ganymede noticed it. Fear in the air, solid and real, the same Fear he'd seen before and learned to dissolve.

He raised both his hands. Slowly, as he struggled to pull his attention from the gun, he remembered his English.

"There's...no need for this. Let me pour you something to drink. If you...shoot someone here, you'll only make more trouble for yourself down the road, right...?" On light, short steps, he made his way closer to the bar, still with his hands raised, pulling the man's gaze and the gun's barrel along with him.

In a blur of modern Greek behind him, he made out one word. "Help." As soon as it was uttered, the man's attention snapped back to where it was, the gun moving unsteadily this way and that.

Ganymede pulled a glass across the counter, leaned over into the well to grab the tap, and slowly brought it over the bar, keeping his left hand in plain view. Then, holding the image of Fear in his mind, feeling its shape and its sound, he pressed the button. A bright cascade of water poured out of the tap, ringing out against the glass and pulling the gunman's attention back toward Ganymede as the Fear on the air dissolved into nothingness and was swept away by the sound.

The other feeling remained like a stone in a drained pond. That unnameable almost-hatred sat heavy on the air. It hadn't been Fear.

While the gunman looked away, one of the men at the table hurriedly produced a cellphone and began pressing against its screen, free of the Fear that had held him back.

"Here," Ganymede offered, and, with his left hand still open in the air, brought the glass of water to the gunman.

Something had changed in his expression. The wildness in his eyes was gone and something cold and calm had taken its place.

And, as Ganymede crossed the floor to bring him the drink, he risked a glance to one side at the men he'd meant to hold at gunpoint. By now the phone was lowered, but Ganymede could still see a blue sliver of light against a dark hand.

"Why's that phone on?!"

"I'm getting a call," lied the one with the richest accent.

The gun moved toward them again. No jerking, now that Fear had been removed.

"Now, there's...there's no reason...please, let's..." Ganymede, as always, failed to sweep away his own fear, left himself stammering.

Could he try and clear away Hatred? Was this just Hatred in a different shape? It smelled different, and sounded different, but he couldn't think of anything else it could be, not while that weapon drew his focus.

He couldn't get another drink, of course, but he held the water in his hand.

So, he breathed in, and tipped the glass slightly. With his mind on the shape of Hatred, he listened to the drum-beats of water on hardwood floor, felt its song trying to break down the Hatred on the air and clear it away.

Before he got more than a spoonful of water out, the song was torn in two by another sound, and pain stopped him. Before he noticed anything else, he noticed the pain, a burning pain in his ribs. Then he saw his field of view change as he fell, and noticed the echo of a loud banging noise. As he slipped to the floor, he saw the black muzzle of that gun, pointed squarely at him.

When he thought to look down, he saw that he was bleeding.

Somewhere in the shine of the floor, he saw the reflection of blue and red lights, and beyond the ringing in his ears, he heard shouting voices and more shots. They didn't sound anything like TV had taught him to expect. Things started going cold around him, like, he thought, the winds around Olympus.

"There you are, sweetheart!"

"Carolyn!" Ganymede tried to push himself up into a sitting position in his tight white hospital bed, but his midsection completely failed him. It was stitched up and bound tightly with white cloth. Today, he hadn't bled through it, but the day before, when he woke from the surgery, it had been red.

"Don't sit up. If you don't heal right, I'll have to keep Jeremy on your shifts for even longer. Evan's already so mad he's closed the kitchen early two days in a row."

"Yes ma'am." He groped about for the button that would operate his mechanical bed, found it, and started the whirring that slowly lifted him so he could watch her set a big shiny balloon and bouquet of blue irises on the table by the window.

"Are you okay there?" She draped her raincoat over the back of the nearby chair, sending little raindrops to spatter against the floor. "You need anything?"

"...not really. Carolyn? What happened?"

She sighed. "I don't know what to tell you. The guy was crazy. You weren't the only one he shot, but the other two should pull through. Those Lebanese guys you helped said they'll be coming by to visit you and say thanks, by the way."

"I'd like that. But, Carolyn....what happened?"

"I said I don't know what to tell you, sweetheart. You want me to talk feelings with you?"

He nodded. "It was kind of like Hatred, wasn't it?"

"I guess it's not the kind of hatred you usually see around here. The kind that causes fistfights. That's....I don't really have a word for it. You know personal hatred, like when one guy hates another one because there's been a slight or something."

Ganymede nodded. "But this was different."

"Yes. Hate that's not about what you've done, but about who you are. When that hate mixes with fear, desperation, stuff like that...it makes people do terrible things. Things like we see on the news." She reached over to stroke his hair with that odd little smile of hers. "I still don't know what you are, but you can't ask me to make sense of ordinary humans for you all the time."

"I need to give it a name, Carolyn. Please."

"I suppose you could call it Terror," she said with a shrug. "It's not quite right, but...it's going to have to do. Now, here, stop being depressing." Carolyn pulled her hand from his head to rummage in her purse for a little stuffed lion, which she nestled in against him. "Cheer up. If you couldn't stop him, then nobody could expect you to."

Ganymede reached up to stroke the toy's soft head. There had been nothing he could do at the time but fumble for distractions and clear the wrong pain from the air. Forty years he'd been learning the names and shapes of the world's ills, and forty years he'd been easing minor pains and doing no good for the world outside the bar, until Terror had appeared and frozen him in his tracks.

But now, he understood it, could name it and recognize its shape. And it wouldn't defeat him again.

ACKNOWLEDGEMENTS

"Finders and Keepers, Its and Not-Its" by J.G. Formato was originally published in The Colored Lens, January 2017.

"Palimpsest" by Kevin Cockle was previously published in Winter 2013 On Spec; Vol 24; no.3; #91.

"Larkspur and Henbane" by Sara Cleto and Brittany Warman is original to this anthology.

"Lupa" by Susan MacGregor is original to this anthology.

"The Tale of King Edgar" by L.S. Johnson was originally published in On the Premises, Issue #26 in 2015.

"Better Angels" by Angela Slatter was originally published in *The Review of Australian Fiction*, December 2017.

"Thorns" by Gabrielle Harbowy is original to this anthology.

"Anime Gamelle" by Sara Dobie Bauer is original to this anthology.

"The Marriage of Ocean and Dust" by Alexandra Seidel was first published in *Postscripts to Darkness* in 2015.

"The Hermit" by Joseph Halden is original to this anthology.

"The Mysterious East (Fredericton, NB)" by Greg Bechtel was first published in *The Fiddlehead*, no. 246, 2011 and subsequently reprinted in *Boundary Problems*, Freehand Books, 2014. Reprinted by permission of Freehand Books.

"One More Song" by Eliza Chan was originally published in *Sirens*, from World Weaver Press in 2016.

"'Till Death is Done" by Chadwick Ginther is original to this anthology.

"Vestige" by Annie Neugebauer was originally published in *The Beauty of Death* in 2017.

"Gift of the Kites" by Jim C. Hines was originally published in Clarkesworld Magazine in October 2008.

"Surveying the Land" by BD Wilson was previously published in *Dark Pages*, Blade Red Press, May 2010.

"Rooks" by Dan Koboldt is original to this anthology.

"Cold Spells" by Diana Hurlburt was originally published via Patreon in 2018.

"The Moon" by C.S. MacCath is original to this anthology.

"The Words of the Sun" by Sarena Ulibarri is original to this anthology.

"My Brother's Keeper" by Beth Cato was originally published in Fantasy Scroll Magazine in 2014.

"Age of Aquarius" by Cat McDonald is original to this anthology.